MY LAND
HAS
A VOICE

Jesse Stuart

MY LAND
HAS
A VOICE

McGraw-Hill Book Company
New York   Toronto   London   Sydney

FIRST PUBLISHED IN *Esquire Magazine:*

"Beyond the News in Still Hollow," copyright © 1943 by Esquire, Inc.
"As a Man Thinketh," copyright © 1955 by Esquire, Inc.
"He's Not Our People," copyright © 1939 by Esquire, Inc.
"A Stall for Uncle Jeff," copyright © 1943 by Esquire, Inc.
"Uncle Jeff and the Family Pride," copyright © 1955 by Esquire, Inc.
"Both Barrels," copyright © 1964 by Esquire, Inc.

FIRST PUBLISHED IN *New Mexico Quarterly:*

"Nearly Tickled to Death," copyright 1962 by the University of
    New Mexico Press
"Judge Ripper's Day," copyright 1965 by the University of New
    Mexico Press

The author wishes to acknowledge with gratitude the cooperation of
the following additional publishers and publications in whose vol-
umes the material herein first appeared. "Corbie," *Philippines Free
Press;* "Yoked for Life," *University Review;* "Red Mule and the
Changing World," *Chicago Magazine;* "A Mother's Place Is with
Her Son," *Ball State Teachers College Forum;* "Lady," *Progressive
Farmer;* "The Rightful Owner," *Walther League Messenger;* "Re-
member the Sabbath Day and Keep It Holy," *Arizona Quarterly;*
"Here," *University Review;* "Another Thanksgiving," *Southwest Re-
view.*

To Jane and Julian

Contents

Contents

MY LAND HAS A VOICE

Corbie

The first day I went to Plum Grove School, a little one-room school on a hilltop where one teacher taught all the first eight grades, I met Corbie. This was his first day of school, too. He and I were the same age. I went to school barefooted, since our school began in July. All the other boys and girls came barefooted, too. Corbie was the only one in school who came wearing shoes. Corbie's two brothers, Seymour and Kim, and his two sisters, Ellie Marie and Kate, came to school barefooted.

Corbie was the different pupil among us. He was the best-dressed pupil in Plum Grove School, and there were fifty of us. I wondered why he was so much better dressed than his sisters and brothers. And I wondered why somebody didn't call Corbie a "dood." Well, no one did. Just about everybody liked Corbie.

3

On our first day of school, I walked up to him and looked him over. He looked me over, I smiled at him, standing there in his corduroy suit, his white shirt and black bow tie, his black stockings and well-shined shoes. When I smiled at him he smiled back at me.

"You're all dressed up," I said. "Why do you wear shoes to school? We don't wear shoes here until frost comes in October and the weather gets cold."

"Yes, but you see, I dance," he said. "I can't dance very well barefooted."

"Let me see you dance," I said. "I'll bet you're just telling me you can dance."

"No, I'm not just telling you this, either," he said. "I can dance and I play my own music when I dance. Have you got a penny?"

"Yes, I've got a penny."

"If you give me a penny, I'll dance. I don't work without pay."

"But dancing isn't work. It's fun."

"It is work for me, but I like to do it. And I don't like to dance unless I get paid. You give me the penny and I'll dance for you."

"Here in the schoolyard?"

"Yes, what's wrong with dancing here? I dance anywhere people want me to dance, if they will pay me a penny."

"I'll give you a penny to dance 'Turkey in the Straw.'"

"Pay me now," he said. "People say they'll give me a penny, and after I dance, I don't get paid. People won't always do what they say they will."

I gave Corbie a penny.

When he opened his little coin purse, I had never seen so many pennies. He didn't have any other kind of coins. Then he reached into his inside coat pocket and pulled out a harmonica.

"Now I got this French harp," he said. "And I got a jews-harp. I can play either one. Which would you rather hear?"

"I got another penny," I said. "Play the French harp when you dance 'Turkey in the Straw.' Now can you play and dance 'Corinna,' 'Stackoles,' or 'Sourwood Mountain'?"

"Yes, all of them," he said. "And I can dance a lot more, too."

Corbie took off his coat and laid it on the grass. The white sleeves of his shirt were held up by armbands. He was really a well-dressed dancer. Now he walked over to a place in the schoolyard where there wasn't any grass. It was a place where the ground had been trampled by many feet until it was too hard for the grass to grow. Here Corbie began to play his harmonica and dance. I don't know how much he weighed, but he seemed to float, and his body was as limp as wilted pods of oak leaves hanging in the July heat. He played "Turkey in the Straw" until I felt like dancing too. And when he played and danced all the Plum Grove pupils, plus our teacher, Mr. Clarke, came running. They formed a circle around Corbie where the dust rose up from his flying feet. It was a yellow dust, and it settled on our clothes and on Corbie's shoes. But Corbie danced on, and he gave us a penny's worth of music and dancing. I thought Corbie was great.

"Now, 'Sourwood Mountain' on the jews-harp," I said, and I gave Corbie another penny.

His breath was coming a little fast after dancing and playing that number. He took his time putting the penny away, he went over to his coat and put away the harmonica in a pocket, then took his jews-harp from another.

"It's harder to play the jews-harp and dance," he said. "I have to use both hands to play it. But I can do it."

When he had played the harmonica, he had to use only one hand to hold the harmonica to his mouth. His other arm was down by his side, and it had moved and swayed to the rhythm of his dance and song.

When Corbie put the jews-harp to his mouth, he held it tightly with one hand and with the index finger of the other hand began to play a tune that went like a buzzing bee. Again the yellow dust came up from the ground as we listened to "Sourwood Mountain." Then he went back to the jews-harp before he finished his dance. And when he finished, all of us clapped our hands. Little Corbie knew we liked to hear him play his music, sing his songs, and dance to the tunes.

We were still clapping our hands and telling him how well we liked to hear him play and watch him dance when he went over to get his coat. The morning sun was very warm now, and Corbie's face was damp with sweat. His damp shirt was sticking to his body. But Corbie put his coat on.

And Mr. Clarke went back in the schoolroom and got his bell. He came to the door and rang the bell. And we formed lines, boys on one side and girls on the other. The girls marched in first, and we followed. I was behind Corbie. Since his name was Corbett Sinnett and mine was Shan Stringer, we sat together. Mr. Clarke arranged the seating that way.

So Corbie and I sat in the back of the schoolroom by the window. He wanted the side next to the window, where he could hear the wind blow and could watch the birds. I let him have the side he wanted. I liked Corbie and he seemed to like me. But everybody liked Corbie. And everybody understood about Corbie. But they didn't understand why he came so well-dressed when his brothers and sisters didn't.

Corbie had brought a new book to school with him. I'd brought one too. We had brought our new primers. Each of us had brought a slate, a tablet, and a pencil. When the school day began, Corbie sat and looked at the picture in his primer. Then he looked out the window. Acorns were falling from the oaks and the bluejays flew down to the ground and picked them up in their short bills. They flew back up to the tops of the old trees and stored these acorns in the hollow branches for winter, when snow would lie on the ground and food would be scarce.

"Funny how birds will work like that," Corbie whispered to me. "But I like to watch how they fan their wings and work their feet when they fly."

I sat beside Corbie my first year at school. All Corbie ever did was watch the bluejays in summer, storing acorns in the hollow branches of the trees. And he looked at the Jim Young farm and the cattle in the pasture. When autumn came, he watched the crows flying over. From the window he watched the leaves come down from the trees. And in the wintertime he watched the snowflakes zigzag down to cover the Plum Grove hills.

Corbie never looked at his primer except, perhaps, once a month. Then he opened his primer and looked at the pictures. I learned my ABC's in a short time until I could say them from memory. I could recite them backwards and forwards and I could print them with chalk on the blackboard.

"Wish I could learn my ABC's like you." Corbie said to me once.

He looked at me and smiled.

"I wish I could dance and play like you, Corbie," I said.

Then I looked at him and smiled.

Before our six-month school term was over, I could read everything in my primer. I was ready for another book. But my seatmate, Corbie, couldn't say his ABC's, and Mr. Clarke never said anything to Corbie. He was very nice to Corbie. Often he looked at Corbie and smiled, and Corbie smiled

back. And when Corbie danced, Mr. Clarke would come to
the schoolyard and watch him. He didn't mind us giving
Corbie a penny to dance.

The school year passed, and Corbie never learned his
ABC's. He didn't get promoted from the Chart Class and the
Primer. And until school began the next year, I never saw
Corbie but once. I was in Blakesburg. Corbie was dancing
and playing his harmonica in the street. A man had given
him a penny to dance. Everybody liked Corbie. Some man
stepped up and said, "How would you like to dance for
this?" He held a quarter in his hand.

"It's too much," Corbie said. "I just want a penny."

Everybody laughed when Corbie wouldn't dance for a
quarter, but he danced again and again for pennies.

In my second year in school at Plum Grove, I was the first
pupil on the schoolground the day school began. Then Corbie came up the hill ahead of his brothers and sisters.

"I want to sit with you, Shan," he said.

"Then we'll sit together, Corbie," I said. "I want to sit with
you too."

Corbie couldn't get a prize in spelling or in arithmetic, or
in handwriting. Mr. Clarke gave us prizes for these things.
But if there had been a prize for the best harmonica player,
or the best jews-harp player, Corbie would have got it. And
if there had been a prize for the best-dressed pupil in the
Plum Grove School, Corbie surely would have taken it. And
he might have won a prize for being the best-behaved boy in
Plum Grove School, if such a prize had been given. He didn't
get into any mischief. He never said a bad word, and when
Mr. Clarke told Corbie to do something he always tried to
do it. He didn't do anything wrong in school, just looked out
the window at the hill slopes in their changing seasons and
watched the animals and the birds.

"Another year has passed at Plum Grove," I told my father

and mother. "And my seatmate, Corbie Sinnett, hasn't learned his ABC's. He can't read in his primer. Honest, Mom, I don't believe Corbie can learn. Maybe he doesn't want to learn. I'll be in another grade next year. But I can't dance," I told them, "and I can't play music like Corbie."

My mother and father didn't say anything.

"And he comes to school better dressed than anybody," I said. "He wears shoes in the summertime when everybody else in school is going barefooted."

"Yes, I know," my mother said. "He wears shoes, a suit of clothes, white shirt, and a hat. He even wears armbands to hold up his shirtsleeves. But Corbie isn't a dood. I think he wears shoes so he can dance. That's what he told me."

My parents didn't say anything when I told them we had to pay him a penny every time he danced.

"Does anybody ever tease Corbie at school?" my mother asked me.

"Oh no, everybody likes Corbie," I said.

In my third year at Plum Grove, when Corbie, who stood up front with the beginners, said all of his ABC's, there was great rejoicing among us at Plum Grove. When Mr. Clarke came to the letter "I" on the old chart that stood up against the wall, I saw him point to his own eye when Corbie was having trouble. Then, very suddenly, Corbie said "Eye." This got the attention of everybody in school. We put our books down. We stopped whatever we were doing. Mr. Clarke didn't say anything to us. He knew we wanted Corbie to go all the way through the alphabet. Mr. Clarke wanted him to go too, or he wouldn't have been helping him. And when he came to the letter "T," Corbie stumbled. Mr. Clarke picked up a cup, and Corbie started to say "coffee," but Mr. Clarke shook his head real quick and Corbie said "T." And when Corbie went all the way through, we all clapped our hands.

So Corbie was promoted to the first grade. Corbie would get to use a new book. He'd worn out two primers. He carried his primer in his pocket, and one just lasted him a year. His third primer was about worn out when he got promoted.

My father and mother didn't know that I was hearing them talk. They were in the little dining room and I'd just come in at the kitchen door. When my father said "Corbie," I stopped to listen.

"Yes, I picked up Felix Sinnett today," he said. "He rode out to the turnpike with me in my express wagon. And we got to talking about the Plum Grove School and he was telling me how well his boy Corbett likes our boy Shan. And he was braggin' on Mr. Clarke, the teacher. You know, Marth," he said to Mom, "this boy Corbie, he just can't get learning, his pappy Felix said. He don't have everything he should in his head. He said they bought the best of everything for Corbie. They wanted to do this while they lived to show their love for this child. I've been thinking about what old Felix said. He is a big coalminer with big fire-shovel hands and shoulders as broad as a corncrib door. How that big Felix can ever crawl back in one of those little joltwagon mines and lay on his side and dig coal from a twenty-four-inch vein, I don't know. But he does it, and he buys Corbie good clothes, fine shoes, harmonicas, and jews-harps."

Not all there in the head, I thought. Now I knew why Mr. Clarke, our teacher, was so nice to him. And I knew why his brothers and sisters never kicked about his going better dressed than they did. And I understood why all the older pupils at Plum Grove in the seventh and eighth grades were so nice to him.

I was ten years old and in the fifth grade when Corbie raised his price for dancing. Corbie was ten years old too. "Too many people ask me to dance," Corbie said. "A penny is not enough. I've got to raise my price to a nickel." And when he raised his price, fewer people asked him to dance. But he made more money dancing for a nickel than he did for a penny, and he didn't dance as much.

I was thirteen years old when I finished the eighth grade at Plum Grove. And I was still sitting with Corbie. But Corbie hadn't finished the first grade. He liked our old seat by the window, where he could look out at the landscape when it changed from summer to autumn and from autumn to winter. He liked to sit there where he could watch the birds and the animals and he could watch the autumn-colored leaves zigzag down from the trees after the first frost.

The next year I went to Blakesburg High School. I don't know how far Corbie got in school. Maybe he got to the second grade. I don't know. But I do know that if grades had been given for dancing, playing the harmonica and the jews-harp and for going well-dressed, Corbie would have made the highest grades in school.

In my four years in Blakesburg High School during noon hours I often walked through the town with some of my classmates. Once we heard a fiddle in the courthouse square. And we heard the tapping of shoes on a concrete sidewalk. The dancer was keeping time to the music. And when we got there I saw Corbie. He didn't see me, for there was a crowd gathered around. Some man was playing a fiddle, and Corbie was dancing to its music.

"Here, I like the way you dance," a man said. "I want to give you this."

The man had a dollar bill.

"No, no," Corbie said. "That's too much. I used to dance for a penny. Then I danced for a nickel. Maybe sometime I'll charge more. Not now."

Then the man put the dollar in his pocket and gave Corbie a dime. The fiddler wasn't ready. But Corbie reached into his inside coat pocket. He pulled out his harmonica and began to play "Turkey in the Straw." And as he played, his feet tapped out the tune on the concrete. His harmonica playing was better than the fiddle. And everybody applauded Corbie.

This was the last time I ever saw Corbie. When I returned from college Felix Sinnett and his family had moved away from the Plum Grove hills.

And later I read a piece about him in the paper, where it said he had been preceded in death by a brother, a sister, his father, and his mother. I threw the paper. For I wondered how Corbie had fared after his father Felix got too old to work in the mine and the family had moved to Auckland.

Yoked
for Life

"But you must not shudder and quiver when we talk about the living things of God's creation," Uncle Jeff said. "I know the subject of snakes is not a very polite one. And I know people don't want to hear about 'em. But why I brought up the subject of snakes is that it fits into a defect in our human society."

I didn't know what Uncle Jeff's line of thought for the evening conversation was going to be. But I knew when he got to talking about a favorite subject it was hard to get him stopped. He liked to talk, and when he started telling one of his favorite stories he wouldn't stop. Well, he might have stopped if we had got up and left the room.

"Now you take old Seymour Pratt," Uncle Jeff said. "He's our neighbor and friend. How many wives do you think he's had?"

"Well, I can remember three," Sister Mary said.

"I remember four of Seymour's wives," I said.

"I'm older than you, Shan," Sister Sophia said. "I remember five."

"I remember Seymour's wife Bertha," Pa said. "I'm not nearly as old as Jeff. Bertha made six wives."

"He had one more," Uncle Jeff said. "Tillie Pruitt was his first wife."

"What happened to all of his wives?" Brother Finn asked. Now my brother Finn was nine years younger than I was. "I didn't know Seymour Pratt had so many wives. What did he do with all of 'em?"

"Uncle Jeff, what has this got do with snakes?" Sister Glenna asked.

"It's got a lot to do with snakes," Uncle Jeff said.

"Stop interrupting your Uncle Jeff," Mom said. "Let him continue with his story. When Brother Jeff talks, he always has something to say."

When Mom said this, Pa turned his head and smiled. And often when Uncle Jeff was talking at his best to us on the long winter evenings before the fire, he had had a little nip from his bottle. And Uncle Jeff's nipping was another story which he never told. But this was why he was living with us. He had been married and was the father of eight children. They were all married now and had homes of their own. And his wife, Aunt Mettie, was dead. But before her death, she and Uncle Jeff had lived apart for twenty years. They were never divorced, but they were separated. She stayed in their old home, and Uncle Jeff came to live with us.

"Now you asked about old Seymour's wives," Uncle Jeff continued. "Three are dead, and four are living. I guess old Seymour and his seventh wife, Hattie Sprouse Pratt, are having some awful battles. I hear they've been in court, but Judge Rivercomb shamed old Seymour and told him he'd had enough wife trouble and to settle down and behave himself. Now, old Seymour's troubles have caused me to think of the snakes. And right now I'm thinking of the copperhead."

"Oh, Jeff," Mom said, "one bit me once and I lived. And one bit you once and you lived. Why bring up the copperhead?"

"Because the copperhead is the meanest snake, the most dangerous and deadly of all snakes we have in these parts," Uncle Jeff said. "Remember, Mollie, when the copperhead bit you, you disturbed him, didn't you? You reached your hand under a tobacco stalk to pull the grass away and you put your hand right on him. He was under the cool leaves away from the summer sun, taking his afternoon nap. You scared him, and he bit your hand. Once I was plowing tobacco and stepped on one beside a rock in the tobacco balk. And he jumped up from his sleep and grabbed my leg. But we lived, Mollie! And I like to think we lived for a purpose. See, we look at any kind of snake as being something evil. And we think there is more evil in the copperhead, because he's the meanest of all snakes."

"I agree with you, Jeff," my father said.

My father seldom agreed with Uncle Jeff on anything. And maybe the reason was, he could never tell a story like Uncle Jeff. We liked to hear Uncle Jeff talk, but not about snakes. Uncle Jeff was a big man. He weighed three hundred seven pounds. He was six feet two, and there were no bulges on his powerful body. He was a muscular man with arms as big as small fence posts, legs at the calves as big as gate posts, and hands as big as shovels. His big head sat almost squarely on his shoulders, and a stranger had to look twice to see if he had any neck. He had a kind face and big blue eyes. His head was bald on top and there was a rim of white hair around the base of his head. He had to have shirts shoes, gloves, pants made for himself. The only ready-made clothes he could buy to fit him were a necktie and a hat. We had to make a special chair for him to sit on, and once one of our beds broke down with him in it asleep.

A person who had never seen Uncle Jeff before might have thought he was as mean among men as the copperhead snake was among snakes. But Uncle Jeff didn't hunt. He wouldn't kill anything. He wouldn't even kill a poisonous copperhead. Once in the field I saw him shoo one away.

"Why did you do that, Uncle Jeff?" I asked.

"It was put here for a purpose," he said. "Besides, the copperhead has his own enemies."

"Who are his enemies?" I asked Uncle Jeff.

"The blacksnake and the terrapin," he replied. "And man isn't exactly friendly to the copperhead."

I didn't know a blacksnake and a terrapin could kill a copperhead until Uncle Jeff told me.

"Now the copperheads wed for life," Uncle Jeff said, looking up at the ceiling. "Oh, I'm not sure whether a pair might separate or not. I suppose they do. But when the old he-copperhead gets killed, the old she-copperhead becomes a widow. And if the old she-copperhead gets squeezed to death by a blacksnake, or chewed to death by a stud terrapin, then the old he-copperhead becomes a widower. The love life is all over for them. See, our Creator put them here to point the way of deep and abiding love for our human family."

"Now, Jeff, you're going too far," Pa said.

"Mick, let Jeff tell his story," Mom said. "He has more to tell. If you give Jeff time, he will prove the point."

"Yes, I have more to tell, and I will prove my point," Uncle Jeff continued. "And . . ."

"But I don't believe copperheads love like that," Pa interrupted.

"Just listen until I finish, Mick," Uncle Jeff said.

"Yes, let Uncle Jeff go on," I said.

"We do want to know about snake-love," he said. My oldest sister, Sophia, was old enough to be having dates now. She could hardly keep from laughing at Uncle Jeff.

"Now back in Elliott County a young couple got married," Uncle Jeff said. "You remember John Porter and Ann Cox."

"Yes, Jeff, I do," Mom interrupted him. "I know what you're going to tell now. Go ahead and tell us."

"Well, John Porter was our fourth cousin and Ann Cox was some distant cousin to us—eighth, ninth, or maybe a tenth cousin," Uncle Jeff said. "Before they married back in them days, it was always customary to have the house built so they could move in. So the parents of the young couple cut trees to make logs for the walls. They rove clapboards from tall straight oaks to make a roof. They split chestnut puncheons for the floor. They built the house in about a week. And after the belling, John and Ann went straight to their new house. One of their parents had given them a feather bed, pillows, and quilts—and the other's parents had given them a stove! You know how it used to be, Mollie. The parents of the bride and groom gave them the base necessities to go to housekeeping on. Their parents gave them a cow for milk and hens to lay eggs. See, in them days people had to dig a living from the ground or starve, and it wasn't easy to live farming the steep Elliott County hills.

"Well, John and Ann were a nice-looking couple," Uncle Jeff said. "John was a tall, powerful man and handy with an ax, and Ann was a medium-size buxom woman with real blue eyes. I'll never forget her eyes as long as I live. I was a sapling of a boy then, and I thought she was the prettiest young woman in Elliott County. They were married in April and moved into their new house just after the wedding and after we belled them there that night. I remember the house wasn't finished but it didn't matter, for they were in a hurry to move into their new home. And back in them days, people weren't afraid of a few cracks between the logs—especially in April when the wind was warm and fresh. And of course they had planned to have the cracks chinked and mud daubed over the chinking before the cold autumn nights.

"Well, John cleared the ground, planted a crop of corn, tobacco, and wheat the first spring," Uncle Jeff continued with his story while we listened eagerly to every word he said. He spoke words we could catch and hold just like somebody putting rocks into a bucket. They were there, and they were solid things. No one could write down what Uncle Jeff said as well as he could tell it. "April, May, and June passed. There was consistent love between them, John and Ann. I remember seeing them ride all hugged up in a little hug-me-tight buggy to Bruin to the store. They traded eggs for groceries. And they had some money to spend. Their corn grew tall and their wheat grew up, and ripened until a high slope looked like a sheet of gold. Their tobacco grew tall and the leaves were broad and dark. John was a good farmer. And Ann helped him some in the fields. She helped him until their first child was on the way.

"Now August came, and if you don't know it, I do know, that August is a bad month for snakes. The old hot sun beamed down in Elliott County in August, and every living thing and just about everybody hunted shade. The minnows in the mountain streams found a shady pool of water, the groundhogs went back into their dirt holes where it was cool. They stirred early in the morning before the sun was up, or in the late afternoon when the sun went down. And the squirrels stirred early and late too, and slept in their nests in the shade or deep in holes in the hollow trees when the sun was up. The snakes found cool places to coil and sleep too, and they stirred mostly at night when it was cool. They foraged for food at night in the dense dark woods and weed fields.

"One August night when the weather was very hot and the wind didn't come through the cracks and windows in John and Ann's house, John thought he heard a noise like a broom swishing over the puncheon floor.

" 'Ann, do you hear something?' John whispered.

" 'Yes, I'm awake listening to it, John,' she whispered. 'Couldn't be somebody here, could it?'

" 'I'll see,' he whispered.

"Since John kept a kerosene lamp on a chair beside his bed, and a box of matches by the lamp, he struck a match and lit the lamp. 'Ann, Ann,' he said, 'don't look!' But Ann did look at the big copperhead crawling slowly over the puncheon floor toward the bed.

" 'I told you not to look, Ann,' he said. 'See, when a pregnant woman looks at a snake, the snake will go blind.'

"The snake stopped suddenly after Ann looked at him, held his head in the air, and moved it around and around like he was addled. Then John got out of bed and shined the lamplight in the snake's eyes, and sure enough, he was blind. His once beady black eyes in their lidless sockets were like clots of phlegm.

" 'Sorry, darling,' he said to Ann, 'but you blinded him.'

" 'But you plan to kill him anyway, John,' she said.

" 'No, I planned to shoo him out with the broom,' John told her. 'I'm afraid to kill a snake. I let the snakes kill each other.'

" 'John, that's crazy talk,' she told him. 'You are a big strong he-man! You've got too much sense to think like that.'

" 'Haven't you heard, darling, that the copperhead is filled with the damned souls of evil men? There is more evil in that snake than you might think. Since you have blinded him, I will have to shoot the snake. Stop your ears with your finger, darling.'

"John lifted the squirrel rifle down from the joist where he kept it hanging above the bed. He took aim at the copperhead's neck when it stopped moving. He fired and the snake went limp on the floor. The bullet almost severed its neck and passed on through the green chestnut puncheon floor and went into the ground under the house.

" 'I never saw a snake bleed like that one,' John told Ann. And if you don't know this, when a snake bleeds a lot, it's not exactly the snake's blood that pours forth," Uncle Jeff said. "That blood is supposed to be the blood of all the damned that has become a part of the snake. John Porter knew this.

"So, that night John took the snake over to Clem Worthington's shack," Uncle Jeff continued. "Clem, an old man whose wife was dead, now lived alone. Many people thought he was a Wise One. He read the stars, coffee cups, studied nature; and he read Hosea, the Prophet, until he had begun to think he was a prophet. He told the people he was a prophet and they believed him. And to tell you the truth," Uncle Jeff said, with a sigh, "it was old Clem that first put me on to the constancy of snake-love. And it was old Clem who said the snake was more sacred than people thought and that the Creator put him here for a purpose, or he wouldn't be on this earth. Well, what he had said made sense to me. I can see old Clem yet in his little two-room house with weeds growing high as the porch was tall. He sat in a little room with his books around him, and he took long walks the four seasons of the year. He observed 'the Creator's handiwork' and he tried to figure things out to his own satisfaction, and for his people. He called us his people, and I guess we were. Old Clem has long gone to his reward. He sleeps on an Elliott County hill without a marker to show where he lies. Well, I went back there, and I couldn't find his grave. And this reminds me of a truth he said once, that man wasn't as immortal as a grain of sand. He said a grain of sand went on forever, but man disappeared from the earth. And poor old Clem, by dying, has proved his point.

"But the night John shot the copperhead, he took him to old Clem and told him how Ann, who was with child, looked at the snake and how its eyes turned to clots of phlegm, as she looked, and how he shot it instead of shooing it out with a broom as he had planned. He told old Clem that he was scared after the way it bled.

" 'You had better be scared,' old Clem told him, 'You and Ann are in for serious trouble. I could mention a half dozen evil men, cutthroats, murderers, and robbers, who might be hidin' in this snake.'

"John Porter, who was young, big, and powerful, and un-afraid of man or animal, now stood before old Clem, shaking like an oak leaf in the night wind.

" 'Rufus Johnson, who knocked old Jerry Bruck in the head for his money, was in that snake,' old Clem told John. 'Old Mary Howes, who tolled Flem Berry to the rock cliff where Tom and Boz Bean were waiting to murder him, was in that snake. Old Fose Jones, so mean to an animal he'd beat his mule's eye out with a stick—I'm sure he was there too. Thurmond Turnipseed, who killed four men for the love of killing, was surely in him. Erf Springhill, who shot his own father, was there. It was their blood, John, that spilled when you shot the snake,' old Clem told John. 'You've unleashed all this evil upon us. The copperhead holds the evil, and should be left for other snakes to kill.'

" 'I told Ann that,' he told the wise old Clem. 'She didn't believe.'

" 'She will believe,' old Clem told him. 'She might be killed and you might be killed with her, since you are yoked together by the Creator's Divine Law.'

" 'What will I do with this dead copperhead?' John asked old Clem.

" 'It won't matter now,' he told him. 'As you ride back, throw him off in the weeds. All the evil he held has gone into his mate. She will take up the fight.'

" 'You may be the wisest of all men around here,' John told old Clem before he left, 'but I can hardly believe all this. How can evil go from evil back to evil?'

" 'You will see,' old Clem warned him. 'Throw the dead snake away. It isn't as much as a grain of sand now. It won't go back to a little grain of sand, but it will go back to loam, and nothing will grow from that loam for three years. It will kill everything close to it. Take that evil carcass out of here, John.'

"John took the snake and threw it in a weed patch beside the path as he rode his mule back home."

"Jeff, you're making all this up," Pa said. "It's the wildest story I ever heard. No man in his right senses will believe that stuff."

"No, Brother Jeff isn't making it up," Mom said. "I know the story. I left Elliott County when I was twelve years old. Everybody up there used to know this story."

"All right, if I am making up a bunch of lies I'll stop my story, Mick," Uncle Jeff said. "I don't like to speak before an unbeliever."

"Go on with the story, Uncle Jeff," I said. "I believe you, Uncle Jeff, because I want to believe you. I want to hear all the story."

"Yes, Uncle Jeff, tell the rest of it," Sophia said.

But Uncle Jeff sat there for a minute. Brother Finn begged him to tell the rest of it. Mary begged him to go on, and then Glenna, our baby sister, wanted to hear all of the story. We liked to hear Uncle Jeff tell stories. We'd seen copperheads, and I had killed them. But now I wondered whether I would ever cut one's head off with a hoe again, and unleash all that powerful evil. I had killed them because I was afraid of a copperhead. But now I thought of all the evil I might have unleashed as I thought back; each time I had killed a copperhead something dreadful had happened in our neighborhood. About the time I'd killed one, a man was stabbed to death. And at another time, a neighbor's barn burned with all his livestock in it. I thought the evil men were sealed up in a copperhead like poison was sealed in a bottle.

"Now, what started all of this was old Seymour Pratt and his seven wives," Uncle Jeff said. "I said that the copperhead snake was put on this earth for a purpose and that purpose for mankind might be to teach constant love. See, there is the frivolous love like old Seymour has, or he wouldn't have had seven wives. Now when the copperhead takes his bride, it is a lifetime proposition with him! Now Mick, if you won't interrupt me again, I'll continue . . ."

"All right, Jeff, you win," Pa said. "The children want to hear that crazy stuff, and I don't think it will contaminate their minds to listen to you. But my mind is closed to it."

"Contaminate their minds?" Uncle Jeff repeated in a surprised tone of voice. "It should help them. All of your children, Mick, my little nieces and nephews gathered around their old uncle listening to his voice now, will be proud someday they had the opportunity to listen. They will be choosing mates someday. Let's hope your sons won't be Seymour Pratts when they and your daughters choose mates for all eternity."

Pa shook his head disgustedly and leaned back in his chair.

"The news of Ann's blinding the snake and John's shooting it and its bleeding and his going to wise old Clem in the night with the dead snake was norated all over that community the next day," Uncle Jeff said. "John told the story to

Bill Wilcox, and when he went to Bruin to Jeff Harper's store Bill told the story to old Jeff, which was like putting it in the Elliott County *News*. And that very night when John and Ann went to bed, John lit the lamp.

" 'John, I can't sleep with the light on,' Ann said. 'I like to lie in the dark and feel the night wind come through the cracks, and then I can sleep.'

" 'Darling, something else might come through the cracks,' John said.

" 'What are you talking about?' she asked.

" 'The mate to that snake I shot last night,' he replied.

" 'John, who told you that?' Ann asked. 'That old bag of wind you call wise old Clem?'

" 'Yes, old Clem told me,' he said. 'When I left here last night with the dead snake you were asleep,' he said. " 'Old Clem told me the mate might take revenge. And now, since the snake bled like it did, it was carrying the souls of the damned and the evil. No fewer than seven, according to what old Clem said. He even named them last night.'

" 'John, are you losing your mind?'

" 'I hope not.'

" 'Well, I can't sleep with that light on,' she said, 'besides we have to be rested to do the work ahead of us tomorrow.'

" 'If we don't keep the lamp burning, that copperhead's mate might come back to undo us. She will take her revenge, for I killed her mate, and copperheads wed for life.'

" 'I'm going to blow the lamp out so I can sleep,' Ann told John. 'I'm not afraid, because all that crazy talk goes in at one ear and comes out at the other.'

" 'You are taking a chance,' John told her. 'And since you and I are yoked by the Creator's Divine Law, I am in danger with you.'

"Ann blew out the lamp and she went to sleep in the dark while John lay on the bed and tossed, so he told me the next

day when I went out there to borrow a hoe. What I wanted
to find out was about his killing the snake. He told me the
story and he said he felt tired to go to work in the tobacco,
pulling suckers from the stalks. He said he'd not had enough
sleep. And he told me how Ann had got up that morning
laughing. And at the breakfast table she had said to him,
" 'Well, the mate of the constant lovers didn't get us last
night, did she?'

"And John told me his wife accused him of being 'teched
in the head.' 'But I told Ann the mate could still come back
on the second or the third night. And she laughed more than
at any time since we've been married. And she even said her
looking at the copperhead hadn't blinded him, but that this
was a season called 'dog days,' and all snakes went blind in
dog days and regained their sight after the season was over.'
I remember every word John told me that morning.

"Well, this was the last time, Mick, I ever talked to John
Porter, my fourth cousin," Uncle Jeff said. "Next time I saw
John Porter, he was lying beside Ann, and they were dressed
in their wedding clothes, side by side in a big double coffin
Pap and the other men made for them. Not just the two of
them, but there was a third one, too. Their unborn went
with its mother, Ann. It was on the third night that the old
she-copperhead followed her mate. She crawled through the
crack of the cabin and found her mate's bloodstain on the
puncheon floor. Then she sought revenge. She crawled up in
the bed with John and Ann, and she must have bit one and
then the other. Birdie Crump went over to help John sucker
his tobacco, the next morning, since they were exchanging
work. And Birdie knew John got up early. Well, he waited
around outside, from six until seven. He watched the flue
from the cookstove for smoke, too. There was no fire in the
stove. Ann was not up getting breakfast. So Birdie knocked
on the door and no one answered. In those days, every man

kept his hunting gun handy by his bed, but no one ever locked a door. It was a disgrace and showed a man's cowardice. Then Birdie just eased the door open and went in. He saw John and Ann still in bed. He spoke to them, but there was no answer. And he walked back to the bed and looked at their pale silent faces. They weren't breathing. And just as he was about to touch John's forehead to see if he were really dead, the old she-copperhead poked her head right up between them from under the cover. Birdie said, 'I jumped three steps backward in one hop. I took off to notify the neighbors.' I remember when Birdie came and told Pop, he was short of breath from running and he was scared—a scared man," Jeff continued. He shook his head sadly. I thought he was going to cry.

"When Coroner Waterfield went to the cabin, the old she-copperhead had gone. She had come to the cabin with all her evil intent, and she had done her duty. John had been bitten four times, and Ann had been bitten six. They had been bitten early in the night when they were asleep and the dose of poison injected in them was so much they were dead before morning. Well, we had a big funeral! You remember the funeral, don't you, Mollie?"

"Yes, I was a little girl, nine or ten, but I went to that funeral," Mom said. "That was the first and only time I ever saw a man and his wife buried in the same coffin."

"Now, Mick, what do you think of that?" Uncle Jeff asked Pa. "Do you believe copperheads are yoked for life? Do you believe in the constancy of their love?"

"Jeff, it doesn't matter what I believe," Pa told him quickly. "I keep a good sharp hoe for the copperheads. I think a man's greatest problem of staying married to the woman he loves is her relatives. I wonder if the copperhead snakes have relatives that are as big pests as we have among the relatives in our human family?"

Pa got up from his chair and rubbed his sleepy eyes. "I believe I'll turn in after that one, Jeff," he said. "You've really told one tonight."

"Mick, you don't appreciate Brother Jeff," Mom said.

"I'm sure glad it's wintertime, and the copperheads have hibernated," I said. "If it was summertime I'd light the lamp upstairs and keep it lit all night, too."

"Yes, they're put here for a purpose just like old Clem used to tell us," Uncle Jeff sighed as he got up from his special chair Pa had made for him, so he wouldn't break all Mom's chairs down. "The Creator had in mind a purpose for every living thing. And I believe the copperhead was put here to point the way to the constant and abiding love."

"What about Seymour Pratt, Uncle Jeff?" I asked. "Since he's had seven wives, will he join the six evil men and one woman in that old she-copperhead?"

"Son, I can't judge," Uncle Jeff sighed.

"I'm never sure of many things," Pa said, "but I'm sure of one thing. If old Seymour is confined with the six evil men and one woman in the belly of that old copperhead, evil or no evil—not one of the six men would have a chance, for old Seymour will get old Mary! You can bet on that! I know him. Come on, and let's everybody get in bed before Jeff spins another one."

Beyond the News
in Still Hollow

Sheriff Enic Bradley thought he knew Melton County, deep in the mountains of Kentucky, better than he knew the pages of the old McGuffey Fourth Reader which was his highest scholastic attainment. He was born in Melton County, had lived in it all his life, had seen the WPA roads come to the county, government electricity to the county seat, and a WPA stone jailhouse. Before these new improvements came there wasn't an electric wire, a stone building, or a road a car could be driven over in the county. Not yet was there a telephone, a foot of railroad or a foot of surfaced highway. Now he sat in his car at the end of the WPA road, baffled as he looked over the warrant. The name of the young man he was to arrest was Crooks Cornett. The post office where the young man got his mail was Piney Point. But someone had scribbled a note on the warrant, "You'll find him in Still Hollow." He knew county sheriffs and revenue men, those that returned, had many occasions to remember Still Hollow.

The road beyond the WPA road was a wagon road; filled with deep ruts and chuck holes. It was impossible for him to drive his car, though his car was built as high as cars were built in the late twenties, over rocks, stumps, and rutty roads. This wagon road was too much for his old car, and he made up his mind to lock the car and walk to the first house to inquire for Piney Point and Still Hollow. He had not walked a mile until he came to a shack beside the road, where he decided to inquire. Two children playing in the yard saw him first, dropped their playthings and ran into the shack as fast as they could to warn their parents a stranger was coming. When he reached the shack door he knocked.

The door opened enough for a man to stick his head out cautiously.

"Sheriff Bradley," the beardy-faced man greeted him, opening the door the rest of the way.

"Ollie Hendrix," Sheriff Bradley said, "I didn't know you lived here. I'm tryin to find Piney Point and Still Hollow."

"I haint never been thar," Ollie said in his slow way. "Years ago it was a dangerous place. 'Spect, Sheriff, it's twenty-five miles to Still Hollow! Ye haint a-tryin to walk thar, air ye?"

"I planned to," Sheriff Bradley said. "You don't have a good saddle horse I could hire for a couple of days?"

"Nope, but I got a gallopin mule," Ollie said, laughing, showing his yellow, discolored, tobacco-stained teeth. "He's as easy a saddler as a body ever rid."

"I'd like to hire 'im," the sheriff said. "I'll pay you well for the mule. I'd like to pay you to watch my car too."

"Where is hit, Sheriff?"

"It's parked at the end of the WPA road."

"I'll do hit, Sheriff," Ollie said happily.

Ollie bridled and saddled his mule for the sheriff and helped him mount, for the mule was as wary of strangers as the mountaineers themselves.

"Follow this road until ye reach Blue Creek," Ollie directed the sheriff. "Follow Blue Creek until ye reach Rocky Branch. Ye'll haf to ast the rest of the way."

"Many thanks, Ollie," Sheriff Bradley said, riding away.

He galloped the mule where the road was suitable. Soon he and the mule were almost covered with mud. But he followed the road to Blue Creek; then he followed the Blue Creek road, which was impassable for any sort of wagons, until he reached Rocky Branch, where the road simmered down to a mule path. He rode wearily up Rocky Branch until he came to a shack that was crowded between the road and a high wall of cliffs. When he stopped his mule and laid the bridle rein over the gate post, children playing in the yard dropped their playthings and ran into the house. When he knocked on the door a beardy-faced man opened the door enough to stick his head out and say, "What do ye want, stranger?"

"How do you get to Still Hollow?"

"Ye haint a revooneer, air ye?"

"I'm goin to visit Cornetts. They're my kinfolks."

"Right good people they are," the man said, holding the door. "Ye're 'bout eleven miles from thar. If ye ride fast ye'll make it by sundown. Follow Rocky Branch road to the ridge. One road turns right, one turns left. Take the road to the left."

"Thank you," Bradley said.

When the sheriff mounted his mule he saw the man looking from the door at him and his many children's faces peeping from behind the curtains of the only window in the shack. He rode away thinking these people were strangers to him, though he lived not more than twenty miles away.

Before sundown Sheriff Bradley asked a man walking along the path, carrying a pole of stovewood on his shoulder and an ax in his hand, if he could tell him where Cornetts lived.

"What do ye want?" the stranger asked.

"Just want to see my kinfolks."

"See that shack against that cliff," the man pointed with the handle of his ax.

"Thank you."

He rode to the shack and hitched his mule to the garden palings, walked over rocks laid down for a walk to the front door and knocked. A big man opened the door part of the way; he was barefooted, wore overalls and his face was unshaven.

"Do Cornetts live here?" Sheriff Bradley asked.

"They do," he said. "I'm Jarvis Cornett. What might yer name be?"

"Enic Bradley."

"Haint ye some sort o' law in this county?"

"I'm the sheriff."

"We don't make moonshine any more."

"I've come to see your son, Crooks."

Jarvis looked worried. "What's he done?" he asked.

"The Melton County Draft Board has sent him three notices."

"Come in, Mr. Bradley, and explain this thing to me," Jarvis Cornett said.

Sheriff Bradley walked into the shack, where there were four girls and four boys who looked at him suspiciously and didn't speak. Then a small wrinkled-faced woman came into the room smoking a long-stemmed pipe.

"What's the sheriff want, Jarvis?" she asked.

"It's something about Crooks," Jarvis told her.

"What's Crooks done?" she asked Sheriff Bradley.

"He's evaded the draft, Mrs. Cornett," Sheriff Bradley said.

"Which one of these boys is Crooks?"

"Crooks is out a-huntin a mess of land turtles," she told Sheriff Bradley.

"What's land turtles?" Sheriff Bradley asked, rather hesitantly.

"Maybe ye call 'em terrapins."

"I didn't know they were good to eat," the sheriff said.

"Better 'n water turtles," Jarvis said.

"Mr. Cornett, did you get the cards notifying Crooks he was called?" Sheriff Bradley asked.

"We never go to the post office," Jarvis said. "We never git any letters. We don't take any kind of papers. No ust to. Not one here can read."

"Then you've never been to the post office?"

"When did ye go to Piney Point last, Ma?" he asked Mrs. Cornett.

"One of the youngins was over thar last Christmas," she said.

"The cards have been sent since then," the sheriff said.

"Who sent the cards?" Jarvis asked, looking at Sheriff Bradley suspiciously.

"The U.S. government," Sheriff Bradley said.

"What does the govern-mint want with Crooks?" Mrs. Cornett asked, looking directly at Bradley.

"Wants 'im for a soldier," Sheriff Bradley said.

"We haint at war again, air we?" Jarvis asked.

"You don't mean to tell me you don't know we are at war?"

"I didn't know hit. Who air we a-fightin this time?"

"Germany and Japan."

He's trying to make me think he doesn't know, Sheriff

Bradley thought; he knows this country is at war. He doesn't want his boy to go. Thinks we won't find him.

"When have you been to the county seat, Mr. Cornett?"

"Hit's been over two year."

"How do you live?" he asked.

"Raise what we eat, eat what we raise," he said.

"Don't you buy anything?"

"A few clothes and shoes."

"Where do you buy them?"

"At Bert Vaughn's General Store down on the creek," he said. "Sometimes we don't go thar fer clothes and shoes. When roads air good the huckster wagon comes to the foot of the hill and we all go down and have our winter shoes fit on our feet."

"How do you make money to buy shoes?"

"Sell hides, chickens, eggs, young calves to the huckster man," he said. "Ye see the boys and me do a powerful lot of huntin."

"And you never go to the county seat?"

"Let me tell ye, Sheriff Bradley," Jarvis said, pulling a tobacco leaf from his pocket and cramming it into his mouth, "I'm the only one of my fambly that's ever been out'n this county."

"You don't have a radio to get the news?"

"Heerd one play once," Jarvis said. "My youngins haint heerd a radio."

"And you didn't know that we'd been at war over a year?"

"Not until ye come fer Crooks and told us about it."

While they sat talking in the small room the door opened and a tall red-cheeked boy with long uncombed hair walked in. He carried a basket on his arm, filled with terrapins.

"Look, Pa, at the land turtles," he said before he noticed the stranger sitting among his people.

"They air fine-lookin land turtles," Jarvis said to his son, who shied away to the far side of the room when he saw the stranger. One of his brothers whispered something to him.

"Sheriff Bradley has come all the way from the county seat to see ye," Jarvis told his son. "He says our country's at war and Uncle Sam wants ye fer a soldier."

"When does Uncle Sam want me?"

"Right now," Sheriff Bradley said.

"When did the war start?" the boy asked, knocking the terrapins back into the basket when they tried to crawl out.

"Over a year ago," Sheriff Bradley said.

"If I'd a-knowed hit I could a-been fightin a year," Crooks said. "Do ye want me to go tonight?"

"In the mornin," the sheriff said.

"Will Uncle Sam have ye if ye'r fifteen?" the boy second in size asked Sheriff Bradley. "I'd like to go with Crooks," he said. "Would ye keer if I'd go, Ma?"

"Not if Uncle Sam needs ye."

The sun had set, and twilight was brooding over Still Hollow.

"I'll have to spend the night with you, Mr. Cornett," Sheriff Bradley said. "My mule is tired and I can't get back tonight."

"Wouldn't think about lettin ye go back tonight," Jarvis said. "We've got a bed fer ye, maybe hit's not as good as ye're ust to; we've got grub for ye; such as hit is. Did, take his mule to the stable and stall and feed 'im for the night."

"All right, Pa," Did said.

"Clean the land turtles," his father commanded. "Ye'd better be a-cookin us a bite o' supper, Ma!"

The skinny mother left the front room at her husband's command. The children followed her into the kitchen while Sheriff Bradley and Jarvis Cornett talked as darkness engulfed the twilight. Jarvis lighted a pine torch and stuck it in a wooden holder on the mantel.

"Crooks won't sleep tonight," Jarvis told the sheriff. "He'll be a-thinkin about leavin in the mornin."

"I thought he was dodging the draft," Sheriff Bradley said.

"Honest, we didn't know about the war until ye told us, Sheriff," Jarvis said. "Thar haint a house in seven miles o' here. We never hear any news, only what people tell us, and we're suspicy of strangers in Still Hollow."

While the men talked in the torch-lighted room, Enic Bradley observed the scanty furniture. There were two crudely made beds in the room, an old paintless dresser with a broken mirror, a small table made of puncheon boards. There were pictures of two old men with long beards and two wrinkled-faced old women. There was a picture of Jesus Christ and below it these words were framed, GOD BLESS OUR HOME. The walls were papered with newspapers turned yellow with age and punctured in many places, letting Enic see the rough log walls. Over the ceiling, newspapers were circled where the shack had leaked. And in one corner, a ladder was placed from the floor to a hole in the loft.

"Supper's ready, Jarvis," Mrs. Cornett announced.

"Let's eat, Sheriff," Jarvis said.

In the small kitchen there was a table covered with oil-cloth in the middle of the floor. There was a cookstove in one corner and a cupboard in the other. Pots and pans were hanging to nails over the newspapered walls. Pods of peppers and leather-britches beans hung from nails behind the stove.

"Welcome to our table," Jarvis said as they sat down.

Jarvis and Mrs. Cornett sat at one end of the table and the sheriff at the other. The boys sat on a bench on one side, the girls sat on a bench at the opposite side. There was a dish of land turtle fried brown in the middle of the table, a dish of corn pone cut in squares and stacked high on a plate; there was a dish of fried brown potatoes, mouse's-ear greens, and wild strawberries for a dessert.

"This will be my first land turtle," the sheriff said when Jarvis passed him the dish. "You don't have a ration book to buy meat, do you?" he continued.

"What's a ration book?" Mrs. Cornett asked.

"It's a book put out by the United States government that entitles you to guy your share of certain foods," Sheriff Bradley said.

"We manage to git along without that book," Jarvis said.

While they ate and the sheriff explained the ration books, the early summer wind blew in at the broken window panes and cooled the hot kitchen. The pine-torch flame that lighted the kitchen fluttered in the wind but did not go out. And above the sound of the wind and the voices around the table, Sheriff Bradley could hear the who-whos of the horned owl on the distant mountain. The sheriff ate many pieces of fried-brown land turtle legs. He was eating a rare delicacy, he thought. He never knew they were good before he visited Cornetts.

Soon as they had finished supper, the men went into the front room while the girls and their mother remained in the kitchen. While the sheriff was telling Crooks Cornett about the war, he picked up the well-worn family Bible from the crude home-made table. When he turned to the flyleaf, he found a name written in beautiful English, "Jarvis Cornett, Yorkshire, England, May 17th, 1797."

"I see this Bible's come from England," Sheriff Bradley said to Jarvis.

"Hit was my great-grandpappy's Bible," Jarvis said. "Hit was handed down from him to his oldest son, who was my grandpappy, and my grandpappy gave it to my pappy, who was his oldest son, and my pappy gave it to me because I'm his oldest son. I'll give hit to Crooks, since he's my oldest son," Jarvis said.

"We ust to have a lot more books that come from England but used 'em to start fires with, since we couldn't read them."

"Then your people are of English descent?" Sheriff Bradley said.

"Yep, they all came from England long ago and settled in these mountains," Jarvis said, spitting ambeer into the open fireplace.

My people came from England too, Sheriff Bradley thought as he fondled the old Bible and laid it back on the table. We used to have a Bible like this that came from England. Nearly all of our neighbors did, but now most of them are gone. They were the last things we lost that we brought from England.

"Sheriff, you'll have a long ride tomorrow," Jarvis said. "Don't want to rush ye to the hay, but 'spect ye's better be a-hittin' hit since ye're tired."

"I'm ready to hit the hay," the sheriff said.

"Ye'll haf to sleep upstairs with Crooks, Sheriff," Mrs. Cornett said. "Hope ye haint got no objections."

"Mrs. Cornett, I'm so tired and sleepy I could sleep on the floor," Sheriff Bradley said.

"Then take Sheriff Bradley to bed, Crooks," Jarvis said softly.

Next morning at four o'clock Jarvis and Mrs. Cornett were out of bed. She got breakfast while he fed the mules. Sheriff Bradley, Crooks, and Did Cornett were awakened for breakfast. They sat down to a breakfast of hot biscuits, wild honey, roasted turtle eggs, butter and coffee.

"You've sure got good things to eat here," Sheriff Bradley said. "First time I've ever tried a roasted turtle egg."

"Glad ye like 'em, Sheriff," Mrs. Cornett said. It was the first time she had smiled.

"It'll be yer last breakfast fer a while with us, son," Jarvis spoke across the torch-lighted table to Crooks. "Did can go with ye and ride one of the mules and lead yer mule back tomorrow. They air waitin when ye air ready to go."

Soon as they had finished breakfast Sheriff Bradley asked Jarvis what the care of his mule and his night's lodging would be.

"Ye insult me trying to offer me pay." Jarvis laughed. "Was glad to have ye and yer mule."

Crooks took a few personal belongings tied up in a pillow-case that his mother had packed for him. There wasn't a sign of emotion. There was only that deep, shy, sensitive look his mother gave him as he stood trying to say something to her. There was not a farewell kiss, as mountain people do but little kissing in parting.

Jarvis, his wife, and their children watched them mount their mules, ride away waving goodbye. They watched them follow the narrow path single file until mules and riders had disappeared into the dawn of morning in a region where the war hadn't reached.

Hand That
Fed Him

Rusty hopped like a rabbit ahead of us. He must have been glad to get away from the old fields where the snow had drifted. Soon as we reached the white-oak grove we didn't find the snow as deep. The dead leaves still clinging to the tough-butted white oaks had served as a leafy roof against the snow.

"It's better here," Finn said. "We'll find birds."

"Rusty can hunt better too," I said as Rusty held his head high in the air, sniffled a few times; then he took off like a red flash under the timber.

"Birds," Finn said, holding his gun ready.

"He's windin something," I said.

Rusty was out of sight. We stood there under the white-oak trees where the December wind rattled the leaves. We heard Rusty bark. Then we heard him growl. Then we heard a strange foxlike snarl.

"He's gone down there and jumped on another dog," Finn said.

"He's never been bad to fight other dogs," I said, following Rusty's tracks down the hill in a run. I saw Rusty standing at the edge of the tough-butted white-oak grove. His hair stood straight on his back. He growled viciously. Another dog growled, but I couldn't see it. Where Rusty was standing, the snow looked deeper.

The snow had covered a hollow black-gum log. Rusty was sniffling at the end of the log. I got down on my knees on the soft snow, looked back into the log; there I saw a pair of eyes.

"Come, Finn," I yelled. "It's a fox in a hollow log."

Finn came plowing through the snow under the trees.

"Can't be a fox," Finn said. "Fox is too smart to hole up in a log."

There weren't any tracks around the log, only the fresh tracks we had made. What ever it was in the log had gone there before the snow had fallen three days before.

"Come, doggy, come, come," I said coaxingly.

The dog whined, then Rusty growled.

"It's a dog," I said. "Take Rusty away. Maybe it'll come out."

Finn held Rusty away from the log.

I put my hand back in the log until I reached the dog's head. I patted its head and spoke kindly to it. I could feel it shivering, though it was resting like a possum on a bed of dry leaves. The log was warm inside, while the cold December wind whistled over the snow, carrying it like waves of white sand into drifts ten feet deep. I coaxed and coaxed until the dog came from the log.

"Look at this pile of skin and bones, Finn," I said. I held the skinny hound dog in my arms. Its skin was so mangy I couldn't tell the color of the little patches of hair left on its bony, trembling body.

"Let that mangy starved-to-death hound go back in the log and die," Finn said.

"I can't let a dog like this die," I said. "I'm takin 'im home."

"It'll give Rusty and Jerry-B the mange," Finn said.

"Not if I keep it in the woodshed."

Finn carried my gun while I carried my new-found dog over the mountain slope where snow drifts were often waist-deep.

"Go bird-huntin and ketch a starved-to-death hound dog," Finn laughed.

"After I've fed him and killed his mange, you'll see a different dog," I said. "I'll have a good huntin dog for next season."

When we reached the house I was wet with sweat.

"Where'd you get that thing?" Pa asked soon as we reached the wood yard where he was carrying wood to the house.

"Rusty found 'im in a hollow log," Finn said.

"What are you a-goin to do with him?"

"Keep 'im," I said.

"But not that mangy thing around here with our dogs," Pa said.

I didn't care what Pa said; I was going to keep my dog. I hurried toward the woodshed with him.

"When you feed a starved-to-death dog," I heard Pa tell Finn, "he'll turn around and bite the hand that fed 'im."

I'd heard Pa say this so much it made me laugh to hear him say it after I'd found a starved-to-death dog. I was afraid that after I'd fed the dog, killed his mange, that some-one would come to claim him. I wasn't afraid of his biting me, a dog that would have died if I hadn't found him. I fixed him a warm bed of coffee sacks. Then I shut the woodshed door and started to the cellar to get sweet milk for my dog.

"What are you a-goin to call 'im?" Finn asked.

"Friday," I said. "I found him on Friday."

It took me until late January to get Friday's sides filled out until his ribs didn't show. I doctored Friday for the mange; I tried everything for it. It was March before I got it killed. By April the hair had grown over the bare spots on Friday's hips and shoulders.

I let Friday run about the place. He was a pretty hound that barked at strangers when they came. He acted as if he had always lived with us and I had been his master. He was a light-tan hound with brown spots above his eyes. He kept his tail wound proudly in a semicircle above his back as he trotted about where I worked. His tail was dark brown with a white wisp of hair on it's tip.

"How'd you like to have half interest in my dog, Finn?" I asked him one day when we were working in the cornfield. Friday ran a rabbit up the mountain slope across the valley from where we worked.

"He's got a good nose," Finn said. "He never made a miscue on that track."

"Ivan Sneed offered me twenty bucks for 'im last Saturday," I said.

"Why didn't you take it?"

"Circumstances," I said.

"What do you mean?"

"The way I found that dog and saved his life," I said. "It was plain fate."

Finn laughed; but the smile left his thin lips as he watched my dog dig for the rabbit. He listened to his pretty deep bark. That was music to Finn's ears.

"Half that dog belongs to me by rights," Finn said.

"I'd like to know how you get that," I said. "You wanted me to put him back in a log and let 'im die."

"He's a nice dog," Finn said. "He's a good hunter. But somebody'll come along yet and claim 'im. Wait and see!"

"No one will get 'im," I said.

Everywhere I went, Friday went with me. Friday seemed nearer to me than my bird dog. I gave him the best bones and bread just for the kind of loyalty he showed me.

Finn offered me before the summer was over his double-barrel shotgun for half interest in my dog. I wouldn't take it. I knew hunting season would soon be here. I'd have a dog to hunt with. I could tell that Finn liked Friday more than he did Rusty or Jerry-B. Even Rusty and Jerry-B growled at Friday when I petted him.

"Rusty has never liked Friday," Finn said one August morning when we went to pick beans. "Rusty has never trusted him."

"He's jealous because Friday gets the most attention," I said.

"Pa's never trusted 'im either," Finn said.

"Pa won't trust any dog unless he's a tree dog," I said. "Wait until I carry home a sack of possums some night, then Pa'll trust 'im."

I waited until middle September before I took Friday possum-hunting. It was a good night for possums to stir, a dark night when the wind was laid, a night of warm silence when we felt the soft mist in the moonless midnight darkness. That's the kind of night when the possum stirs. That's the kind of night that all living things stir in the woods—a night when there isn't the sound of wind rattlin the dead leaves, brush, briars, and treetops.

When Friday treed the first big fat possum up a little persimmon bush, Finn offered me his double-barrel and five bucks to boot. When Friday treed the second possum up a pawpaw sprout, Finn offered me his double-barrel and ten bucks to boot. When Friday treed the third possum up a sassafras, Finn offered me his double-barrel and a yearling calf. I just laughed at Finn's offer. When Friday treed his fourth possum, Finn offered me his double-barrel and yearling calf and fifteen bucks for half interest.

"It's not enough, Finn," I said. "Half interest in Friday is worth a hundred bucks."

"He ought to be half mine," Finn said. "If you's the right kind of brother you'd give me half interest."

After he'd treed the fifth, sixth, and seventh possums, Finn said, "I'll tell you what I'll do. I'll give you my double-barrel and yearling calf and twenty-five bucks for half interest in Friday. That's all I'll give you."

"I don't care about selling half interest," I said. "What would we ever do if we took a notion to divide Friday?"

"We'll keep 'im," Finn said. "I'd never want to sell my half of 'im. We'll go halvers on the fur we ketch this season."

"I'll make two hundred bucks on that dog this season myself," I said.

Pa looked at the possums in the sack next morning.

"Ketch 'em with that dog?" Pa asked.

"Yes," Finn said.

"Tell you what I'll do, Shan," Pa said. "I'll give you any cow on the place for half interest in your dog."

"Finn offered me more than a cow last night," I said.

"I'll give you two cows," Pa said, "providin you let 'em stay on the place so we can milk 'em."

"I'll just keep both halves of Friday," I said. "It's one time that the starved-to-death dog didn't turn around and bite the hand that fed 'im."

Pa's face got red as he walked toward the barn with Finn.

I heard Finn tell Pa, "It's sweet music to hear that dog bark up a tree."

I knew that made Pa want my dog more than ever. He tried to buy half interest twice that day. I wouldn't sell. Then he told me that it was his grub that I'd fed Friday and that he ought to have something for that. I told him that if he charged me for the grub that I'd fed Friday, he'd have to pay me for working for him. That silenced Pa.

Cane Highlander offered me a hundred bucks for Friday soon as he heard that Friday treed seven possums in one night.

"He ain't sellin that dog," Pa told Cane.

"But he's your boy's dog," Cane told Pa.

"That's all right," Pa said. "That dog's not leavin this place."

Rusty grew more jealous of Friday. He tried to start fights with him.

"All a damned bird dog's fit fer," Pa said one morning when Rusty growled at Friday, "is to fight a good dog. I'll unjint Rusty's damned neck with a rock one of these days when he picks a fuss with that tree dog."

We could rabbit hunt durin the day with Friday; then take him a possum-hunting that night and get a sack of possums. He never tired. One night he killed two coons. Pa said right then that Friday was the best dog that we ever owned. Said he was enjoying life more than he had ever enjoyed it since he was a boy. He said that Friday was worth more cows than we had in the whole community. I was glad to hear Pa say that. It was almost impossible for him to admit when he was wrong.

When Finn and I started rabbit-hunting one November morning, the ground was white with frost. The leafless frost-covered trees on the timbered hills looked like multitudes of ghosts that had been resurrected from unmarked mountain graves of the ancient dead. It was a wonderful morning to kill rabbits. It was the kind of cold November morning that made rabbits ripe to kill. This kind of weather always ripened them, Pa had told us, just like it would ripen the persimmons. We knew persimmons puckered your mouth until a frost hit them. Pa was right too. He was always right, except he had made a mistake about Friday.

Friday circled away from us that morning like he was hunting a rabbit. But he never put his nose to the frosty ground to strike a cold trail where the rabbits had played that night. He looked at me with strange soft eyes. Then he circled up the hill, came back and followed me as we climbed the steep hill toward the briar thickets where we had always found rabbits.

I'd taken a step when I felt something tear into my hip like Number 20 nails. I wheeled around to look; Friday was yankin at me with a mouthful of my hip. He didn't growl or bark. He was just biting me.

"What's he playin with you for?" Finn asked, looking back when I screamed.

"He's just playin rough," I said, as he let his hold go to grab me again.

I couldn't believe it. I couldn't shoot him. I was too close. Besides, I couldn't have shot 'im if I'd wanted too. Finn stood above me; he couldn't believe it was happenin either.

"Let loose, Friday," I screamed, as he almost pulled me down the hill. "Let, loose—loose—"

I dropped my gun as I slapped at his head. I beat him loose. My overall leg was bloody where he'd bitten me.

"Was he playin?" Finn asked.

"No—he's bite—"

"Watch out," Finn screamed—"he's comin at you with his mouth open—"

I grabbed a white-oak limb and swung myself into the air. Then I locked my legs around the tree, holding there, weak as a cat and almost ready to drop. Friday ran above me, then jumped high as he could to bite me. He nipped my other hip as he leaped headlong through the air.

"Must I shoot 'im?" Finn screamed.

"You can't hit 'im for me," I said.

"I hate to kill a good dog," Finn said. "He might've been playin with you."

"It's a rough way to play," I said.

It seemed that Friday had slowed down the way he trotted up the hill with his tongue out. He eyed me in the tree. He walked past me toward Finn. Then he jumped at Finn—grabbed him by the shank bone. Finn let out a scream. He couldn't shoot, for the dog's head was over his foot. It was such close range Finn struck him with the gun barrel—knocked 'im down the hill. Then he aimed his double-barrel at his head and pulled both barrels. He snuffed his life out. Friday rolled over the hill; I dropped to the ground.

"That dog's mad," Finn said, his face red from excitement.

"Must be," I said.

"What must we do?" Finn asked.

"Have to cut his head off and take it to town," I said.

Finn severed his neck with his hunting knife. We limped home on bloody legs, carrying our guns and Friday's head.

"What's the matter, boys?" Pa asked. "Why'd you kill that dog?"

"He's mad, Pa," I said.

"He bit us both," Finn said.

"My God," Pa said. "I told you about that damned dog."

"What will we do?" Finn asked Pa.

"Take his damned head to town fast as you can get there," Pa said. "See a doctor soon as you reach town."

We limped hurriedly five miles over the hill to town. Each took his turn carryin Friday's head that we had put in a coffee sack. My legs were a little stiff; my overall legs were red with blood. Finn's sock was red with blood above the shoe-top.

"That bite hurts like hell," Finn said as we reached town. "He damned near stove a tush in my shank bone."

"Boys," Doc Madden told us, "that dog had to be mad to do a thing like that. I won't let you leave here without takin treatment for rabies."

"Are you goin to send Friday's head off?" I asked.

"Yes, I'll send it off to be sure," Doc Madden said, looking from behind his black-rimmed specks, "but I'd advise you boys to take the treatment right now."

"If we don't take it, Doc?" Finn asked, "what will happen to us?"

"You'll go mad like the dog," Doc Madden snapped.

"My Lord," Finn said. "Let's take it, Shan."

That day Doc Madden sent the head to the State Health Department. He gave us a shot in our legs for rabies.

"Now you'll have to come back to this office every day," Doc Madden said soon as he had given us our shots, "until I give you twenty-one shots."

"My God, but Pa was right about that damned dog," Finn said. "Look what we're into now."

"How much will these shots cost us?" I asked, wondering about the doctor bill.

"The vaccine for each one of you will cost $18," Doc Madden said. "That will be $36 for the vaccine. I'll have to charge you $2 apiece for each shot."

"You'd a-better sold that dog to Pa, Shan," Finn said. "It's a-goin to cost you over a hundred bucks before we get outen this."

"You will have to pay for your—"

"No, I'm not payin a cent for my shots nor my vaccine," Finn spoke like quick thunder. "He was your dog and he bit me! You've got to pay the bill!"

"Are you boys indigents?" Doc Madden asked.

"What's that, Doc?" Finn asked.

"It's somebody that can't pay me for my work."

"Hell no, Doc," Finn said. "My brother's got a little money."

"All right then," Doc Madden said.

For nineteen more days we walked five miles to town to take our shots. Each day we asked Doc Madden if the head had come back. Each day he told us it hadn't. On the nineteenth day Finn said, "Whoever you sent that head to, Doc, is pretty slow about findin out whether Friday was mad or not. If he's that slow with all the heads, you've got to give everybody shots that's bitten by dogs."

"They're all mad, son," Doc Madden said seriously, "that jump on a man and bite 'im like that dog bit you boys. In my forty years practicin medicine not more than five heads were negative outen the five hundred heads I've sent away. That dog was mad sure as I'm stickin this needle in your leg."

The day I had my last shot, Doc's wife brought him a letter. He read the letter, looked at us, then read the letter again.

"I'll be damned," he said. "Negative report."

"Then the dog wasn't mad!" I said.

"That's right," Doc Madden said.

"Then I wish I hadn't paid you in advance for these shots," I said.

"But I bought vaccine and gave you the shots to be sure," he said.

"Then I won't be cheated," Finn said. "Give me my last shot."

Doc Madden gave Finn his twenty-first shot. Finn cursed because the needle hurt him.

We hurried home to tell Pa, for he was worried. He'd had a fifth cousin bitten by a mad dog in Lawrence County and the "madstone" that Doc Felty used didn't do him any good. He'd gone mad anyhow. Pa'd often told about his cousin's horrible death, how it had taken four men to hold him in the bed before he died and how he slobbered and come at 'em with his mouth open. He had told us this same story every night since we'd been taking shots.

"Find out about the head, boys?" Pa asked soon as we reached home.

"We did," Finn said.

"Mad, wasn't he?"

"No he wasn't, Pa," Finn said.

"Doc Madden said Friday's head was the fifth outen five hundred heads that he'd sent away that wasn't mad," I said.

"It was damned meanness workin outen that dog," Pa said.

"Shan, you's offered too much for Friday," Finn said. "You's offered more than he's worth and wouldn't take it. You can't worship anythin and have luck with it."

"It wasn't that," I said.

"Just as I told you boys," Pa said with a smile. "I was right. What did I tell you about feedin' a starved-to-death dog?"

"That he'd bite the hand that fed 'im," I said.

"Then I was right," Pa said, laughing a wild laugh like he thought it was funny.

He's Not
Our People

"What do you say, Alf," says Jim, "let's get rid o' Whirly. He's come out here to see Tessie. If he marries Tessie you know that you'll have 'em both to keep."

"Yes," I says to Jim. "I can't keep Bessie, myself and our three youngins, Whirly and Tessie too. We'd better put th' sled runners under his shoes.

"Now just how can we put th' sled runners under his shoes," I says. Jim is turnin our hound dogs loose. We had our lantern lit. We's ready to hunt th' fox. Our hounds were standin on their hind feet and chargin!

"We'll run 'im like a fox," says Jim. "Th' damn devil's from town nohow. Out here tryin to spark th' prettiest woman in th' country. We'll get 'im in front and I'll pull my little pistol and burn the wind close to him a few times. We'll run that dood through th' red-brush and dirty his pretty clothes he's struttin around here in."

"Jim, you're a smart man," I says, "to think of that. You're sure you won't hit 'im and leave a corpse on our hands?"

"Oh hell no," says Jim; "I'll just shoot a little close. When I start shootin you cut drive with a rock. Make 'im think he's hit with a pistol. Make 'im think he's plugged! We'll run 'im until he drops in his tracks."

"All right," I says to Jim. "I know you love Tessie. You just ain't been able to pop th' question to 'er. You'll haf to get braver. You'll haf to have th' heart o' a lion. Women love brave men!"

"I don't mind fightin a man," says Jim, "but talkin to a woman and tellin 'er you love 'er is hard to do. My heart comes right up in my mouth. I can't do it. When I see Tessie th' blood all runs right to my face."

It is a night in January. Just a few brown leaves are clingin to th' winter oaks. Th' ground is dark. Th' high dark hills stand up before us. Th' dogs take to th' hills to start th' fox. It won't be any time until they'll have th' fox goin.

Jim says. "Now to keep down suspicy you go in and say: 'Whirly, don't you want to go out and hear my hounds run with me awhile?' He can't turn you down, for he wants to be your brother-in-law. I've got th' pistol ready."

"Just as you say, Jim," I says. "We've hunted many a night together. We've had many a good time together. I'll do anything in my power to help you. You know I'd rather you'd be my brother-in-law as Whirly. God knows he couldn't plow. He can't do anything. He's not used to our ways. He's not our people. He's from town."

I go in th' house. Here sits Whirly in front o' a good warm fire. He has on a high white collar. If a fly lit on it the fly would fall off and break its neck. He has on a striped tie that shows between his collar and vest. He wears a silk-striped shirt. His blue serge suit is pressed so th' creases in his pant-legs would cut you like a razor if you run against them.

Tessie and Whirly are drinking coffee. They have th' coffee on a stand-table in th' front room before th' fire. Just as I go in Whirly says, "No, honey, I don't want sugar in my coffee. Just put your finger in it. That will make it sweet enough."

I just thought to myself: "Poor old Jim, in love with Tessie and can't put th' question to 'er. A good boy to work if there ever was one! Out there in th' cold January wind waitin with his pistol in his pocket."

I says, "Whirly, I just wondered if you wouldn't like to go out with me and hear my hounds run th' fox. You ain't never heard th' hounds run, have you?"

"W'y no, Alf," says Whirly, "I've never been fox-huntin in my life! I'd like to hear th' hounds run if it's all right with Tessie."

Whirly gets up and grins. He says, "Honey, I'll see you later. I want to hear th' hounds run th' fox. You don't mind, do you, honey?"

"Oh no, darlin," says Tessie. "But ain't you afraid you'll ruin that good suit o' clothes out in th' brush?"

"Oh no, honey," says Whirly, "and they's plenty more where these come from."

"Whirly, this is Jim," I says, "th' boy that fox-hunts with me and lives on adjinin farms!"

"I'm proud to meet you," says Whirly. He reaches his hand to Jim.

"I'm glad to meet you too," says Jim. "We're glad to take you a-fox-huntin and let you hear th' hounds run. I told Alf it'd look bad not to invite you out for one night."

"That's nice of you, Jim," says Whirly. "I appreciate that. I've heard a lot about fox-huntin. Where are the horses?"

"What horses?" I says.

"Don't you ride?" says Whirly.

"No," says Jim, "we walk. I never heard o' ridin horses to fox-hunt."

Jim laughs. He bends over and slaps his knees and laughs.

"I might be fox-huntin a lot with you boys," says Whirly.

"That's fine," says Jim. "You may not like it. We've been run outen th' woods a few times. You know Alf and me's got th' best bunch o' foxhounds among these hills. The best to ever sniff a track! It's that crowd o' Hewletts after us all th' time. Trying to run our dogs outen th' woods."

"Oh," says Whirly, "you're havin trouble in th' woods."

"Trouble ain't no name for it," says Jim.

I can see Jim by my lanternlight. His face is brown. His eyes are sparklin as he looks at Whirly.

"You see, our dogs have winned all th' chases here lately and th' Hewletts can't take it on th' chin," says Jim. "They got a pack o' old starved foxhounds. A lot o' half-breeds among 'em. We got th' real Blue-Tick breed o' hounds. All they know is th' scent o' fox. You just wait a few minutes and you'll hear one open up on a hot track."

We walk down th' hill under th' cherry trees. I carry th' lantern. Whirly walks in front o' me. He can get th' benefit o' th' lanternlight. Jim walks behind me. There are a few big stars in th' sky. But they don't make enough light.

"Wow-wow-wow—"

"That's old Lead," says Jim. "Got a hot track on th' Jurdan pint. Let's be off."

"Yeppppppp."

"Old Drive right in there with 'im," I says. "Just in a minute, Whirly, and you'll hear th' prettiest music you ever heard in all your life. Wait until all seven o' our hounds get lined out on a hot track!"

"All in but old Scout," says Jim. "Listen to old Drive comin in there! Listen to 'em drive that fox! Listen to Fleet!"

"Yes," I says, "listen to Rags, Speed, and old Belle!"

"If th' Hewletts'll stay outen it," says Jim, "and let us have peace for one night. This comin outen th' woods and runnin us in, I'm gettin tired o' it."

"Fellars," says Whirly turnin around and speakin to me, "I'll like this life. I think the music of barking hounds is pretty."

"Ow-ow-ow-ooo!"

"Old Scout," I says. "He's right in there now. Listen to 'em go, won't you! Right toward th' Barney Tunnel and Buzzard Roost."

"Turn to your right, Whirly," I says. "Take up this path so we can get on top o' th' hill. We can hear 'em better up there. We can hear 'em go down in th' deep hollers and come out on th' ridges again."

It is a long path to th' top o' th' hill. Whirly walks in front o' me with a big checked overcoat on over his blue serge suit.

I hold up my hand for the signal.

"Pow-pow-pow-pow!"

"They're behind us," says Jim, "I felt th' wind from a bullet. Right behind us. It's th' Hewletts! Go!"

"Which way?" says Whirly.

"Up th' hill," I says. "Follow th' path in front o' you!"

"Pow-pow!"

"Did th' get you," I holler to Jim.

"No," says Jim. "A bullet grazed my ear. Oh Lord!"

"Come on," I says, "Whirly is a runner!"

Whirly is in front. His big overcoat is hittin his heels every jump. He is pantin like a horse. Right up th' hill—a path with big greenbriar patches on both sides. Sprouts among th' greenbriars and a big wall o' brush no man can get through!

"Pow-pow-pow!"

"Oh, Lord," says Whirly as he pulls his overcoat off on th' run. He throws it down in th' middle o' th' path.

I pull a round rock from my pocket. I let th' rock go. I holler, "Rocks! Watch out!"

"Oh," says Whirly, "I felt th' wind."

"Keep goin, boys," says Jim. "To your left at th' top o' th' hill."

I pull another rock from my pocket. I cut drive at Whirly.

"Crack," goes th' rock on a oak tree right above Whirly's head. We cannot hear th' hounds now. We do not listen for them.

Just as Whirly tops th' hill he hollers, "Thank God! God be praised."

He makes a sharp turn to th' left for th' big timber road. I cut drive with another rock. It pops Whirly right on th' leg.

"I'm hit," says Whirly, "oh my Lord!"

"Pow-pow-pow!" Jim is behind us banging away with his .32 pistol. Th' bullets wheeze in th' brush.

"I'm scinted by a ball," I holler. "Oh heavens on earth! Let's go, boys!"

Jim is right beside me. Whirly is gainin ground on us with one lame leg. Jim says to me, "Let me nearer until I can get one good crack at 'im with a rock!" Whirly pulls his coat, throws it in th' road and keeps goin. I cut drive with another rock. It hits in th' brush-tops above Whirly's head. We run right out th' ridge. Whirly is still in th' lead. Jim passes me up like a streak o' wind. We're headin straight toward th' Jurdan pint and th' old Three-Mile house where we used to meet and play poker. Th' ridge road leads down th' pint and straight to th' old Three-Mile house. Just one creek to cross when we get near th' old house.

Whirly pulls his vest. He throws it on th' road. He keeps goin. His white silk shirt is filled like a balloon in th' wind. Right down th' pint—he is gainin ground all th' time even if his leg is lame.

Just as Whirly gets to th' creek Jim elbows his arm and

whirls a rock like a bullet. He pulls his pistol and shoots once. I see two dark long things like th' prongs o' a tree turn up in th' air above th' creek and th' balloon white shirt go down to th' ground.

"They got Whirly," says Jim. "Come quick. Th' Hewletts got Whirly."

We run down to th' creek. Whirly is lyin there in th' water. Th' blood is pourin offen his temple.

"Th' Hewletts have knocked Whirly cuckoo sure as God made little green apples," says Jim.

We carry Whirly outen th' water and throw 'im down on th' creek bank. I says, "Jim, I feel sorry for Whirly. Knocked cold as a cucumber. He don't know th' ways o' these woods."

"He wanted to marry Tessie and be a great fox-hunter," says Jim.

Jim brings his cap filled with water and pours it on Whirly's hot face. Whirly begins to squirm like a snake on th' ground.

"Where am I plugged?" says Whirly.

"You ain't plugged, Whirly," says Jim: "you've been scint on th' temple. Come nigh as a pea gettin you though. If th' bullet had cut in a quarter o' a inch closer you'd a-been a dead man."

I get Whirly by one shoulder. Jim gets 'im by th' other. We hobble over to th' Three-Mile house with Whirly. When we get in th' house Whirly falls on his knees. Of all th' pitiful prayers you ever heard a sinner pray Whirly prays it. It is to save us from th' Hewletts. I hang th' lantern on a nail. Jim builds a fire from some old boards in th' house. I take a white handkerchief from my pocket and bandage Whirly's head when he finishes his prayer.

"Do you feel all right now?" says Jim.

"I feel a lot better," says Whirly.

"We're safe in this house, Whirly," I says.

"How about a little poker, boys?" says Jim.

"It suits me," I says, "while Whirly's gettin all right and we're waitin for th' dogs."

"I don't mind a little poker," says Whirly.

I'll declare if Whirly doesn't sit right here by th' fire with a blood-soaked bandage around his head and lose twenty-seven dollars and fifteen cents. Jim takes it. Old Whirly tries to be a good sport. Jim takes th' last dime I have.

"How about puttin in this seventeen-jeweled Elgin watch that stands railroad inspection," says Whirly, "at twenty dollars, and winner of this hand takes th' pile."

"Suits me," says Jim, "I'll play you twenty dollars against it."

Whirly's watch is th' prettiest turnip you ever laid two peepers on. It has Tessie's picture in it too. Jim's eyes get big as he looks at the watch. When Jim pulls his card from the hold he has four aces. He takes th' watch.

"I've had bad luck," says Whirly, "but I can take it. I can take it on th' chin."

"You can't tell what'll happen before th' night is over," says Jim. "Th' Hewletts are a sneakin bunch o' people. They won't come to this house, but they're liable to be hid in th' brush waitin."

It is three o'clock in th' mornin. We leave th' Three-Mile house. When we walk outside Jim whirls a rock over our heads. It buzzes through th' air. Whirly starts like a shot outen a gun. Right down th' Old Line Special wagon road that leads back to town.

Jim says, "It's th' damned Hewletts again. Let's be off, men! Let's be off."

"Pow-pow-pow!"

"Damned funny," says Whirly, runnin in th' January wind without a coat.

He is thirty yards ahead of us. I am stiff from th' run we've just had.

"Any damned fellar," says Jim, "that would pray to God Almighty then set down and play poker ought to be shot."

He turns th' pistol toward Whirly. He empties it. Whirly beats it down th' road toward town. He is hollerin every jump. Jim just burns the wind close to Whirly.

"Don't want to kill 'im," says Jim, "but just want to make 'im think he's shot."

We turn up past the Three-Mile graveyard to th' road that leads us home.

"If he ever comes again," says Jim, "I'll feed 'im th' genuine hot lead."

"A shame," I says, "we did not get to hear more o' th' chase. They've done their runnin tonight around Buzzard Roost."

"A hunt lost," Jim says, "but I'll get Tessie. I don't think Tessie'll turn me down when I show 'er Whirly's watch with 'er picture in it. Whirly give it to me because he'd found out he didn't love 'er."

"Yes," says I, "it's a shame he's got a girl so much prettier in town. He ought not to have come out here and made love to 'er."

We walk slowly home through the early morning mists. Jim has a smile on his sleepy face.

South America
and Tiger Tom

When I left my four brothers and five sisters to stay with Grandpa Watson, my pa said, "Adger, it will be lonesome for you there, but Pap and Mom are gettin old and they need you to help them in the store." But my pa sure made a mistake when he said the place was lonely. There was more noise in Grandma's and Grandpa's house and store than anywhere I'd ever been. I had been to some noisy Sunday baseball games between the Tiger Bottom Boys and the Mount Ebo Indians where the fans stood on each side of the ball diamond and called each other names. They threw small rocks and clods of dirt at each other. But the Sunday afternoon noise there couldn't equal the noise in Grandpa's and Grandma's store.

Maybe I'd better tell you that the store was the front part of the house. And the house-and-store was between the

Tiger River Road and the Tiger River, right where the Three Prong Valley Road came in. "Best location in the world," Grandpa said. "Get the Three Prong Valley trade and the downriver and upriver Tiger River Valley trade." And my grandpa did get about all the trade. Chad Harris, Billie King, and Troy Evans had all put up stores, but they couldn't compete with Grandpa. Grandpa thought he brought everybody in to buy from his store. Well, he didn't bring them all himself. He had help.

It was before I went there to stay that Grandma got her a kitten, and he grew up to be a big bushy-tailed cat. She named him Tiger Tom. She'd feed old Tiger Tom canned salmon right in the store until he'd lay on the floor and stretch his full stomach. Then he'd get up and go outside and run up on the side of the smokehouse or barn and catch himself a sparrow or a wren. "I hate that old s.o.b.," Grandpa would shout.

Grandpa would not more than say these words about Grandma's cat than South America would poke his head through the cracks of the cage, look down at Grandpa, Grandma, and old Tiger Tom and then say, "I hate that old s.o.b. He wants something for nothing."

Now South America was about the biggest parrot anybody had ever seen, and he belonged to Grandpa. When my Uncle Tim, Grandpa's youngest boy, operated a bulldozer in Brazil for a South American company, he brought this big parrot home to Grandpa. Grandpa, who liked all birds, loved South America.

"South America's got sense," Grandpa told Grandma. "He can talk, and your old Tiger Tom can't. All that cat can do is catch my pet birds all over the place. Dollie, your old Tiger Tom is a killer and you know it!"

"Dollie, old Tiger Tom is a killer and you know it," South America would repeat.

"All that blasted old parrot can say is 'You want something for nothing' or 'He wants something for nothing,'" Grandma said. "Dave, he's heard you talking so much about people that he's getting just like you."

"Well, he hears other people who come in here to talk too," Grandpa said. "And you can't deny South America isn't telling a few North Americans the truth. I'll say he's a truthful old bird, and I like him as much as any flesh-and-blood thing I've ever seen."

"Because he speaks for you, Dave," Grandma said. "He's listened to you until he's just like you. He can almost repeat everything you've said."

"A smart bird," Grandpa said. "Old Tiger Tom can't even thank you for the salmon and mackerel you feed him, can he?"

South America stuck his head through the crack of the cage and looked down at Grandma and said, "Old Tiger Tom can't thank you for the salmon and mackerel you feed him, can he?"

"Shut your bill, you nasty bird," Grandma shouted. "You've listened to Dave so long you've memorized his words!"

Oh, there was lots of noise in Grandpa and Grandma's house and store. Sometimes on a Saturday afternoon when everybody came to the store and Grandpa, Grandma, and old Buck Stevens who helped us out were all working to fill the orders, there'd be more shouts of laughter than I'd ever heard around the merry-go-round at the Greenwood County Fair. South America, sitting up above the crowd in his big cage so Tiger Tom couldn't get to him, just seemed to know what to say. "Dollie feeds old Tiger Tom salmon and mackerel, and he can't even thank her!"

Then everybody would laugh and slap the counters with their hands. And they'd look at old Tiger Tom, his stomach so full it looked like a small keg of nails, lying on a rug snoring in a deep sleep.

"Old Tiger Tom wants something for nothing," South America would say. And everybody would laugh again.

Now every one of our customers knew that old Tiger Tom belonged to Grandma and that she dearly loved this old cat. And everybody knew that South America belonged to Grandpa and that Grandpa loved this bird. And everybody knew that old Tiger Tom was waiting his chance to catch South America. If South America got out of the cage and Tiger Tom was in the room and he caught Grandpa's parrot (I'd heard the customers talking among themselves), this would cause a separation between Grandpa and Grandma. They had been married forty-five years, had raised all their twelve children now married and gone, and yet if Grandma's cat killed Grandpa's bird there might be a separation.

The house was a divided one, and Pa said that when he was growing up in this house sometimes the roof almost went straight up in the air when Grandpa and Grandma argued over religion and politics. Grandma was a Democrat and a Methodist, and Grandpa was a Republican and a Baptist. Now they didn't argue so much over religion and politics, but they argued over old Tiger Tom and South America. And maybe this was one reason why Grandpa and Grandma had raised their dozen children with this country store and a hundred acres of land that my father and his brothers farmed while Grandpa and Grandma and my aunts ran the store.

People used to come to argue politics and religion. The Democrats came because of Grandma and the Republicans came because of Grandpa. The Methodists and the Baptists came, and this took about everybody in Tiger Valley and a clean sweep up to the head of Three Prong Valley. I'd heard my pa tell about the big arguments that went on in the store when Grandpa refused to wait on the Democrats and Methodists and Grandma waited on them. But Grandma wouldn't wait on the Baptists and Republicans, so Grandpa waited on them and would let them have anything, whether the credit was good or not.

My pa had told me about all of this before I came. And when he'd tell these stories he'd laugh and slap his thighs with his big hands. "Nobody ever had parents like we had," he said. "We had the best parents in the world even if the roof did raise about every night above our divided house. A dozen children, and Ma got six Methodists and Democrats and Pa got six Baptists and Republicans. And now, Adger," he explained, "they've got that old parrot and old cat and still a divided house. They're old and need help, and you've got a good eighth-grade education and you can figure and help them in the store. But don't you take sides. Stay neutral."

But how could I keep from taking sides? It was one of my jobs to climb up on a stepladder and feed South America. I had to clean his cage and give him food and fresh water. First, I was afraid of him. He was such a big bird with a hooked bill and rusty-looking legs, and about the longest toes and toenails I'd ever seen on a fowl. He had longer toes and toenails than a rooster or a turkey gobbler. And his spurs were almost as big as a young rooster's. He had a wicked-looking bill and a mean eye. He had feathers greener than the leaves on the willows along the Tiger River banks in the springtime.

South America was a pretty bird. And when he said to me when I first opened his cage, "They want something for nothing," with a voice just like Grandpa's, I liked him. Old Tiger Tom never talked to me. He was just what Grandpa said, a lazy old cat that never even thanked my good grandma for the wonderful salmon and mackerel she fed him from the cans.

Then another thing happened. It was just after I went to stay with Grandpa and Grandma. "Adger, early Sunday morning before I take you to church with me," Grandpa said, "I want you to look over this store . . . look every place . . . and see that old cat is not around. . . . I want you to clean South America's cage, and when you do it, let him exercise his wings by flying around over the store. When the weather gets warm we'll let him out. He flies all over the place and roosts in the trees sometimes, but he knows his home. He always returns."

Well, I did what Grandpa told me. I went up the stepladder, unhooked the cage from the chain that was suspended from the ceiling, and I brought the cage down. Before I opened the door to the cage, I looked for the second time all over the store for old Tiger Tom. I looked under the counters and in the back storage room among the baling wire, sacks of feed, sugar, and beans. I looked in the salt barrel . . . every place a cat could be hidden.

Then I opened the cage door and let old South America out. I started cleaning and scrubbing the cage. I was working away when I heard a scream and wind from fanning wings. Old South America was rising up above the counter toward the ceiling, and old Tiger Tom's eyes flashed fire as he stood on the counter on his hind legs, his forepaws working like pistons, for he was trying to climb up the wind to get South America. And he had almost got him, for he had his mouth full of green feathers.

"Tiger Tom, the old s.o.b., wants something for nothing," South America chanted as he clumsily circled the ceiling trying to find a place to alight. "Tiger Tom can't thank Dollie for his salmon and mackerel."

I ran up and grabbed Old Tiger Tom and I made for the door.

"I threw him out," I shouted.

"I threw him out," South America shouted. I felt the brush of his wings as he went over my head and out into the brisk autumn air. He alighted in a yard maple that had shed its leaves.

When Grandpa and Grandma heard the commotion they came running. Grandpa and Grandma were dressed in their Sunday clothes ready for church.

"Watch that s.o.b.," Grandpa screamed.

It was too late, for old Tiger Tom had sneaked past me and was on his way up the tree. His eyes were on old South America and he climbed in a crouch.

Grandpa grabbed a rock and threw it at old Tiger Tom, but the rock missed by ten feet.

"Look out, South America," I shouted. I picked up a clod of dirt and threw it at the parrot. The clod burst in the air and the fragments of dirt sprinkled him. He flew over into another tree just before old Tiger Tom pounced on him.

"That infernal cat is after my bird," Grandpa said.

"The s.o.b. wants something for nothing," South America said.

"I'll say he does," Grandpa said, "and if he harms you there'll be plenty of trouble in this house!" Grandpa then turned to Grandma. "You'd better put that cat up."

"You'd better keep your parrot in the cage," she told Grandpa. "Tiger Tom was a pet kitten here when Tim brought you that old foreign bird."

"Yes, but I love him," Grandpa said. "If that old s.o.b. gets my bird he'll die a horrible death."

On one Sunday I went to the Methodist Church with Grandma and on the next Sunday I went to the Baptist Church with Grandpa. What puzzled me was that if I stayed on with them I didn't know which way I would register when I got old enough to vote, since I couldn't register Independent here. I'd have to take sides when I registered. But right now we had a cat up in one tree and a parrot up in the other, and everybody who was coming down the Three Prong Valley Road or up or down the Tiger Valley Road stopped to help us. I know the attendance fell off in both Methodist and Baptist Churches on this Sunday.

Grandpa threw rocks at old Tiger Tom, but he didn't have much power heaving rocks straight up. "When I think of that cat, it's enough to make a good Baptist lose his religion," Grandpa said. Everybody who had gathered around understood the situation. And even under these two leafless trees, the people took sides. Some gathered around Grandma and some gathered around Grandpa. No one was doing any thinking. They just took sides.

"Grandpa, don't run old Tiger Tom out of the tree," I said. "Make him stay up there. He can't leap over into the other tree. And maybe I can climb up and get South America."

"Adger, my boy, you got a head on your shoulders," Grandpa said. He was pleased. "Maybe it will work. I feel like going in the house and getting my hardware piece. I can fetch him down from that tree."

"You shoot my cat and that bird won't live," Grandma said. "I warn you, Dave!"

"No, don't shoot the cat and don't kill the bird," I said. "Give me time to climb the tree."

I pulled my shoes off and put my arms around the big trunk. I knew if I could climb twenty feet where the limbs began then I could go on. Well, everybody watched me in silence. I had caused the trouble, and now I was trying to solve the problem. Honest, it was hard climbing and I rested three times, hanging on to the tree for dear life, but I finally got my hands on the first branch of the tree. The rest of the way up was easy. South America didn't try to fly. I don't think he could have flown down, because he was so cold in this chilly October air that his wings were stiff. So I just lifted him from his perch, put him on my shoulder, and I felt his long toenails grip me like a vise through my sweater and shirt. It was painful, but I gritted my teeth and scooted down the tree with him. And when my feet hit the ground, Grandpa ran up and lifted South America from my shoulder. "My South America," he said, "old Tiger Tom wants you."

"Tiger Tom is an s.o.b.," South America chanted in words plain enough for everybody to understand. "Tiger Tom wants something for nothing."

"But he won't get you, South America, if I can help it," Grandpa said.

"There must come a showdown between that old bird and Tiger Tom," Grandma said. "One has to go."

Old Tiger Tom was coming down the tree backwards, his claws tearing up the bark, and Grandma went over and got him in her arms.

"I say there must be a showdown," Grandpa said. "And I'm praying a Baptist prayer that my South America will win."

"Ah," Grandma said with a wink and a chuckle, "when the weather gets warmer I'll let South America go scot free and his wings will get stronger."

It was almost noon before we'd got the parrot from the tree. It was too late for the crowd gathered around Grandma, who was holding Tiger Tom in her arms, and the crowd gathered around Grandpa, who was holding South America, to go on to their churches.

"Grandpa, let me have South America," I said. "I'll put him back in his cage." Grandpa let me take South America back inside the store.

South America was happy to get back into his cage. I took

the cage up the stepladder and hooked it on the chain. "Tiger Tom wants something for nothing," South America chanted. "The people want something for nothing."

That's Grandpa all right, I thought; he's even got Grandpa's voice. No wonder Grandpa likes him. There's no other bird like him.

When I went back the last of the crowd had just left, and Grandpa and Grandma had started back into the house. They weren't speaking to each other, but Grandma had old Tiger Tom up close, holding him with one arm and rubbing his furry back with her hand.

For days after this trouble between Tiger Tom and South America Grandpa and Grandma were not on speaking terms.

"You don't have any competition, Dave," Frank Meenach said on a Saturday. "And I'm glad since you're a man of our party."

"Frank, you just don't know about it," Grandpa said. "I've got more competition than I ever had in my life."

"Not another store in ten miles," Frank said.

"It's not that," Grandpa said. He put a bag of beans in Frank's basket. "That's last on your list, Frank. Your basket is ready."

"What is your competition, Dave?"

"You mean you don't know, Frank?" Grandpa leaned over the counter, and he looked Frank in the eye and pointed a trembling finger. "Commodities in Greenwood, Frank, is my competition," he shouted.

"Commodities in Greenwood, Frank, is my competition," South America shouted in the same voice.

"People want something for nothing," Grandpa said.

"People want something for nothing," South America said.

"My trusty bird-friend, South America, even knows this,"

Grandpa said. "The squirrels and jaybirds who gather food for winter know it. Every living thing but Dollie's old Tiger Tom knows this."

"Tiger Tom wants something for nothing," South America said when Grandpa mentioned his name.

"Now they don't drive from here in big cars like a lot of people say," Grandpa said. "But they drive from here in pretty good old cars. They drive twenty miles to Greenwood on the first Tuesday in the first week of every month. They come back, Frank, loaded." Grandpa was shouting, shaking his fist.

"They come back loaded, Frank," South America shouted in Grandpa's voice.

"Commodities is my competition," Grandpa shouted for emphasis. "They drive to Greenwood and they come back loaded."

"Commodities is my competition," South America shouted from his cage above. "They drive to Greenwood and they come back loaded."

After Frank had gone and Grandpa closed the store for the day, I said to South America, "Commodities is Dave's competition. They drive to Greenwood and they come back loaded."

South America repeated what I had said, but his voice was still like Grandpa's. I said it over and over again to him. And every time I said it South America would say it back to me.

Now South America told all the customers when they came in," Commodities is Dave's competition. They drive to Greenwood and they come back loaded." A lot of the people laughed and thought South America was a smart bird because he could talk just as well as Grandpa. But Grandma was against everything South America said.

And then South America added something more. When

he'd sit up in his cage and say, "Commodities is Dave's competition. They drive to Greenwood and they come back
loaded," Grandpa would say to his parrot, "And Dave pays
taxes too."

So South America began saying, "Commodities is Dave's
competition. They drive to Greenwood and they come back
loaded. Dave pays taxes too."

And Grandpa would say, "South America is telling you the
truth. The birds and the squirrels know it even if the people
don't."

October passed and November came and went. Then December came, bringing the Christmas holidays. I wouldn't
have cared if a few more people had gone to Greenwood for
commodities. We had more work than we could do. Business
grew with every passing day. The toy and candy trade in
December was something. Poor old Buck Stevens carried so
many loads to trucks and waiting cars that he complained of
lumbago in his back. And old Buck, who was as big and as
strong as a bull, said, "It's that sensible bird up there in the
cage and not that infernal old cat that brings this trade."

Grandpa told Grandma, "People know my bird speaks the
truth."

We welcomed January and the New Year. Grandpa said
he thought there would be some letup in our trade in January, but instead trade picked up. South America sat in his
cage, looked down and told the customers, "Commodities is
Dave's competition. They drive to Greenwood and they
come back loaded. And Dave pays taxes too."

And when old Tiger Tom came in the store, alone or with
Grandma, South America would look down and say, "Tiger
Tom is an s.o.b. He wants something for nothing."

Customers thought this was the funniest talk they'd ever
heard. They thought Grandpa was talking, and they'd look
up to see where the voice was coming from. Sometimes

South America would laugh just like Grandpa after he'd spoken about Tiger Tom, commodities, and taxes. Our business increased as our house became more divided over Grandpa's and Grandma's arguments in the store about his bird and her cat.

February passed; March and April came and went. Then came the warm balmy days of May.

"All right, Adger, it's time to let South America out among the green leaves and flowers," Grandpa said. "Let him exercise his wings riding on the balmy breezes of spring." Grandpa pointed his skinny index finger at me. "But I want you to keep your eye on that infernal cat."

"If that old bird had any sense it would keep out of Tiger Tom's way," Grandma said. "He's got wings—there should be no problem."

Well, this raised another big fuss. Grandpa said South America had the right to sit on his shoulder at the table and not be molested. He said he had the right to sit on the counter in the store and not be molested. He told Grandma his bird had the right to walk any place he chose—in the store, house, or yard—and not be molested by old Tiger Tom.

South America sat around in the trees a few days. Every day he'd fly in at the open door to his cage, where I'd feed him. He knew old Tiger Tom wanted him. After a few days, when South America had exercised his wings, he flew out to meet the crows. When they saw him they took off. He tried to make friends with the cardinals, and they went away from him on whirring wings that looked like red streaks on the blue. Grandpa had about the only redheaded woodpeckers left in the country. They dined in the timber on a steep Tiger River slope on a hill north of the house. South America flew up among them, and they took off in a hurry. "He wants a mate," Grandpa said. "He wants company. But he's a lone bird in this world. Sorry he ran my redheaded woodpeckers away.

"They're a vanishing bird, and they lived where the hunter's guns never found them. I'm afraid now they will all vanish."

"Dave, why don't you get rid of that old bird?" Grandma said.

Well, Grandma couldn't have said a worse thing to Grandpa. It wouldn't have hurt him more or made him madder if she had told him to strike a match to the store and house and burn them to ashes.

"Get rid of yer damned cat," Grandpa shouted.

"If I did get rid of him, you wouldn't get rid of that bird!"

"You're right, I wouldn't! I'll keep South America as long as he lives!"

"I'll keep Tiger Tom as long as he lives too," Grandma told him.

"I keep on praying for that showdown," Grandpa said.

"There won't be any showdown," Grandma said. "I don't have to pray over such a pagan thing. If the showdown comes, I know my cat will do the showing."

Right now South America was flying from tree to tree like a crow. He was flying to the hilltops like a hawk. He was trying to find himself a wife-bird. Maybe he was trying to find company. But when he told the crows, the cardinals, chicken hawks, owls, redheaded woodpeckers, "Old Tiger Tom wants something for nothing," or "Commodities are Dave's competition. They drive to Greenwood and they come back loaded. And Dave pays taxes too," the birds he tried to communicate with took off in all directions. Here was a strange bird among them speaking a strange language. And he spoke just like Grandpa. He scared the wits out of every flesh-and-blood thing on wings.

"There'll come a showdown," Grandpa said.

"I hope it'll be soon," Grandma said. May came and went, and June followed. July came and the roads were dry and dusty. When a car went up or down the Tiger River Road, clouds of dust swirled after it. The Three Prong Valley Road was covered with four inches of pulverized dust. But the dust following the cars didn't bother South America. He lived in treetops, and he soared through the blue while the clouds of dust rose above the earth and then settled back down.

Well, I was the only one who saw the showdown. I wish Grandpa and Grandma could have seen it. South America was sitting perched on a top branch of the tree where old Tiger Tom had once gone up to try to get him. Old Tiger Tom came walking from the store, twitching his tail and meowing like he had something on his mind. He didn't see South America up in the tree. He walked across the Tiger River Road and started up the Three Prong Valley Road, twitching his tail, meowing and shaking the dust from his feet.

"Old Tiger Tom, you s.o.b. You want something for nothing."

South America had no more than spoken these words until he left his perch, went down like a dive-bomber and his sharp claws went into old Tiger Tom's back. Tiger Tom let out a squall that could be heard a half mile away as he clawed at the wind, and South America came up with the tomcat in his claws. He was lifting a load, but he was a big bird with a wide wingspread. And when he rose to about forty feet with the screaming cat that couldn't reach up to bite him for looking at the dusty road below, South America stalled on the wind, and then he let his old enemy slide from his claws while he flew higher and began to circle. But I watched old Tiger Tom coming back toward the earth with his feet spread out, his bushy tail riding on the wind, his head thrust forward like he was trying to run.

When old Tiger Tom hit the four inches of pulverized dust on the Three Prong Valley Road, he hit running. I couldn't see too well for the cloud of dust. There weren't two inches of space between his belly and the dust on the road. He didn't take time to shake the dust from his feet, and he didn't meow and work his tail now. His feet looked like they were stepping on the wind. He was running up the road faster than a blowing wind, while South America circled back and alighted on his perch in the topmost branch of the elm tree. The last anybody ever saw of old Tiger Tom was a small wisp of dust that rose up in the first bend of the Three Prong Valley Road.

"Old Tiger Tom, the s.o.b., wants something for nothing," said South America high in the elm tree above me. "Commodities is Dave's competition. They drive to Greenwood and they come back loaded. And Dave pays taxes too."

I walked slowly into the store to tell Grandpa and Grandma what had happened.

April

I just couldn't go to sleep last night. Spring of the year here, and the moon came in at the window and fell across my bed. There was a bright strip of moonlight across my head. The whippoorwills kept hollerin to one another in the apple trees by the well. I could see the apple blossoms in the moonlight. I could hear the beetles.

"Roll out, Arabella," Shuttlefoot said as he got out of bed and lit the lamp. "Tater's goin to be here today to help me plant corn. Got to get out of here if we get anything done."

I was a little drowsy but I jumped up and got my dress. I went to the dabblin pan and washed. Then I started makin biscuits. Shuttlefoot always puts a fire in the stove for me. That's the first thing he does after he gets up of a mornin.

I fixed a good breakfast for Shuttlefoot. I had hot biscuits, black coffee, peaches, wild honey, fried eggs, bacon, and milk gravy. You ought to watch Shuttlefoot eat. He can clean up a whole table of food. This mornin he was in a hurry. "Tater's not here yet and it's broad daylight," Shuttlefoot stormed.

I heard Tater coming. I was out on the porch when Tater came up the road. "I'm a little late," Tater said to Shuttlefoot.

"I see you are," Shuttlefoot snorted.

"We caught a big fat possum last night and we had a time gettin 'im cooked for breakfast," Tater said.

Catchin possums out of season and eatin one for breakfast! That's the Risters for you! They take a split-bottom basket and pick up the terrapins and eat 'em! They eat all kinds of berries and a lot of roots and barks. They are strong people. Shuttlefoot says Tater is the strongest man he has ever hired to help do a day's work. He's the only man Shuttlefoot can't run to the shade.

While Tater and Shuttlefoot were in the field workin today, a rooster stepped upon the doorstep and stuck his head in at the door and crowed. "That's a sign somethin is goin to happen around this place," I thought. "First time anything like this has happened in twenty years around my house. A rooster stepped up and crowed in Ma's door once and Brother John was shot the next day."

I went on with my work, mouldin my butter and puttin it in crocks on the cellar rocks, gettin bread on the stove for supper and the pone bread for Tater and Shuttlefoot and the hardtack for Shuttlefoot's nine foxhounds. I had my sweepin to do and my cleanin up the house. It's a lot of work around this place to keep everythin goin.

It was Tuesday. Bob barked at the gate. When Bob barks, someone is comin. I ran out to the gate that faces the road in front of the house. I wish you could have seen. She just walked right in!

"I have to find a home," she said.

I could understand. I wouldn't have run her off for anything. But somehow I was jealous of another woman under my roof. She was bigger than I was. She was a strong woman with red cheeks and eyes blue as the sky. She was a pretty woman.

"Somebody get you in trouble and wouldn't marry you?" I asked.

"Yes," she said.

She didn't answer me. She was in a world of trouble.

"Honey, whatever made you come here and stop in the head o' nowhere?" I asked her. "Where did you ever come from and why didn't you make the man marry you? Any man ought to jump at the chance of marryin you."

"I couldn't get him," she said. "He's married. I've been on the road a long time. I saw this house and I just had to stop. Where is your husband? Will he run me away when he comes home?" She looked up at me so pitifully.

"Honey, if he does, he'll have to run me too," I said. "We have no children. We've always wanted a baby. You can stay here and have your baby. I'll take care of Shuttlefoot."

"Honey, what is your name?" I asked.

"My name is Gracie," she said. "Just call me Gracie! That's all the name I have."

I thought it was funny. I never asked her to tell me her last name. I wondered what Shuttlefoot would say. I put her in a room by herself. I told her if she wanted anything just to call. I wouldn't be far from her reach.

I heard the trace chains rattle. I heard Bob bark. I saw Shuttlefoot comin up the road, ridin the big mule. His dinner bucket was in one hand and he was ridin sideways with his feet hangin halfway down the mule. He rode up to the gate and slid off. I just had to run out and throw my arms around his neck and say, "Shuttlefoot, a strange woman stopped in at the gate this mornin after a rooster stuck his head in the door and crowed. And this woman is goin to have a baby. I'm so tickled."

"Why are you tickled?" Shuttlefoot asked. "A woman here goin to have a baby! Why didn't you send her on?"

"I couldn't send her on," I said. "She can't get on. It's goin to happen soon."

"Let me see her," Shuttlefoot said.

We went into the back room. Gracie was layin down on the bed. Shuttlefoot looked at her. He never spoke. I guess he felt sorry for her. She looked at him. She never spoke, but her lips curved like they wanted to speak. Shuttlefoot walked back out. I could see tears come to his eyes. He couldn't turn her out. He would have to keep her. We would have to see her through her trouble. I never spoke to Shuttlefoot about it. He never spoke to me. It was just understood.

"Don't fix Tater's dinner," Shuttlefoot said. "He brings his dinner from home now. I give him more on the day. Now you've got all you can do to wait on Gracie."

It was on the third night after Gracie came when I called Shuttlefoot. "Come out of that bed quick, Shuttlefoot," I screamed. "Get on the mule and go after a doctor!"

You ought to have seen Shuttlefoot. He yawned and rubbed his arm across his eyes. He put his pants, shirt, and shoes on. He went out the door without sayin a word. He wasn't gone three minutes. He came back on the mule. "Arabella, which doctor do you want me to bring?" he asked.

"Bring Doc Miller," I said.

Shuttlefoot acted like a crazy man. He reined the mule one way and then he took back across the yard. He cut back across the yard by the pine tree and made a beeline for the road that leads to town. I heard the mule's feet beatin a tune on the hard path. It kept gettin fainter and fainter till it was no louder than a drizzle of rain beating on the washtub at the drain.

Doc Miller came just in time. He rode a big sorrel and he beat Shuttlefoot here. The mule just couldn't run with the horse. When Shuttlefoot got here the baby was born. It would cry like a mouse. I felt the baby belonged to me. Its little hands and feet! It was a girl! I thought Shuttlefoot would want a boy. Why was I thinkin all this? The baby didn't belong to us.

Just as soon as Shuttlefoot came in the house he asked, "Everything all right, Doc?"

"Can't you hear the baby cryin?" Doc Miller said. "One of the prettiest little girl babies over there you ever saw in your life."

"I always wanted a girl," Shuttlefoot said.

His eyes got bright as ten-dollar gold pieces there in the lamplight. Gracie just laid there. He didn't know what to do. He was about to forget and then he asked, "Doc, how much do I owe you?"

"I get twenty dollars for a case like this," Doc Miller said. "Due to the circumstances I'll only charge you ten dollars."

"No, you won't," Shuttlefoot said. "You'll get your full amount."

Shuttlefoot reached in his pocket and pulled out two ten-dollar bills. He danced around and around in the room. "What is the matter with you, Shuttlefoot?" I asked. "This isn't our baby. What are you dancing for?"

"I don't know," Shuttlefoot said.

I walked over to the window. I looked out at the moonlight on the fields. It was midnight and the whippoorwills were hollering. "Holler all you want to now, whippoorwills, about your nest with two eggs in it," I thought. "Just sing all you want to. I've got a bird in my nest."

She was my baby. She was Shuttlefoot's baby. She belonged to us. I guess it was wrong for a person to feel that way. It was the way I felt, though, and I couldn't help it.

Shuttlefoot was the proudest man I ever saw over a young baby. I went into the room where Gracie was asleep. I looked at the little thing. She made me think of a little mouse in a fodder shock. I was afraid to pick her up; I was afraid I might hurt her. I left her there with Gracie.

I waited on Gracie. I cooked for Shuttlefoot and did my housework. Gracie laid in bed with the baby. "You love my baby, don't you?" she asked. "You just love her to death. You love her like she was your own."

"Yes, I love your baby," I said. "I do love her to death. I feel like this is a different place since she's come to this house."

"I want you to give her a name," Gracie said.

"I've already got the name for her," I said.

"What?" Gracie asked.

"April," I said. "She was born in April."

"Arabella, you are so nice to me," Gracie said. "I love you for it. I'll soon be ready to get up and go."

"Gracie, I'm not going to let you go," I said.

"I'm goin to give her to you. I'm going to make you a present of her. When I leave, I'm going far away," Gracie said.

I put my arm around Gracie's neck and hugged her. The tears came from her eyes and from mine. That evening when the whippoorwills began to holler, Shuttlefoot came riding the big mule up to the gate. He stopped to see the baby before he took the mule to the barn. Just as soon as he stopped I ran out and put my arms around his neck. "Gracie gave me April for a present," I said. "She gave her to me. She's mine! She's yours! She belongs to us!"

Shuttlefoot was the happiest man I ever saw.

It was just three weeks till Gracie disappeared. She left

the baby with us. "That baby belongs to me if this isn't a dream," I said to Shuttlefoot. "It's too good to be true. I believe it's a dream. I just can't wake up and make myself believe I've got a baby, Shuttlefoot!"

Spring passed. The pretty green leaves that were on the sassafras sprouts by the barn soon turned to tough leaves. The corn by the barn started tasseling and silking. The wheat turned golden on the hills and the wind ruffled the wheat. The wheat looked so pretty with the black stumps sticking their heads above the golden waves. I never was so happy in my life.

Summer passed. You know how lonesome summer can pass. Beetles were crying in the dying grass. The whippoorwills hollered lonesome-like to each other when the leaves started turning brown. The winds ruffled the dead grass on the slopes. Summer's passing always made me want to cry. I saw the summer pass and the fall-time come. Little April was growing fast. Her hair was light and curly and her cheeks were red. Shuttlefoot made a high chair. I told him she was too little for it, but he wanted her in it. He could look at her across the table. And she'd look up at him and try to talk.

Autumn went into winter. The barn, the pigpen, and woodpile were covered with snow. Shuttlefoot had to cut a path through the snow to the woodshed, well, smokehouse, pigpen, and barn. He sliced the snow with a shovel. I stood at the window and held little April in my arms. She looked at the window and said, "Yah-yah."

That's when I discovered she had cut a tooth. I ran out where Shuttlefoot was. "Look here," I said. "Our baby has cut a tooth."

"Are you crazy?" Shuttlefoot said. "Get that baby back in the house out of this snow. Can't you see there's not enough clothes around her?"

First, the greenbriars leafed a little. Then the percoon

started blooming in that ditch at the back of the barn where the scrub white oaks grow. Spring was here all right, for Shuttlefoot saw a blacksnake in a hen's nest at the barn. The hollyhocks started coming back of the chimney. I had a feeling something was going to happen. "Something is going to happen, Shuttlefoot," I said.

It was just as I expected. I was out in the yard with April. I had a little blue dress on her and a red ribbon on her curly hair. She was taking tiny steps on the grass and going "yah-yah" at the chickens and waving her little hands. Bob barked at something back of the house. I went to see. It was Gracie. I hated the sight of her. I nearly went crazy when I saw her.

"Pretty baby you have there," she said. "I've come to get her."

"You can't have her," I screamed. "Stay on the outside of this gate. Stay out or I'll hiss the dog on you." She was dressed up so she didn't look like the same woman.

"Where did you come from?" I asked. "Where do you live? Who are you, anyway? I'd like to know."

She just smiled at me. If I ever hated a woman in my life it was now. If she had come through the gate I would've knocked her down with the apple-butter stirrer that was hanging on the well box.

"You don't love this baby like I do," I said. "I'll never give her away like you did. I'd rather be dead than to see her go."

I was afraid Gracie would run in at the gate and grab the baby. I called to Shuttlefoot. April held to me like she was afraid.

"I know a little bit about this baby," Shuttlefoot said as he came running out of the house. "I've a right to hold her. I am going to hold her."

"I'll get the law, too," Gracie said. "I'll get my baby."

"Gracie is not your name," Shuttlefoot said. "You are Heather Rister. You are Tater Rister's gal from over on Shelf's Fork. I am the father of that child." I was so glad that the child was Shuttlefoot's I didn't care about anything else. I could understand now why he went for the doctor and why he let her stay. I could understand it all. I hated Heather Rister but I loved the baby.

"The child does not belong to you," Gracie screamed.

"It belongs to me," I said. "What are you doing, having babies by my husband? I'll get you for that."

I wanted through the gate to her. Shuttlefoot kept me back. I was so mad I don't remember. I remember Gracie said, "How can you prove the child is yours?"

"You remember Peachy Applegate, my mother, don't you?" Shuttlefoot asked me.

"Yes, I remember her," I said.

"Every August a peach came on each side of her cheek. She was marked with peaches. Grandpa Baritt came in one day drunk as an owl before my mother was born and he had peaches rubbed all over his cheek. My mother was marked by a peach on each cheek. And last August two little peaches, one on each cheek, flushed on April's cheek. I know she is my child. She is my baby. Wait until August and you look at my cheeks and look at her cheeks. Ain't that proof?"

Gracie ran off the hill. She ran away from us. I saw her turn around the cowpath at the foot of the hill. I had always thought the baby looked like Shuttlefoot. I went over to where Shuttlefoot held her in his lap. I picked her up and went into the house with her.

Shuttlefoot followed me into the room. The morning sunlight came in at the window. Its golden rays fell on my little girl.

Red Mule
and the Changing World

"Scrappie, you're goin' to make a real teamster," Red Mule said as I stopped Dick and Dinah to let them rest. "You like mules and they like you."

"Gee, I'm glad to hear you say that," I told him. "You taught me to like mules."

Just across the street Milford Royster was making his tractor hum. He had two plows and he was turning the dark dirt over. His tractor made so much noise Red Mule walked up close so we could hear each other.

"Do ye reckon old Milford likes his tractor as well as you and I like these mules?"

"I don't see how he could," I replied. "The tractor can't put its mouth on your shoulder and nibble when it wants something. The tractor can't talk to you."

"Then you've learned mules can talk," Red Mule said. "That's when you really fall in love with 'em. You'll be a real

85

mule man when you grow up. People will be calling you Mule, too. Only you don't have red hair like mine. They might call you Blond Mule."

Dick and Dinah had their second wind and I shook the lines.

"We've got to finish this lot before noon," I said to them. "We can't let Milford finish three lots before we finish one."

Dick and Dinah understood what I told them and their small feet went down into the dirt as they pulled against the disk harrow. Mules are powerful things, even if they have got little feet and slender bony legs. They have long ears, too. Their ears can catch the sound of what anybody says about 'em even if he just whispers. They can hear a gnat's wings on the wind five feet away and they can hear a snake crawl over plowed ground thirty feet away. They can bend their ears in any direction to catch sounds. Red Mule told me once he wished he had mule ears like Dick's and Dinah's so he could hear what people in Blakesburg were saying about him.

I worked with Red Mule every day I wasn't in school. I liked him. He never looked ornery and run-down to me. But once right before Christmas when Red Mule walked down the street, everybody looked at him and laughed. He thought people were just being friendly. But somebody had pinned a sign on the back of his coat: GIVE RED MULE A FREE SHAVE AND A HAIRCUT FOR CHRISTMAS. I ran up and jerked the sign from his coat and wadded it up so he wouldn't see it.

Milford Royster had finished plowing his three lots and had disked them before we finished one. But I didn't rush Dick and Dinah to beat Milford. Red Mule told me never to rush mules. He told me to let them walk in their own slow gait and they would be going when the tractors and the trucks had broken down. And I never forgot these words, because I liked the way Red Mule talked. When I had finished disking the lot, Red Mule walked over.

"Scrappie, you can disk more ground than I can," he said. "You're lighter on the disk."

Just then Milford raced down the street on his tractor, grinning at us as we unfastened the trace chains and wound them around the backbands. Red Mule and I led Dick and Dinah over to the wagon. Here, Red Mule poured feed from a sack into their feedboxes.

"I'll water them before you get back, Scrappie."

"But where's your lunch?" I asked, looking inside the wagon bed.

"I didn't bring any today."

"Won't you get hungry?"

He looked at me and grinned. "Oh, sometimes I get hungry," he said, "but I've not worked any this mornin."

"But you'll get hungry," I said. "Go home with me and eat."

I invited Red Mule before I thought. Mom had heard too much about his being dirty. She had heard women talk about having to hold their noses when they met him on the street. But Red Mule didn't have that kind of smell. He smelled like a mule.

Red Mule stood there looking at me. Then he said, "I'd better not go. Thank you, Scrappie."

When I got a few steps away I turned and looked back. I watched Red Mule dip his big hand into Dick's feedbox and come up to his mouth with a handful of feed. I knew he was hungry to do this. As I walked toward home my hunger went away.

"Get ready for lunch, Scrappie," Mom said. "You're late."

"Mom, I'll wash my hands and face," I said, "but I'm not hungry."

Mom looked strangely at me, for I had always been hungry when I worked with Red Mule. I'd come home and Mom and I had eaten together. Pop ran a store in Blakesburg and he took only a few minutes at noon. He ate at Uncle Bus Burton's restaurant just across the street from the store.

"What's the matter, Scrappie?" she asked me. "Something gone wrong?"

"Red Mule's not got any lunch," I said.

"Well, he could have had, couldn't he?" she said, looking at me with her soft blue eyes. "He gets paid for every garden he plows, doesn't he? He's never paid you yet for helpin him, has he?"

"But he's got mules to feed, Mom," I said. "He doesn't get as many gardens to plow as he used to. Milford Royster, Jad Warnock, and Sylvester Lybrooks have all got tractors, and they're getting the work. Red Mule's had a hard winter and not much to do. I don't care whether he pays me or not. I'll stick with him and the mules."

Mom didn't frown, but I thought she was going to.

"Come on now, Scrappie, and eat your lunch," she said.

"Mom, I can't eat," I said. "I can't eat when I know Red Mule's hungry."

"How do you know he's hungry?"

"I saw 'im eatin mule feed from Dick's feedbox when I looked back. A man has to be hungry to do that."

"But he's so . . ."

"He's not dirty, Mom," I interrupted. "I work with Red Mule. I know he smells like a hot mule. But I like mule smell."

"I've got plenty cooked," Mom said. "Go tell him to come over and eat with you."

Then I ran back across the street and told Red Mule Mom wanted him to eat with me.

"That's wonderful, Scrappie," he said. "But I ain't hungry."

"If you don't eat with me I'll quit workin for you," I said.

It was funny to see big Red Mule in our little dining room. It was almost like bringing Dick or Dinah in and setting one up to the table in a little chair. Red Mule towered over the table. And he was careful with Mom's little dainty dishes, cups, and saucers. He and I ate up everything there was on our table. We sopped our plates with bread just like Dick and Dinah always cleaned their feedboxes and sopped up the fine grains of feed with their long tongues. Red Mule thanked Mom for the fine meal, as he looked at Mom's clean, snow-white, tie-back curtains. He eyed our house so much it made me wonder where he lived. He lived somewhere out of town.

That afternoon we went back to the wagon and took Dick and Dinah to Town Branch and watered them in a deep hold shaded by willows. Then we came back and plowed Barry Kendall's garden. Jad was through with Mrs. Smollett's garden in a couple of hours.

"I'll tell you, Scrappie," Red Mule said, walking over where I was letting the mules rest, "a tractor-plowed garden ain't as good as a mule-plowed garden. You look where Jad's plowed and look where we're plowin."

It was sundown before he had finished with Barry Kendall's garden. Then we hitched Dick and Dinah to the wagon. We loaded the plows and Red Mule drove down the street as cars whizzed past. Our wagon and mules were a little out of place, and our load made a funny noise. When we drove down past our house Pop had just come from the store. But he stopped to look when he heard our noise. When Red Mule stopped to let me out, Pop took one disgusted look and turned toward the house.

"Go home with me, Scrappie," Red Mule said.

That was the first time he had ever invited me.

"I can't go now, but maybe I can tomorrow night," I said. "I'll have to ask Mom."

"Tomorrow we'll plow the potato patch for Dave Bishop," he said.

That evening when I asked Mom if I could go spend a night with Red Mule, she said, "You're goin to turn to a mule, Scrappie; you're goin to be like old Red Mule if you keep on. His red hair comes down to his shoulders and the beard on his face is as long as the hair on your head. I looked at him today and I wondered how you could have taken up with him."

"You don't know 'im, Mom," I said.

"Just a fleeting fancy," Pop interrupted. "These dreams never come to a boy but once in his lifetime. I say, Ruth, we let Scrappie go home with Red Mule tomorrow night."

Pop lit a cigar and walked over to his big chair and picked up the afternoon paper. "He'll never meet another man like Red Mule anywhere in the United States," Pop mumbled as he opened his paper. "He's just about a beggar."

I didn't say what I wanted to say to my father. He was like Mom; he didn't know Red Mule. And he'd never worked with mules.

It was a wonderful thing to me. I was never happier in my life than when I sat on the wagon seat beside Red Mule with the checklines in my hands. We had plowed the potato patch for Dave Bishop, and Red Mule had got the pay. We were on our way to his home. In Blakesburg, Dick and Dinah shied at the automobiles. The disk was making an awful noise behind the wagon. But soon we were out of town, and we went up a winding dirt road between a couple of low hills. We drove up a little road that forked up another little hollow where the hills were rising up. We came to a big barn that looked like it was ready to fall. Here we drove into the barn entry and stopped.

"Well, here's the place," Red Mule said.

"But where's the house, Red Mule?"

"Up there in the hay," he said. "Dick and Dinah and my other mules have their stalls down here."

"Gee, this is wonderful," I said. "I'd like this kind of life."

We unhitched Dick and Dinah and took the harness from them. Red Mule turned them loose in the lot so they could wallow in the dry dust and then get water from the stream in the barnlot. Then Red Mule put feed into their boxes and I threw down hay into their mangers. Red Mule had me fork more hay down into a long manger where there weren't any mule stalls.

"What's all this hay for?" I shouted down at Red Mule.

"You just wait and see," he said.

He walked to the upper end of the lot, opened a gate. Then he started calling, "Cope, boys! Cope, girls! Cope! Cope!"

I heard the pounding of hoofs and I looked up the hollow through a crack in the barn and I saw the mules coming. I lost count when some mules jumped in front of the others. They came running into the big stall which took up nearly all of the barn.

"What do you think of 'em?" Red Mule asked, following the last mule in.

"I didn't know you had this many mules."

"I've got thirty-five."

"But you can't work all these mules?"

"But I can save 'em!"

"From what?" I asked.

Red Mule didn't answer me. He climbed up the ladder into the loft.

"Now we got the mules fed," he said. "We'll eat our suppers and we'll talk."

In one corner of the barn with the hay all around us, Red Mule opened up a wooden box. He fetched a box of crackers, a block of brown cheese and a box of brown sugar from the box.

"This is our supper," he said. "In the morning I'll have a cup of coffee at Bus Burton's restaurant. And I'll let you go home for breakfast."

Red Mule sliced the cheese with his pocket knife and we ate crackers and cheese and brown sugar on crackers. I'd never had a meal like it before. And I never ate anything in my life that tasted better.

"See, I'm older, Scrappie, than your father," he told me. "I lived with my mother until she died fifteen years ago and then I've lived with my mules ever since. I never married. Some people say I'm married to my mules. I guess I am."

"Gee, I'd like this kind of a life," I said. "How come you ever to find such a good way to live?"

"Scrappie, I found it by circumstance," Red Mule said as he laid a big cracker loaded with brown sugar onto his tongue. "Trucks come first and replaced the joltwagon and mule teams. Then we got tractors with plows and disks. We've even got tractors to haul logs from the woods. So our mules didn't have any work. Men started buying 'em up to butcher 'em! Ever heard of anything like it?"

"I never did," I said. "Is that where the truckloads of mules I've seen on the highways are going?"

"They're going to the cannery," Red Mule said. "When I see a truckload of 'em, I turn my head and cry. I really cry, Scrappie. It's hard for me to cry, too. No more work for these good mules. It breaks my heart, Scrappie."

Tears came in Red Mule's big blue eyes. He sliced more cheese for me and for himself.

"I grew up at a different time," he said, eating dry crackers and cheese without water to wash them down. "Mules belonged in my world and I'm tryin to save as many as I can."

"Does it take a lot to keep 'em, Red Mule?"

"All I can make and more too," he said. "If I had the money to buy 'em and enough land to pasture 'em, I'd own two thousand. It ain't the mules' fault that this happened, Scrappie. Mules are as good to work now as they ever were. Mules are industrious. They've lost out."

"I hate to hear that."

"In a hundred years, boys like you will be askin what a mule used to look like," he said. "I used to have money in the bank. But I bought this barn, a hundred acres, and all these mules, and that's why I have to buy hay for 'em. It's about broke me, Scrappie, but I'm still fightin for mules in this changin world."

That night Red Mule and I slept on the hay with a quilt over us. I could look up through the cracks in the barn and see the stars in the blue April sky. And down under me I could hear the music of the mules eating hay. Now and then two mules would fall out and one would squeal and bite the other. Red Mule would raise up from his bed of straw and yell, "Cut it out down there!"

Next morning Red Mule stopped at Uncle Bus's restaurant and I went home for breakfast. I brushed the hay from my clothes carefully before I went inside. Mom was getting breakfast, but she stopped when she discovered more hay in my hair.

"Scrappie, where did you sleep last night?" she asked me.

"Last night was the best night I ever spent in my life," I said as we sat down at the table. "Red Mule and I slept in the loft on the hay, with Dick and Dinah and thirty-five other mules below us."

"A wonderful experience for you, Scrappie!" Pop said. "Don't you think so, Mother?"

"You got three hundred acres all fenced and nothing to eat the grass," I said to Pop. "Why don't you let Red Mule put his mules there this summer? He's got a hundred acres of woods—not enough to pasture ten mules. He has to feed 'em hay. He's trying to save them, and he's got thirty-five. He plows ground to make money to feed mules. He says there's something left that mules can do that tractors and trucks can't."

"I'll think about the pasture, Scrappie," Pop said, laughing. "I know what mules can do that tractors can't. They can eat their heads off when they're not working."

Before the pear, plum, peach, and apple trees had shed their blossoms in Blakesburg we had thirty-three of Red Mule's mules on Pop's three hundred acres.

Pop was even nicer to Red Mule. He gave him our meadows on another farm to cut for winter hay.

It was good that Pop did this for Red Mule. For the rest of the spring and all through summer, work was slack for Red Mule and me. The tractors did most of the plowing and trucks the hauling. We seldom got a day's work. Red Mule mowed the meadows with Dick and Dinah, and I helped him rake and haul the hay to his big barn. We saved plenty of hay for the winter. Red Mule saved the money he would have spent. So we went to the Blakesburg stock sales the first Monday in each month and Red Mule saved five more mules.

September passed without much work for us. I was back in school but free to help on Saturdays. Then October came, and it was a big month for Red Mule. Big River had flooded in summer and had left piles of driftwood seasoned by August and September suns. Years ago Red Mule had first started hauling driftwood to the people in Blakesburg for wood and kindling. But now Milford, Jad, and Sylvester had taken this business from him too. Then on a Saturday in mid-October something really happened.

Jailer Adam Linwood wanted sixteen cords of kindling.

Since my father, Red Mule, Jad, Milford, and Sylvester belonged to the same party, he gave the order to all of us. So each of us tried to get more than his share. The tractor drivers were getting most of the order, competing among themselves and overlooking Red Mule and me. Then it happened. Milford got too close to Big River. His tractor started spinning and the wheels sank. When Jad tried to pull him out, his tractor stuck too. Sylvester tried to pull Jad's tractor and he bogged down.

"Now we'll get the order," Red Mule said. "Let 'em set there in the mud. We won't stick. It's not neighborly, but trucks and tractors have never been good to mules. They send them to the slaughterhouse. Let's work while we can get it."

Red Mule and I laid the driftwood onto our joltwagon. We'd let the mules stay in their gait up the river bank to the jailhouse, and when we came back empty we let them trot all the way. We had hauled two loads and raced back, thinking they'd have the tractors out when we returned. But Milford had gone up in Blakesburg and got Dave Attlebury's truck and hooked on to his tractor. But the truck botched into the river and drowned out.

"They'll come to me this time," Red Mule said as we loaded and started back.

They worked most of the day trying to get their tractors out. We let Dick and Dinah walk down the river bank after the last load.

"Say, Red Mule," Milford said, walking over. "We're stuck. We're really stuck!"

"You are?" Red Mule said.

"Do you suppose your mules could pull these tractors out?"

"Yes, but my mules are a little tired," Red Mule said. "We've hauled three-fourths of that big order today. Dick could pull one of the tractors out at a time if the singletree didn't break. My mules will pull in water up to their bellies. Their engines won't choke."

Milford looked down and shoved a round gravel with his shoe.

"How much would you charge to pull our tractors and the truck out?" Milford asked, looking quickly at Red Mule.

"It will be high," Red Mule replied. "Same price I use to get for digging a well and walling it."

"You mean a dollar a foot?" Milford said, color coming to his face.

"That's the least I'll take," he told Milford. "I've got pasture for my mules now, and hay in the barn to feed them this winter. I've got money in my pockets to jingle."

"I won't pay that," Milford said.

"You'll have to have mules for that job," Red Mule said. "Heavy rains above last night, and the water might rise any time. No gasoline-pulled vehicle can pull you out of there. Only the sure-footed, reliable mules can do it. I've got all the mules left around here. It's all right with us, ain't it, Scrappie? What about Dick and Dinah?"

Dick and Dinah walked on to get the last load. We loaded the wood and were starting back when Milford came running over.

"We'll pay you that, Red Mule," he said. "I've talked to the boys. We've agreed."

"I've raised the price, Milford," Red Mule said. "Two dollars a foot."

Milford ran back where a group of men were working with the tractors. And we started up the river bank when Dad screamed for us to stop. We waited and he came running up.

"The water is rising fast," he said excitedly. "Unhitch from your wagon and bring your mules. Maybe you can save us."

"My Dick and Dinah," Red Mule said, "we'll save your tractors. We'll be over soon as we can unhitch and get the drag chains."

"Two dollars a foot," I said. "More than fifty feet to pull each tractor and truck. That's two hundred feet. It'll be over four hundred dollars, Red Mule. That's money!"

"Ah, we'll make them tractors and that truck save some more mules, won't we, Dick?" Red Mule said, rubbing Dick's tired shoulder. "We'll save more mules, won't we, Dinah? See what mules can do in a pinch, Scrappie? There's still a place in the world for 'em!"

A Mother's Place
Is with Her Son

"When a boy is sent home from college, it's a disgrace," Mom said.

"But it wasn't my fault, Mom," Finn said, pushing his chair back from the breakfast table.

"It's never been your fault when something goes wrong for you," Mom said.

Mom sat looking across the table at Finn as she finished her cup of coffee.

"Every woman around here knows what's happened," she continued. "Every time I go to town, neighbors stop me and ask about you. They ask me if you're home and what you're doing. They ask me questions I don't want to answer."

"It's none of their business what happens to me," Finn said to Mom. "What about their boys? How many have ever seen a college? Far as I'm concerned they can keep their noses out of my business."

"You're a failure, Finn," she told him. "You don't have to be a failure at anything. The metal in you can cut the toughest oak. You won't apply yourself. You've lost your ability to get down to work. You've got soft."

"I'd better get the horse harnessed," I said. "It's getting light enough now so I can see. The weeds are taking the corn."

I left Mom and Finn sitting at the table. As I walked toward the barn in the streaks of mornin light, I wondered what would happen at our house. I wondered if Finn would want to leave home. Mom had always told us we should be kept busy doing something worthwhile. She told us that idleness was the devil's workshop. Never a day passed she didn't say to Finn and me, "I want you boys to amount to something. You have one life to give. You must make your life count."

I put the harness on the horse and led him toward the field. It was getting light enough to plow now. I would be able to see the burnt-off stumps in the new-ground balks before the plow hit them. When I passed the toolshed I saw Mom and Finn. Each had a hoe.

"You're not goin to the field, Mom?" I said. "You don't have to do this."

"That's just where I'm goin," she replied. "I'm working with you boys."

"But we can do the farming," I said. "There's two weeks' work over there. Your place is in the house."

"A mother's place is with her children," she said. "I'll be with you until the corn is finished."

"She's even challenged me," Finn said. "Said she could beat me with a hoe."

"That's just what I'm goin to do," Mom said. "When one of my boys is sent home from college there's one thing left for him to do. He's got to get back to his early training. That training was hard work, sweat, honesty, and an ambition to do something worthwhile in life."

"It takes a man and not my mother to challenge me in the field," Finn said. "Mom, go back to the house. You can't last in the field."

I didn't listen any longer. I didn't want to see Mom in the cornfield again. She had worked in the fields when she was a young girl at her father's home. She had worked there after she was married and after we were born, to help feed us. I thought she had worked in the field long enough. She was fifty years old now. Finn was sixteen. How could she, mother of seven children, go to a tough new-ground cornfield and do as much as her son? Mom was like her own father. He had worked until he was eighty-eight. Then he sat in a chair in the yard watching others work. He cried because he couldn't work any longer. Now Mom was on her way to the field. There wasn't any stopping her.

The plowing was very slow, for there were stumps and roots. There were many rocks to plow around. Only last year, virgin trees had been cut from this slope. Giant white oaks, black oaks, and red oaks—beeches, elms, and maples had grown here. The broad mountainside was a graveyard of lost trees. Stumps were their monuments. Giant roots ran from these stumps under the ground. These roots were too big for my plow to break. My plow-point often hitched on these roots; then I'd have to lift the plow over on the other side of the root.

Finally I got two rows plowed for Mom and Finn. I rested my horse to watch them start hoeing. I thought Mom would take the upper row because it would be easier. She took the bottom row. She gave Finn the chance to rake weeds down on her row if he was a good enough worker to do it. She had really challenged him. She pitted her strength against her son's. I watched their hoes go up and down with the rhythm of their bodies. The hoes went up and down in unison. They worked the loamy new-ground dirt where the poplar, oak, and maple sprouts were taller than the corn. And it was barely light enough to tell the weeds and sprouts from the young green corn that grew prolifically from the sweet-smelling new-ground earth. The few minutes I watched them while old Fred and I rested, Mom was barely keeping ahead of Finn.

Before the morning sun edged over the mountain rim, behind Mom and Finn wilting sprouts lay in the corn balks on the slope beneath Mom and Finn. I breathed good wind fresh with the aroma of new-ground earth while I plowed. Often I had to stop plowing to find the row of corn. It was discouraging to look above me at the young green forest that was beginning to grow in our cornfield. The green mass reached to the mountain rim where the sun, a warm, bright fireball, was getting higher in the sky.

Before noon Mom was leaving Finn behind. But I saw his hoe going up and coming down faster. Soon Finn was close to Mom again. Once while Fred and I were resting, I heard Mom say, "Finn, you hoe your corn and clean your balks like I do. Don't leave a sprout around any stump. Don't leave a weed in any row."

By noon Mom and Finn had cleaned the corn rows and hoed the corn high upon the slope. What they had done looked good. The sun had wilted the weeds they had cut. It was good to see the green corn blades waving in the slow-moving wind over the clean soft ground. When Mom and Finn laid down their hoes for lunch Mom was far ahead in her row.

"You certainly have done some hoein here this mornin," I said.

"We got along fairly well," she replied. "Finn is a little soft. But he's doin very well."

When we ate lunch our sister Glenna had prepared for us, Mom, Finn, and I didn't talk much. Finn helped himself to the corn bread, soup beans, fried potatoes, and milk. Since he'd come home from college he hadn't eaten with as much appetite. The food on our table hadn't suited him. Now he was not mincing over the grub on our table we had grown on our hilly farm. This was grub Mom had often told us would stick to our ribs when we worked and would keep us from getting hungry.

After lunch Finn got up from the table and hurried out of the house. I went to the barn to get my horse. When I came back past the house, Mom was waiting to walk back to the field with me. Finn wasn't with her.

"Mom, where's Finn?"

"Look over there in the field," she said.

Finn had hurried back to get his row hoed up with Mom's.

"He can't stand for me to beat 'im," she said. "He's like my father. Pap could never let anybody do more than he could. In a short time I'll have Finn back to his old self. Before this summer is over he'll be wanting to go back to school, too."

"But Finn and I can farm this land, Mom," I said. "You have enough to do at the house."

"Glenna can do the work in the house," Mom said. "Housework won't hurt her. She needs to learn how to keep house. I want her to know what it's like to run a home before she gets one of her own."

Mom had always liked the outdoors more than she had a house. She had always liked to dig in the dirt out in the wind and sun. When spring came, she always wore a bonnet to shade her face, got her hoe, and started to the field. She was determined now to stay in the field to work with Finn.

The afternoon sun beamed down from the blue sky onto the loamy, pungent, new-ground soil. While my plow went slowly through the roots and around the rocks, Mom's and

Finn's hoes beat rhythmically against the dark, rich earth. Sweat ran in little streams down Fred's flanks and dripped onto the loose dirt. There was too much sweat on my arms and face for the sweat bees. They didn't want to try to sting me, for they got all the sweat they wanted. I was sweating enough to drown them. I watched Finn stop long enough to wipe his face with his red bandanna. Later I saw him pull his shirt from under his overalls and wipe sweat from his eyes. His bandanna was too soaked to absorb more. He wrung the sweat from his bandanna and left it on a stump to dry in the sun.

The afternoon was hot, but Mom and Finn never stopped to rest under a shade tree. They kept on hoeing steadily in their long rows around the mountain ridge. Mom was strong for a woman of fifty. She knew where to strike and how to strike to make every lick count. Her experiences, throughout former years of working with her father, had taught her this. She had worked in the hot sun before. That afternoon Mom and Finn reached the first flat of the mountainside. I had gained only a few rows on them with the plow.

When we quit for the day the sun had gone down. We heard cowbells tinkling on the high pastures around us where children had gone to the pastures to bring the cows home to be milked. We heard the mournful songs of whippoorwills on the ridges. Evening shadows were spreading over the land. The cool of evening was bringing new life to the corn Mom and Finn had hoed. Blades stood upright toward the blue sunless sky, unmolested by weeds now, to accept the dew and coolness of the starry night.

"We've done a good day's work," Mom said as we three and the horse walked toward the house together. "I gained a row on Finn."

"Did you let Mom beat you?" I said, looking at his red, sunburned face.

"I think she'd beat you too," he replied quickly. "But she

won't be beatin me when I get used to work again. I didn't know I was so soft."

"My sons should never be soft," Mom said.

Tuesday morning we were in the cornfield at daybreak and we didn't stop work until noon. There was a new swath plowed and hoed around the mountain slope. The young forest of sprouts and briars trying to choke our corn was falling fast. Rows of clean corn were very pretty among the stumps and rocks. Slow, lazy winds beat down the corn blades and let them rise again. Finn had kept his row up with Mom, too.

That afternoon we went back to the field in warmth from a sun that looked like a red-hot ember fanned by wind in the roof above our shut-in mountain world. Finn pulled off his shirt so the lazy winds could blow against his shoulders. Finn had met Mom's challenge. He was having it tough, too, for Mom was strong and a great worker. She had worked in the fields with her father before he got too old to work. I wondered if Finn wasn't sorry he had laughed at her when she told him she could take the bottom row and lead him through the field.

When we left the cornfield on the second day, Mom had hoed a half row more than Finn. She and Finn had left a wide swath around the mountain where the corn could breathe and feel the wind in clean rows.

Finn's appetite was growing. I had never seen him put away so much of the grub that stuck to the ribs before. Glenna had to fetch more and more grub to the table. Finn could have eaten about everything there was on the table by himself. She had to bake an extra pan of corn bread. We were all eating more, but Finn's appetite had increased the most.

Wednesday, Mom and Finn finished the second bluff on the mountainside up to the second flat. On Thursday they finished the second flat up to the rugged part of the field under the ridge's rim. It didn't seem possible when we had started at the bottom of this mountain that we would get to the ridge's rim in a week. But if we kept on going we had a chance to finish it in two more days.

"It's goin to be tough, Finn," Mom said as we went to the field before daylight on Friday morning, "but I believe we can finish this mountain this week."

"I can finish plowin it," I said. "Fred can hold out all right. I think I can. The plow jars my shoulders and arms when the point hitches on a stump."

Every few feet my plow hitched, on a rock or a root. The horse got some rest each time I had to lift the plow over to the other side of the stump. But we kept moving slowly toward the rim. Mom's and Finn's hoes sang a different song as they moved higher with the long rows. By sundown when the evening shadows began to lengthen, they had hoed halfway up the last bluff.

Saturday morning, when the sun popped over the rim into our faces, Mom and Finn were working to finish the field. I had never seen Finn work like he was working now. Finn had worked with me, too, since he was big enough to work.

"We'll get done today," Mom said as we left the field for lunch. "It's a pretty sight to see corn blades wave above a clean field."

"Mom, you didn't gain on me this morning," Finn said. "Think I'll start takin the bottom row."

"Any time you want the bottom row you're welcome to it," she said proudly. "But be sure you are ready for it."

When we came back to the field after lunch, Finn dropped down into Mom's bottom row. Mom looked proudly at him and smiled.

Saturday afternoon at four o'clock we had finished the field. Mom's and Finn's hoes were worn so brightly when they lifted them up in the sun the sunlight on them hurt my eyes. The bull-tongue plow on my sturdy plow beam was almost worn out. It was worn so thin I would have to put on another bull-tongue plow before I could do another field.

Sweat drops the size of early morning dewdrops stuck to Mom's face under the shade of her slat-bonnet. The sun had tanned Finn's back and shoulders until he was losing skin like a snake in the early spring loses its old winter skin for a smoother, newer, prettier one.

"The big field is finished," Mom said. "This is the field you thought would take two weeks to plow and hoe. You see how you can do a job when you get down to work. We've been gettin out at daylight instead of sun-up, too. We've got out early while it was cool. We've worked late, too, while it was cool."

"We've worked in the sun, too," I said.

"I took the bottom row this afternoon," Finn said proudly.

"Wait until later in the season; then see if you are still holding on to the bottom row," she said.

"You're not working with us all summer?" Finn asked.

"I certainly am," she said. "I believe a mother's place is with her sons. I ought to know what you are doing. I ought to work with you."

"Mom, I like to work with you," Finn said.

"You boys must not forget it takes work, sweat, and honesty to make you amount to something in life!"

"Cornfields don't have anything to do with college," Finn said. "But I do want to go back next September."

I drove Fred down the mountainside at the edge of the cornfield, dragging the plow behind him. My tall mother and my six-foot-four brother followed behind me carrying their hoes over their shoulders, looking at the new-ground cornfield which covered a mountain slope from the valley to the rim. The rainbow-curved rows of pretty green corn could feel the sun and breathe the wind.

Lady

The sawmill had moved in to cut the giant trees on the farm we had rented; we were moving out. As we moved down the hollow with the last load, Pa sat on the express-wagon seat with Mom. They looked for the last time at the land they had cleared and farmed. I sat on the end of the express wagon and led Gypsy, our cow, with a long rope. Raggs and Scout, our hounds, followed the wagon.

When we reached the sawmill Pa stopped the mule, climbed from the wagon, and helped Mom down. They walked over to see the sawmill. I tied Gypsy's rope to the rim of the muddy wheel, then slid off the back end of the wagon and hurried down to the dam where several men were standing around the hole of water, a few of them sighing, others laughing.

"I tell ye hit's jist hard to drown a pup," an old man with a coal-black mustache was saying. "I've tried hit. Ye ought to put hit in a coffee sack and put a big rock in th' sack and throw hit in."

"Jist keep throwin hit in the water," said a cleanshaven young man. "Hit'll drown in a minute."

I saw the helpless pup working its front paws in the bottom of the deep hole of mountain water. It worked its way to the top. When it stuck its nose above the water, two tiny streams of water came from its nostrils, shooting a few inches into the air.

"Jist keep shovin hit back," the young man said to the short man with a beardy face. He pushed the pup back to the bottom with a long pole.

"Don't shove it back any more!" I screamed. "*I want it!*"

Mom and Pa walked over to the water hole.

"What kind of a pup is it?" Pa asked.

"It's a lady pup," the old man with the black mustache said right in front of Mom.

"Let 'im have it, Mick," Mom said. "Don't drown it."

"No she-dogs around my place," Pa said firmly.

"But remember, part of the place is mine," Mom said.

As Mom and Pa argued, the men looked at each other. And while they argued, I hurried to the express wagon with the shivering, whining pup in my arms. I pulled my cap off and put the pup in it.

Soon as we reached the house I carried my pup in one hand and led Gypsy to the barn lot with the other. Pa and Mom carried house plunder from the express wagon to the house. "We're in fer a lot o' trouble with that she-dog," I heard Pa tell Mom. And Mom didn't try to answer him.

That evening Mom fixed a bottle for my pup. She put a stopper in a bottle and then put a goose quill through the stopper.

"Poor little pup," Mom said. "She's without a mother."

We filled the bottle soon as we'd milked Gypsy. Then I fed my pup before I carried in wood, got in kindling, and drew water from the well. All the time I worked I thought about a name for her. The name that stuck in my mind was the name that the old man with the black mustache called her when he told Mom and Pa what kind of dog she was. He said she was a "lady dog." So I called her Lady Dog. But that name was a little long when I talked to her and petted her. I started calling her Lady.

The next morning, soon as I got out of bed and dressed, I hurried downstairs to get Lady from her box. She was whining but stopped as soon as I took her in my arms. Now her hair was dry and fluffy. There was a white wisp of hairs on the end of her tail. She was the prettiest pup I'd ever seen.

Mom helped me feed her. She even warmed milk for Lady before she put it in the bottle. And it wasn't long until Lady's eyes opened. She wouldn't stay in the box. She'd jump out and follow me about the house, biting at my overall legs like I was her mother. But the house wasn't a world big enough for Lady. She was soon going to the barn with me. When I started to cut cornstalks and sprouts on the steep hill slopes, Lady followed me. Soon this was not enough world for her; she went into the woods alone.

It was that summer when we were hoeing corn, I heard Lady bark after a rabbit. She ran the rabbit past me—I knew it was a she-rabbit, for most of her soft hair had been pulled out. And I knew just why, too. She had pulled it from her own body to make a bed for her little rabbits. But Lady was too young to catch her.

She often ran after rabbits. I knew her bark when she was running—little fast yelps. But on this day she barked in one place. It was a long bark. It was a sweet bark; it was music to my ears. I dropped my bean basket and took off to see why she was barking. When I found her she was barking up a hickory tree. I saw a gray squirrel right in the top, sticking to a wind-bent limb. I patted Lady on the head. "Stay, Lady," I said.

Lady stayed, too, until I got back with the gun. I laid the gun barrel across a little limb, for it was too heavy for me to hold in the air. I leveled across the barrel at the squirrel. I'd never shot a gun before. I almost closed my eyes when I pulled the trigger . . . then a great sound and a cloud of smoke—and something came tumbling down, hitting the green leaves as it fell. It was the squirrel. Lady grabbed it as soon as it hit.

One day in September when I was cutting corn, I killed seven squirrels that Lady treed on one hill slope. I couldn't cut corn for taking my gun to the hill to kill a squirrel. She smelled in a hollow beech log and barked. I cut the log with my corn knife and there was a big possum. I let Lady fight it—petted her when she did. I knew that after this she'd know I'd want her to catch a possum, and she would go after them. I'd have a possum dog as well as a squirrel dog.

When I carried my game home Pa looked at me and asked, "Where did you get all that game?"

"Caught it with Lady," I said proudly.

"You didn't cut much corn, did you?"

Pa wouldn't admit it, but he was proud of me and my dog.

When October came Lady and I spent nights in the woods together. She would tree possums like she had treed squirrels. Some nights we'd hunt all night. I'd get home at daylight, do my work around the house, then go to school. And I told the boys at school about my dog. Soon everybody was talking about the good dog I had.

"You've sold possum hides and bought your clothes and schoolbooks," Pa said. "If you don't tag her the sheriff will kill her."

I knew Pa wanted me to ask him for the two dollars so he could refuse me. I lay in bed that night and thought about how I'd tag her. I couldn't sell more hides. It was out of season. I told Mom about it. She gave me all the money she had—a one-dollar bill. I sold my marbles to a boy at Plum Grove school for a dime; I cut stovewood one Saturday for Mr. Daugherty for fifty cents; I borrowed a quarter from my sister with a promise of ten cents interest; I borrowed a dime from my cousin, Glenn Hilton. Even then I lacked five cents —but the time was up and I hurried to the county clerk's office to get Lady a tag.

"We won't kill your dog," the clerk said gently. "And I'm not going to charge you that extra nickel."

Lady was a year old when she started having boy friends. It was June when I found her under the crib floor with a family of four. And they were all ladies.

"You'll have to drown 'em," Pa commanded.

"But I can't."

"You will 'r I'll kill her and the pups," Pa stormed at me. "Son, I ain't standing this foolishness no longer. I'm going to town this morning and I want 'em drowned by the time I'm back. Put 'em in a coffee sack with rocks and throw 'em in a hole of water."

After Pa left I put Lady in the corncrib. I took the four pups to a hole of water. But I didn't put the pups in a coffee sack with rocks. I couldn't do that. When I threw the little blind pups in the water, they slowly came to the top. I'd throw them in again like I'd seen the man do at the sawmill. Then Lady passed me like a flash. How she'd ever got between the corncrib logs I don't know. I watched her jump into the water—carry each struggling pup by the back of the neck to the bed under the corncrib floor.

"Did you kill th' pups?" Pa asked soon as he returned.

"I couldn't. Give me a chance to give 'em away."

"I'll give you a chance," Pa said.

I had a time giving her pups away. Everybody wanted a male pup—just like Pa. They said the she-dogs were so much trouble. But I told them what a tree-dog their mother was. I told them the amount of game I'd caught with Lady; I finally gave her pups away.

Winter ran into another spring. Then Lady's lovers came again. This time Pa was furious. He quarreled violently with Mom about my dog.

"I'm going to kill Lady, Mom," I finally said.

Mom wiped her eyes with her apron. She didn't say a word.

I wouldn't shoot her with the gun she loved to hear bark when it rolled the squirrels from the tall trees, I thought. I would kill her with my club.

I went to the corncrib to get her. Lady followed me up on the hill where I was going to get a club. Lady watched me cut it. Tears blinded my eyes until I couldn't see my dog. When I wiped the tears away, Lady stood before me looking straight at me with her keen vixen-eyes. Her little ears stood straight as if she were listening for me to say a kind word to her—but I held death in the club for my dog. I looked at her and didn't speak. Then, like the puppy she once was, she pulled at my overall leg and whined. *I just couldn't kill her.*

"Did you kill her?" Pa asked me soon as I reached the house.

"No, I didn't," I said.

"What are you going to do with her?" Pa asked.

"I'm going to give her away," I answered.

I told the boys near home I wanted to give Lady away. I begged them to help me find a person to take her. My cousin, Glenn Hilton, found a man that would take her, since she was a good tree-dog. Ronald Jenkins, an old hunter with a long beard, came and got Lady.

Another season passed and I didn't hunt. And another season passed and I never took a gun into the woods. We had rented another farm now, and we moved to new hunting grounds.

One day in June I followed my father up the path. We were going to the field to hoe corn. We had to pass the deserted log shack where we used to live when we had Lady.

"Can't believe it," Pa said, as he stopped and turned to look at me.

It was Lady! She ran around him to me. She greeted me by kissing my hands and face. Then she ran toward the corn-crib. We hurried after her and looked under the floor. There we found four pups.

"Can't she have but four pups?" Pa asked. Then he smiled at me. "Shan, if that dog thinks that much of us, she'll never leave again."

I didn't hoe corn that afternoon. I took Lady to the new place where we had moved and fixed a bed for her puppies while she greeted Mom and my brother and sisters.

Each season I hunted with her while I went to Plum Grove school. Each spring she had four pups. But her reputation grew. When I went to high school I hunted less with Lady. When I finished high school Lady was getting gray around the mouth. She was eleven years old.

After I'd gone four years to college Lady was a little slower about greeting me.

When I started teaching school Lady was fifteen. Now she was going blind. She grew so deaf she couldn't hear me speak to her, but she could see my lips work and she knew I was talking to her. When I came home she slowly walked to greet me. She'd kiss my hands and face. She had a time getting up in a chair where she slept on the back porch. We sawed the legs from the chair and put a cushion on it for a bed. At sixteen she had two pups; at seventeen she had one puppy, though she was totally blind, totally deaf, and her hair was white as sheep's wool.

One morning I went out to wake Lady where she was sleeping in her chair. Her head was erect, her white ears pointing upward like she always looked when I spoke to her. But she stared with sightless eyes. Lady was dead. I carried her to a high hill overlooking our farm and buried her. And I put a fieldstone at the head of her grave and carved LADY on it.

As a Man Thinketh

"Our hounds have put Big Foot in the Artner cliffs," Timmie said. "It's time to put out the fire and go home."

Timmie walked into the semi-darkness away from our fire on Seaton Ridge. The February night was cold and there was frost on the pine needles above us. The winds whistled through these frosted needles with a mournful sound. Timmie was fourteen, but much larger than his father. His number-ten brogans whetted on the frosted leaves and made rasping sounds. When Timmie walked away from the fire we knew the chase was over and it was time to go home. The stars and the morning moon were fading from the sky. Daylight was near.

Timmie returned with his water jug and mattock.

"Timmie, what's the matter with you?" Big Aaron asked.

"I never saw anybody as careful with fire. You know there's frost on the leaves. They can't burn. This fire can't get out."

"I'd like to see you set these woods on fire," Cousin Penny said.

Then Big Aaron, Little Ed, Cousin Penny, and I laughed louder than the February winds roaring through the frozen pine needles.

"It pays to be careful with fire," Timmie said. "The earth will be destroyed by fire someday!"

"Fire," Little Ed repeated, laughing. "You like to warm by it. You eat victuals cooked by fire. How can you do without it?"

"It's an enemy," Timmie said as he started digging the frozen ground.

"Now we'll have to wait another half hour," Big Aaron said with a sigh. "I want to get home in time for breakfast."

"You fellows go on home," Timmie said. "I'll come after I've put this fire out. I'll put it out if it takes me until noon."

Timmie was a determined man. His snappy blue eyes were narrow slits. His long sharp chin stuck out like a dead half limb on a pine tree near our fire. Timmie wasn't talking. His lips fit so tightly one had to look close to see his mouth. Timmie didn't do much talking, but when he spoke we listened. We stood there and watched him dig a hole close to the fire. Then he raked the brands and living embers into the hole. He poured water from his jug into the hole. We gathered close to hear the last breaths of fire go when it met its enemy. Then Timmie raked the loose dirt back into the hole to cover the ashes. He stood upon the loose dirt and tramped the frozen clumps.

"If the water can't quench," Timmie said, "dirt can smother it. Fire can't blow out of its grave. I like to put fire in its grave before it puts me in mine."

Little Ed couldn't hold his laughter. He squealed like

Cousin Penny's foxhound, Old Queen, when she was trying to take the lead and her breaths were coming hard on an up-hill run. Cousin Penny chuckled and Big Aaron held his hand over his mouth. I turned my head away because I had to laugh when I thought about Timmie and fire. Timmie wasn't afraid of anything but fire. He was the strongest boy amongst us. Not any two of us could put his shoulders on the ground. He wasn't afraid of copperheads. Once I saw him reach down and pick one up by the neck and choke it to death. He wasn't afraid of fighting bulls, biting dogs, rattle-snakes, copperheads, or men. And the rest of us were afraid of these things. But he was afraid of fire and we weren't.

None of us could ever forget the January night when a big snow blanketed our hills. And in that great white silence, with a blue sky and bright twinkling stars above and a white earth below, we built a big fire and listened to the greatest fox chase we ever heard. There was no wind blowing that night, and we could hear our hounds when they ran in the deep valleys and crossed the ridges. With all this sweet music coming from our hounds, Timmie looked at the fire and said, "I've always wondered what a frozen flame would be like. I'd like to touch a frozen flame, lift it up, and feel its weight. It would be frozen gold."

When Timmie and his father, Bill Phelps, burned brush piles in the spring to grow light burley tobacco in new ground, they raked a ring fifty feet wide around the clearing. We never raked a ring over three feet wide. At night, when the Phelpses went to bed, Timmie shoveled the wood ashes from under the andirons and heaped them over the fire so it couldn't breathe. Big Aaron, Little Ed, Cousin Penny, and I spent nights at his home, but he wouldn't spend the night with us. He wouldn't sleep in a house at night unless the fire was smothered. Uncle Mel, Cousin Penny's father, John Howard, Big Aaron's and Little Ed's father, and Mick Powderjay, my father, all laughed at Timmie. They had never seen such an oddling grow up among our hills.

In the dry autumn and windy spring months, when Timmie saw a smoke-rise on a distant hill, he came running with a rake across his shoulder and told us. Then he ran on and was the first one to the fire. And we never had a man in our hills who could fight fire like Timmie Phelps. Our fathers always warned us never to tease him about frozen gold, and minting it and getting rich, because Timmie had saved more timber, houses, barns, and crops than any man among our hills.

Years passed, and when we reached manhood Timmie was first among us to marry. He married Ruth Hazeltine, and the night Little Ed, Big Aaron, Cousin Penny, and I went to bell Timmie and Ruth, just about everybody from the Seaton Hills was there. Timmie was handsome in a new suit, white shirt, and necktie, polished shoes and silk socks. His blue eyes sparkled above his long pointed nose and chin. Ruth's hair was as black as the charcoal we had left on the ridges where Timmie had put out the fires. Her eyes were snappy black and she was tiny and beautiful. And in that big belling crowd, Big Aaron whispered to me, "Now if Timmie could mint some frozen gold, he could buy fine clothes for Ruth and himself and he could have a fine home and an automobile. He'll never do these things raising light burley on new ground. He can't get enough pounds of tobacco because it is light when it grows in new ground." Then Big Aaron and I laughed.

Our womenfolk remained inside the house while old men, young men, and boys lined up outside like a company of soldiers. We held our pistols, shotguns, and Winchesters above our heads and fired at the sky. We marched and shot, around and around the house, reloading and firing until our weapons were hot. Small boys followed behind us, ringing cowbells, sheep bells, and dinner bells, and beating on dishpans, lard cans, and wash pans with sticks. We wanted to give Timmie and Ruth a loud belling. We wanted to give them one they would never forget. The louder the belling, the more they are loved by their neighbors. We wanted them to know they were the most-loved couple we had ever belled.

Then we paraded inside for our treat. Timmie had candy for everybody. There was plenty to drink and enough food to feed two hundred people. There were cigars for the men. Everybody ate, talked, and laughed. And we kidded Timmie about intending to ride him on a rail, but because he had treated us so well we decided we wouldn't. All went well until we started smoking.

Then Timmie got as fidgety as a June bug on a hot griddle. But everybody knew how he felt about fire. He left his pretty bride and walked among the clouds of smoke. When a cigar stub or a cigarette butt was laid smoking onto an ashtray, Timmie picked it up and rubbed out the fire on the tray. He walked among us watching our fire.

More years passed. Cousin Penny, Big Aaron, Little Ed, and I got married and we had bellings and settled on the land like our fathers before us. When Timmie and Ruth came to my belling they brought three small children. And I was married five years after Timmie. When we went to Big Aaron's belling, Timmie and Ruth brought four children. Big Aaron was married a year later than I was. Two years later they brought five children to Cousin Penny's belling. And three years later they brought seven children to Little Ed's belling. And this was the year Timmie gave up trying to raise enough light burley tobacco in new ground to support his family. Since he didn't smoke, and he was such a good worker and was so careful with fire, he got a job at the Winston Powder Company, five miles away, down in the valley between the folded hills.

He lived on in the house he had built on his father's farm. He raised a big garden, farmed a few patches, kept cows, horses, chickens, hogs, and hounds. He had to grow vegetables, and keep poultry and livestock to feed his growing family. And we never wanted Timmie to move away. Everybody wanted him to stay among us. Because, my father once said, with his long sharp nose he could smell a forest fire twenty miles away. Timmie never missed a day's work at the powder plant for seven years, and he worked seven days a week then. Yet he farmed for himself and saved more timber, autumn-ripened crops, houses, barns, orchards, and wildlife than any man in our community. He was the most valuable man we had!

Once Timmie found a box of matches lying on the ground near the powder magazine. He buried the box of matches three feet underground. If a new man, who had been used to smoking, forgot and pulled his pipe or cigarettes from his pocket, Timmie tackled and threw him to the ground in a hurry. He was powerful enough to have been a wrestler. Then he apologized to the man, let him up, and let him keep his cigarettes or pipe but buried his matches. All of the hundred eighteen men employed by the Winston Powder Company soon knew Timmie Phelps and how he felt about fire. Every year he worked for the Winston Powder Company he won the Safety Award.

The first explosion at the Winston plant blew Timmie twenty-one feet. Timmie was unscathed, and he was the only one close to the explosion. He didn't carry matches and he worked in rubber-soled shoes. But after a careful examination of what had caused the explosion, it was thought to be caused by friction of a belt. Timmie didn't leave his job after this explosion, because he had thirteen children now and he had to have food and clothes. His oldest three sons farmed the patches at home under Timmie's supervision. He worked on at the powder plant and there was another explosion. A new man forgot and struck a match to light a cigarette. The explosion took one life. Still Timmie worked on.

Timmie worked until his foreman was retired. A new man, Bill Miller, an expert in making powder, took over. Bill Miller smoked at home, but never on the job. He had been on the job a couple of weeks when Timmie saw him pull a pack of cigarettes from his pocket and Timmie ran like a tackler in a hard-fought football game and laid Bill Miller down hard. He took the matches from his hand and dug a hole and buried them. This time Timmie didn't apologize. After fifteen years with the Winston Powder Company, he left and found a new job, braking for a railway company.

Timmie had to be away from home most of the time, but his sons were old enough now to carry on the work at home. Timmie went into the mountains on the coal drags. The railroad men he worked with soon learned how he felt about fire. When the giant freight engines, blocked by signals, spit fire from their stacks and often set fire along the right-of-way, Timmie was the only man among them to leave the standing train and run to the fire. He kept a rake and hoe with him for this purpose. He'd get the fire out if the train was held long enough. If he had to climb back on the moving train and leave the fire, he was worried the rest of the day.

When the coal business got bad, railroad men with the least seniority rights were the first laid off. When Timmie was laid off, Big Aaron, Little Ed, Cousin Penny, and I took a day off to fish with him in the Little Sandy. We wanted to get together like in the days before we were married and had families. We didn't fox-hunt any more. We sat on the

Sandy bank fishing and talking. When we smoked, we threw our lighted match stems into the river so Timmie wouldn't get nervous. We remembered Timmie's saying that water was the greatest enemy of fire.

"I'm more afraid of fire than I've ever been," Timmie said while we sat on the Sandy River bank and watched our floats jerk as the little suckers tried to steal our bait. "I'm out of work and Bill Miller has been to see me twice. He wants me to go back to work at the powder plant."

"I wouldn't go back there," Big Aaron warned. "You're too afraid of fire. Can't you make a living raising light burley now that the prices are up? No danger of fire on your farm and it's nice and . . ."

"There's danger of fire on my farm, too," Timmie interrupted. "There's no escape for me."

"It's all in your head, Timmie," Little Ed told him. "You've worried forty years and you're still alive. Get that silly notion out of your head."

"Timmie, your temples are white and the fire hasn't got you yet," Cousin Penny said, grinning.

Timmie's temples were as white as the frost we used to see on the dead leaves and pine needles on the winter mornings when we left the chase.

"Fire is the world's greatest enemy," Timmie began, but he didn't finish. He got a real bite. We rejoiced when Timmie pulled in a six-pound carp. We thought he'd stop talking about fire now. But when the fish stopped biting, he brought up the subject again and we went home.

A week after we had fished together, Timmie was burning trash in his garden. He had raked a ten-foot ring inside the garden, but a puff of wind lifted the fire over to the dead grass between the stream and road. There wasn't any possible way for the fire to get out unless the wind blew it across the valley to the hills. But Timmie got scared and sent his sons after Little Ed, Big Aaron, Cousin Penny, and me. Timmie had the fire out himself before we got there. And when we arrived Big Aaron told a joke so we could laugh at Timmie and pretend it was the joke.

"I fight fire like a copperhead," Timmie said. "That's why I've got a lot of sympathy for this mean snake. A copperhead will strike back at a forest fire until he's burnt up alive and left a gray wisp of ashes on the charcoal-dark ground." When Timmie started his talk about fire we went home.

Timmie went back to work for the Winston Powder Company when Bill Miller came after him the third time. And in the next three years there were two more explosions at the plant, but no one was hurt. Timmie was knocked to the ground both times and in one a shoe was knocked from his foot. Timmie later told Big Aaron and me that the explosions at the plant were tokens to warn him. He said he'd never get another warning signal. And he knew the end was near for him. Big Aaron turned his head to smile and I bit my lips to keep from laughing. He was the same old Timmie. He would never change now. He was too old to change.

In October Timmie was working night shift. One morning he came in and never went to bed. He harnessed his horses and began hauling the hay that Walter and Ernest had mowed, raked, and stacked. The hayfield was a mile beyond his home and Walter went along to help load and unload.

In the later afternoon the blue skies changed to dark clouds that raced across the sky like long, thin-bellied greyhounds. Timmie and Walter rushed to finish the job. When they were hauling the last load to the barn, jets of lightning began to knife the gaunt-greyhound skies. Walter ran ahead of his father, who was driving the team. Timmie, who loved his horses, let them walk in their accustomed gait through the lightning and approaching storm. Walter had turned the bend and was out of sight.

Cousin Penny, who was leaving his timber-cutting in the foothills across the valley, was the only one to hear Timmie's screams. He saw the flames rise up from the wagon, too. He threw his ax to the ground and started running. On his way, he hollered and told me he thought something had happened to Timmie and to come fast. Because of the threatening storm I was getting ready to leave the field where I was shocking corn. I followed Cousin Penny fast as my legs would carry me. Cousin Penny called across the valley to Dollie, Little Ed's wife, and she told Little Ed and he told Big Aaron.

Cousin Penny got there first. But he was too late. Timmie was burning like the dry broom sage we used to gather when wood was too damp to build our fox fires on the ridges. The horses had galloped to the barn in their harness without the wagon. Their tails and hindquarters were singed brown as red-oak ashes. When Walter saw the team running toward the barn, he ran back to look for his father. Walter and I got there in time to see the last flames leaping from Timmie's body. He was as much of a charred ember as the firebrands we'd seen him bury on Seaton Ridge. Walter fled toward the house to tell his mother. Big Aaron and Little Ed came running. They had told others and word was spreading. When Ruth and their children came up screaming, Little Ed, Big Aaron, and I kept them back. We didn't want them to see Timmie now.

Neighbors, men and women, young and old, ran in from all directions. Coroner H. H. Thombs came. Timmie had run a hundred yards from the smoking ruins of the wagon. He had thrown his pocketbook one way and his wrist watch another. Lightning had set the hay on fire and wind before the rain blew the flame forward just as Timmie unhitched his team from the flaming hay wagon. The flames had covered him as he had freed his horses. This was the way Coroner Thombs reasoned his death.

The thunders roared across the sky like heavy joltwagon wheels rolling over frozen potato ridges. Lightning knifed the thin-bellied rain clouds.

"Timmie was right when he told us he'd got his last token," Big Aaron said. "I didn't believe him then, but now I know he was right."

"So as a man thinketh," Little Ed said softly. "He always believed he would go this way."

"Fire from the heavens!" Cousin Penny's words came slow. "Not from the powder plant. This goes to show us Timmie was right all the time."

The lightning lit up Cousin Penny's face. It was the color of copperhead ashes.

Then the rain came down in torrents. But the rain, Timmie's friend, which came from the heavens too, had arrived too late. The smoke rose from Timmie's charred embers like it did when he used to pour water from the jug onto the firebrands. We heard the sizzling sound of the fire's getting its last breath on Timmie.

Both Barrels

Now I was at peace with the world as I lay on my back on the grass under the apple tree and looked up at its green boughs and white blossoms while they swayed gently in the winds of May. There were many things I could be doing on Pa's small hill farm but to know and think of these things while I lay on the grass has always made rest so much better. Just like when I have stacked hay in the pasture and put a little fence around it, just enough so the cattle can reach over and eat hay from the stack. They think they are stealing the hay and will eat the worst hay Pa has. Well, in the same way I like my rest on the grass under this apple tree because I know I am stealing time.

Yes, I lay here enjoying every minute, even each little second, for I could hear my watch ticking in the bib pocket of my overalls. While I lay here flat on my back I could see the

prettiness of the soft green apple-tree leaves and the white
and pink blossoms mixed up there with the green leaves and
on beyond this I could see soft blue sky. If I was out there
plowing a slope for corn or tobacco I'd never notice blossoms
and leaves. I'd never hear a tuneless song of the lazy spring
wind. Right here flat on my back on the green grass was the
place where I liked to be and enjoy myself. This was the
place for me to get a little education, too. Everybody has
talked about my lying under this tree on afternoons of most
every day in the week when I should be here resting only on
the day God rested after he made the world. It has taken me
a long time to learn how to appreciate life. Just about everybody says I am lazy. And maybe everybody is right.

When I was a younger man, I'd traveled maybe a hundred
miles away from home on the train. And I once got a job in
West Virginia at a coal mine. That was when a man was supposed to load fifty tons of coal with a shovel into the mine
cars that hauled it out on a little track and dumped it into a
railroad car under the tipple. Well, for two weeks and three
days I showed the boys how to load coal. I put over sixty
tons into the mine cars in eight hours, not because of the big
money I made, but because my boss, Henry Domino,
bragged on me. He even asked me once if I'd roll up my
shirtsleeves and show him the muscles in my arms. "Are your
muscles made of steel?" he asked me. No finer words were
ever spoken to me than these words by old Henry. And the
rest of the week, my last days at the mine, I wore a shirt
without sleeves. If old Henry liked the looks of the muscles
in my arms I thought everybody else would admire the bulging muscles that heaved every time I came up with a scoop
of coal. One of the reasons I loaded ten tons more than any
man on the job, I had the biggest loading scoop. It took a lot
of fuel for my body to raise enough steam to lift it up loaded
and let down empty for eight hours. I often thought as I

loaded coal how much easier it would be if I could come down to the mine car with a loaded scoop and go up empty to get my scoop filled.

Well, I guess I surprised Bill Prater, Lin Darby, Ross Carter, and old Henry when I left Old Number Seven Mine. Old Henry wanted to know if he hadn't treated me right and a lot of things like that. And I told him he was about the best man I'd ever worked for and the pay was so big it scared me. But I told him how homesick I was to get back to Pa's little hillside farm in Kentucky. I told him the hills were a little too high in West Virginia to suit me. And when he asked me if the hills weren't just about as high in my part of Kentucky, I had to admit they were. Maybe old Henry knew I wasn't telling him the truth. But I was a little homesick. But my being homesick wasn't the only reason I wanted to go home.

I guess it is all right for a man to think one thing and say another. Well, whether it was all right or not, this was my nature. I was born this way. I had big muscles in my arms and all over my body. And I'd never worked to get these big muscles. I guess I'd been born to have them. So I didn't think anything about it except when little boys came up in front of me and stood and looked and often one would ask me which one of the breakfast foods I ate. I guess I sold a lot of breakfast foods for one of the food companies. I thought a lot about going and asking them for a job selling their foods. I could have done this all right. All I'd have had to do was stand before young boys stripped to the waist, inhale on my tiptoes and exhale coming down flat on my heels. Each time I inhaled I would have clinched my fists and contracted the muscles in my arms. I could have sold more of that company's breakfast food to the little boys than any twenty salesmen they could have put on the road.

As I have said, I could have sold this breakfast food and

could have made a lot of money and bought a few extra acres of old hill land that joined my Pa's farm. But, as I have also said, I'd been given my muscles to use and I'd been given a head with a brain in it to do my thinking. And as I have said, I might be thinking one way and speaking another . . . but so what? My brain hadn't been trained beyond the one-room school, for I figured that I didn't need it. Let the brain be as natural as the muscles. I can't see why a man should be partial to parts of his body and do more for one part than he does for another.

Yes, a high school football coach, Martin Purdy, came to see me once and he said, "If you'll go to Gadsen High School and play football for us, we'll make a star out of you." "But why be a football star?" I asked him. "And I don't care for the training of my mind. I don't believe my mind will accept training." "Don't worry," he said, "if you can play football, we'll give you a tutor since you don't have a liking to books. We'll get you by." That kind of talk didn't suit me. I knew what I wanted. I wanted to leave my mind, like my muscles, home-grown, as we say when we speak of corn, tobacco, hay, and sorghum cane, things we grow on our farm. I wanted to let my mind take its natural course like the streams among the mountains. We know that water follows the course of least resistance. So why wouldn't it be natural for a man's mind?

Yes, I'd met a lot of people in my rambles as far away from home as a hundred miles. I might have been farther away from home than this, maybe one hundred twenty miles. Everywhere I rambled people I met tried to change my course. And to change my course is the same as trying to change the course of a mountain stream that has worked a long, long time to cut its channel deeper and deeper into the rock. I think I've cut and am still cutting a channel into my own rock. People wanted me to play football in high school.

Old Henry wanted me to stay at Mine Number Seven in West Virginia and load coal. And when I was bumming around I never worked a day for a farmer or a contractor that he didn't want me to stay and work for him. I never was concerned too much about the wages. I didn't need very much, and if I could earn enough in a week to keep money in my pockets for a month, well, it is all the same. Why should I worry about whether I work to loaf or loaf to work?

Now it's too late for the high schools to want me to play football. I'm twenty-four and unmarried, and I live with Pa and Mom and with my six brothers and three sisters. There are ten of us, and not a one married. Most parents don't want to see their children leave home. I believe Pa and Mom would be glad to get rid of three or four of us. They know they'd have more room in the house and they know they wouldn't have to work so hard. But everywhere over this wonderful mountain country and among these wonderful mountain people where I have traveled, there is one little thing that calls me home. You wouldn't believe me if I was to tell you I couldn't stay away from home in late April or early May, no matter how hard I'd try. And, it's not my Pa, Ma, nor my brothers and my sisters that bring me back. If I was to tell you it was this apple tree that I'm lying under right now you wouldn't believe me. Well, this is the way my natural mind thinks. I wonder if it could have been trained like I've heard a lot of people speaking about the trained minds of men and women in big cities beyond these hills. Well, I wonder if this is the truth! But if it is the truth, could my mind be trained until it wouldn't want to come home to this apple tree?

I'll say right now, while lying here and looking up at the most heavenly things I've ever seen on this earth, if my trained mind told me to stay away and I know my natural mind tells me to return, that my natural mind gives me far more pleasure than it would if it had been trained. I don't think the mind should be trained and the hands educated as I have heard hands could be. I've been told myself that I have educated hands, because they can do most anything. They can fix gadgets and they can load coal. Since my hands are big, my right hand can throw a football half a country mile. And I can reach down and pick up a basketball with one hand. I didn't know until Coach Purdy told me there are a lot of men in the world that like to play basketball and football but don't have the right kind of hands. But so what? What is the difference if you like to play and don't have the right kind of hands or if you have the right kind of hands and don't like to play? All that running up and down a basketball court, for what? Just to make points and have people shouting and screaming if you do make points and cussing you if you're not "hot," as they say. So this is the way my natural mind reasons this out. I do a lot of thinking as I lay under this apple tree. I think things out before I gradually go to sleep and have my afternoons off out here.

Now to tell you more about this tree and why I like it. It has the finest apples on it, and they get ripe in late June. We call them June apples. Back as far as I can remember, Mom has fried June apples in their season for us in a skillet for breakfast. So I guess we like the trees and the ground when they feed us. Now I've never cared for the spot of ground where we raise cane every season for our sorghum molasses. Honest. I've eaten so much of that old sweet sorghum molasses on pone biscuits and corndodger bread that I hate the patch of ground where we raise it. Well, we don't raise so much any more. We get paid to rest the ground. And, since we rest the ground this gives all of us a rest every day. I'm all for this law for getting paid for resting the ground. I wish somebody had thought of it sooner. Might sound a little crazy and unnatural, but still it's a good law.

I've laid here under this apple tree and let my natural mind do some thinking. It's my way and my kind of thinking and I don't know whether anybody else thinks like me or not, but I think a lot of people think like I do. If they do or if they don't this doesn't bother me. I could lie right here under my apple tree without a cent of money in my pocket and no food, and if I got hungry enough I could eat green grass first, then I could change my diet to green apple leaves. Have you ever tasted green apple leaves? They've got a good taste. Well, I could eat green apple leaves and eat the apple tree blossoms. But I don't like to eat apple blossoms too well. Have you ever tasted them? They don't have a good taste for me but they're sweet to the bees. No, I've tasted them and they're not half as good-tasting as the leaves. I could never figure this out since both leaf and bloom came from the same tree. I guess the same thing is true with children in the same family.

None in our family is struck with work, although Pa grumbles and says he has to manage or we would starve. My brothers, Jack and Timmy, are good to help him when he works, and I guess the other boys are more like me. I guess Mom is about the best one in our family to work. She's doing something, cooking or sewing, all the time. You know in a family of ten children and two parents, a dozen people, somebody has to do something at some time. As I've often told them, we can't all lie under the apple tree at the same time. Well, there is hardly a time of day when the spring sun warms the hills and the buds and blossoms come that one or more of us children, and sometimes Pa with us, aren't lying on yard grass under the snowball bushes to keep the sun out of our eyes or under the maple or the poplar in the yard. But

I always come out here to the apple tree which is beside the potato patch and close to the barn. Pa and my brothers never come out here because it's about two hundred yards from the house. They can lie on softer grass, so Brother Adger said, have better shade and not have to walk so far. But I like this apple tree because of its leaves, its blossoms, and its fruit. It's almost like a person to me. It's some sort of dumb living kin. When I come here alone I don't have anybody disturb me. I don't have one of my brothers nor Pa lying close to me and wanting to talk all the time. I can't think when somebody is talking to me.

"Ah, you would come around me," I said. "Begone! I want to lie here and think."

I slapped with my big hand at the bumblebee but I missed him. "Why would you want to fly around my face and disturb me when there are blossoms on the trees? Get up there among them!"

So with slumber gathering in my eyes I watched the old clumsy bumblebee fly up among the branches of the tree. I coursed him like I've coursed wild honeybees from a watering place to a bee tree in the woods. I've coursed honeybees two hundred yards at a time. I can see a bee that far, and a wild honeybee is smaller than a bumblebee. I course the old big honeybee only a few feet up into the tree, then I lose sight of him in the shadows. Now my eyes were getting droopy, for I had laid here and I'd done a lot of thinking. But my eyes are good. Pa never likes to admit that I can do things better than he can, but once he told me I had the best eyes he'd ever seen in a human head. He said I could course a honeybee farther away in the clean blue air on a sunny day than any person he had ever seen.

Now I lost the sight of the bumblebee up in the apple tree not because of the sleep in my eyes but because the wind had swayed the leafy boughs and had covered up the holes where I had been looking up at the sky. The wind played peeky-boo with the apple boughs but I knew that neither wind nor bough had a mind and since neither had any sense they couldn't have fun playing this game. But I liked to wonder why two senseless things like wind and leafy boughs got together and played a game. Why? What was the point? Well, they entertained me. I played peeky-boo with them, first with eyes opened, then half closed, then with one opened and one shut. And I wondered why senseless things played games when I with sense who could play them or at least people thought I could, didn't want to play them.

I could hear that old bumblebee up there among the green leaves and I wondered if he had joined in this game of peeky-boo. That old bumblebee was having himself a right good time up there among the leaves. He was either enjoying the game played by the wind and the boughs or he was in there playing with them. Now, I wondered what went through a bumblebee's little brain. I wondered if he could enjoy himself like I could. Why was he up there gathering sweets from the apple blossoms? Was he making honey and laying it away for an autumn day when the weather got so cold he couldn't fly and had to get in a warm place like a hole in the ground or a hole in the tree to keep from freezing?

I knew I didn't want to be a bumblebee, who had a little brain and worked hard for the cold days when flowers disappeared from the earth and the snows came and it wasn't no season for the bees and I didn't want to be a senseless puff of wind and I didn't want to be a senseless apple bough producing green leaves and pretty blossoms for people to see and fruit for them to eat. Why should I want to do all these things for nothing. I got along all right. I'd rather be just what I was, a big mountain man and lie in the shade and let everything come to me. What is that old saying: "Everything comes to him who waits"? Well, whether it comes or not it doesn't matter. I like to be a man with a mind of my own, one with a natural mind, who can think. I was about to go off to sleep when I heard a loud buzz from the old bumblebee. I'd heard about dive-bombers in the last war but I'd never seen one. We don't have them around here. We don't need them. But this bumblebee came straight down out of the tree toward my face. He was mad or happy drunk on soured nectar from a blossom the way he roared. I put my hands over my face in a hurry. He didn't touch me. But when he pulled out of his dive I felt the wind from his wings on the back of my hands that covered my face. He went back up among the leaves.

"You do that again and I'll knock the hell out of you," I said. "What's the matter with you; are you drunk or crazy?"

He was back up in the leaves buzzing around, and I thought everything was all right now so I took my hands from over my face. I laid on my back on the grass and looked up, because I have never seen much looking down. So it pays to look up and not down. Well, I heard the bumblebee fiddling and fooling around up in the tree and all of a sudden here he came, another dive-bomber at my face, and I covered my face with my hands in time. I felt a little cool wind on the back of my hands when he pulled out of this dive and went back up into the apple tree, where I lost sight of him among the green leaves.

"All right, you pull that again and I'll be ready for you!" I said. "I didn't come out here to fight a bumblebee. You must think you own this tree. Well, you don't! I've been coming here since I was a little boy. Now if you've got a home up there you stay in it and I'll stay down here and we'll not bother one another. Let's have peace. Let's share the same tree—you up there, me down here. I won't bother you and you be damn sure you leave me alone."

I knew he wouldn't understand my words and how I felt toward his nonsense but I talked to him anyway, for I didn't like to be disturbed—especially not now when I was about to doze off into a sweet, peaceful slumber. I enjoyed slumber more under this tree than I did in my own bed under Pa's roof where I had slept, except for my rambling days, since I'd been a baby.

Well, the bumblebee certainly didn't understand me. He regarded me as a foreigner, when I was trying to sleep under my own apple tree. He came down out of the leaves again at me. I struck at him again and missed. I couldn't get my hands and arms up in time. If he'd have carried a bomb and dropped it I would have been blown up. Now, I was getting riled; here was a bumblebee attacking me on my own premises. I raised up and sat on the grass. "Now, damn ye, you come buzzing around me and I'll give ye more than you're looking for," I said. "There'll be a dead bumblebee right here among the fallen petals."

That bee wasn't to be bluffed, for this time he came in behind me. He buzzed around my head and ears before I had time to turn around and swat at him. Well, I had to laugh. Really, this was funny! A thing as small as a bumblebee having enough nerve to attack a big man like me. I was tall enough when the sun shone over my apple tree at noon, if I lay stretched out full length, the top of my head and my feet would be in the sun on the outside of the circle of shade. And this was the reason why I always pulled my legs up a bit, bending them at the knees, or I stuck my feet out in the sun. What I wanted to do was keep my head in the shade and keep my brain cool so I could think better. It's always better to have hot feet and a cool head than it is to have a hot head and cold feet. This doesn't require much thinking. About any ordinary person could think this out for himself. And while I had turned around this bumblebee, who had enough sense to regard my size and the dangerous sweep of my hand striking at him, came in on the back side of me again. I fought that bumblebee for the next thirty minutes. He'd come down out of the green leaves and strike me from the back side every time.

"You're a coward," I said. "Here in Kentucky when men fight they meet face to face! You keep this up and I'll take care of you, foul or fair. You don't own this apple tree! I was here before you were born."

But talking to this bee was like talking to a hickory stick. Why was a bumblebee attacking me? I didn't have sugar in my pockets. I didn't have a piece of candy. There wasn't anything sweet about me. I'd never seen a bole on this tree in winter when it was stripped of leaves. He surely didn't have a nest up among the green leaves. Only hornets and red wasps built nests up in trees. He was neither a hornet nor a red wasp—but he was a bumblebee. Bumblebees build their nests in boles of trees, in hollow legs, and in nests under the ground. Down he came again right at the back of my head.

"All right, Bumblebee," I said. "I've had enough from you. You're not going to go back and stay among your blossoms, and play peeky-boo with the wind and the green boughs and enjoy the fun. You want to fight me. You're not going to leave me alone. I've warned you too many times. I've told your little brain more than once to behave yourself and if you didn't I would get you foul or fair."

I got up from under the tree. And I felt very badly at first to be disturbed of my sleep. And then I felt worse because a bumblebee had done it. Now if it had been another man, one of my kind, who had come here and tried this I would have put him on the go. So I walked two hundred yards to the house. And when I went through the gate to the paling fence around our yard which kept out the chickens, snakes, varmints, and stray dogs, I walked past Pa who was lying under the snowball bush with his eyes closed, and snoring. My half dozen brothers were all lying around under the snowball bush and elm and poplar shades. All were sleeping soundly. I never saw Mom nor my sisters. They might have been taking their afternoon naps on the beds. I didn't disturb anybody. I went into the house and I got Pa's double-barrel shotgun which he kept loaded and hanging on a joist over his and Mom's bed. Pa never locked our doors but he kept his gun loaded. And I opened the dresser drawer and got me a handful of shotgun shells.

I walked out the way I'd come in and I eased back through the gate and let the weights bring it back shut without logchains and plowpoints jingling. I walked back to my apple tree and I laid down flat on my back on the grass and I started looking up. "All right, bumblebee, now you start something," I said. I let him know I was back. I knew he was a vicious bumblebee. Maybe if I hadn't spoken he would have forgot I was down on the grass beneath him. He came down in a dive and when he started back up I raised the shotgun up, aimed, and fired one barrel. I shot right up through my dear friendly apple tree too, for I was trying to rid myself of an enemy that wouldn't let me sleep. Twigs with green leaves hanging on to them, leaves, and pieces of leaves and a few shattered blossoms came zigzagging down, but there was no bumblebee among them.

"I can't believe I missed him," I thought. "And if I did miss him after he felt that hot air and heard that blast, maybe he won't be back."

Well, I broke the shotgun at the breech, took out the smoking empty shell, and replaced it with a loaded one. When a man has trouble it pays to keep his gun loaded and his powder dry. It doesn't take much thinking for this, for any dummy knows wet powder won't burn. So I settled back with the double barrel across my chest, hammers cocked and my fingers on the trigger. "If you're still up there and you come again, if I can't get you with one barrel maybe I can with two," I said. Since I'd taken that shot I'd not heard him buzzing around up there. And I wondered if my shot out here had awakened anybody sleeping in our yard or in the house. Well, if the shot had awakened anyone, no one had come to see who was doing the shooting.

While I lay looking up through the little holes at the blue sky when the winds shifted the green apple boughs, I heard a buzzing sound. "It can't be that bee," I thought. But there was the same old bee, for he came down toward the back of my head and before I could lift my gun and fire he was hidden again up among the leaves.

"So you've not had enough, bumblebee," I said. "You come again and I'll be ready!"

I'd no more than warned him until here he came. I was ready, and when he pulled out of the dive I leveled over both barrels at him and followed him up to the green leaves and just before he entered my world of green I pulled both barrels. It sounded like a cannon. Now I knew I'd awakened all the sleepers out home. But this didn't matter. Not anything really mattered as much as my shooting that bumblebee. I had blown a little hole about two inches across up through the leaves and blossoms and I had a nice peephole to the blue sky.

Well, I broke the gun at the breech and took out the empties and reloaded again. Then I settled back with my head pillowed on the grass and I looked up at the sky. I hadn't awakened anybody out home—not even with the blast of two barrels shooting at once. I never heard another sound from the bumblebee. I got him this time. So now, my eyes began to get heavy and my natural mind must have been a little tired with so much trouble and so much thinking. Last thing I remembered doing was putting my shotgun on the grass and putting my legs over it. I wasn't going to take the gun back until after I had had my rest, for then I could make one trip do it all. If anybody came along and tried to steal Pa's gun he'd have to pull it from under my legs, and this would wake me. In a few minutes I was myself again. My natural mind calls for a puff of wind, a blade of grass, or a petal falling from a tree.

Judge Ripper's Day

When Nadine and I drove through the gate into Greenwood County Park, hundreds of cars already were parked and behind us were cars lined up, bumper to bumper, to a bend in the road about a mile away. How far beyond this bend the line extended we didn't know, for we couldn't see. Impatient drivers were honking their horns for cars up front to move on into the park grounds, so they could move up for the big day.

"Some turn-out for the retirement of the Solemn Old Judge," I said. "I can remember when I was a boy he was called 'Rip, the Ripper.' And he couldn't have been named after Rip Van Winkle, for the Solemn Old Judge wasn't so solemn when he was a younger man. He was up hoeing in his garden at six in the morning. He always liked to use a hoe to chop weeds and hoe vegetables and flowers."

"Yes," Nadine recalled. "We lived across the street from him. I remember Judge Ripper always was hoeing in the garden as my father went to work."

"And, you see, the early bird got the worm," I said. "Look how long he has served as circuit judge!"

When an usher had guided us into a place to park we got out and looked at the throng of people gathered over on the bank of Big River. The river is the northern boundary of our twenty acres of Greenwood County Park.

"The Solemn Old Judge is already over there," the usher told us. "He's been here since daylight. You know he gets out early, and he gets there in a hurry."

"Yes, but who's up in that big elm over there?" I asked.

"Must be the Solemn Old Judge Ripper," he said.

"But what's he doing up in a tree?" I asked.

There must have been five hundred people gathered in a circle around the tree looking up at the man whose long, thin white hair rode on the June morning wind that blew up Big River—rode like a man's white undershirt flapping on a clothesline. Nadine and I hurried across the park to join the outer rim of the circle of people gathered around and under the big elm. We crowded up just like all the others who were hurrying to be a part of Judge Ripper's Day.

It was Judge Ripper up there in the big tree, all right. Two pulleys had been fastened to a big branch in the top of the elm and they came down and fastened to a rocking chair on which sat our Solemn Old Judge. Two men worked the pulley ropes, lifting our judge up a few inches at a time.

"What in the world is going on here?" I whispered to Mort Perry, who was standing beside me. "What's he doing up in that tree?"

"Ah, just getting up there where the people can see him, I reckon," Mort replied in a low tone. "You know, he's been a most unusual judge. He began to wear them big ribbon neckties before anybody else did. He got everybody's attention focused on himself until they forgot all about the trial. Just to look at him sitting up in his judge's seat would make people think he was trying to be God Almighty on his throne."

"Gather up closer to me, my friends," Judge Ripper said in a soft voice that somehow carried out a long way. "Come under the sound of my voice, as I will have no gavel today. I am no longer your circuit judge. The Day of Reckoning has come to me on this Earthly Footstool. Old age has overtaken me, as it will overtake everybody who stands down there and listens to the sound of my voice. I will no longer wield that gavel and you will no longer hearken to the sound of my voice. My days of administering justice in the Greenwood County courtroom are over. You have elected me to eight terms of office!"

"Your honor, Judge Ripper, I beg to correct your statement," spoke a voice down among us, though on the other side of the tree from Nadine and me. "You have served Greenwood County as our Most Honorable Circuit Judge for nine terms, six years for each term, which makes fifty-four years."

"You are correct and I am correct, my friend, Daffy Perkins," the Judge replied. "But I was elected by the people only eight times. I will explain this to you today as I am lifted higher in this tree. But I have served you, my honorable constituents, fifty-four years, as Daffy Perkins has told you. There are many things I wish to say on my last appearance before you.

"Today I appear before you an honest man. Time is fleeting, and with each minute I am nearer the grave. When Death's cold icy fingers grab me by the throat and I depart this life, I want to leave an honest Will and Testament to my fellow man, to my constituents, who have been so kind to me, regardless of what I have done to them."

Above us, our Solemn Old Judge, with his wind-blown white hair, still had the frigid air of the Solemn Old Judge that we had known so long and feared as much as we would fear the appearance of Old Beelzebub among us. His face was pale, his nose long and sharp at the tip, almost like a hatchet with a blunt edge. His cold blue eyes that looked down upon us were similar to those of a predatory hawk. He was wearing the rose-colored ribbon tie, which fluttered up there in the wind like a flag. He wore a black funeral suit. His coat had a pencil, fountain pen, and spectacle case in its front pocket. His long legs dangled, encased in wrinkled black pants, and he was wearing black high-top lace shoes with sharp-pointed toes. Across his middle, from arm to arm of the rocking chair, a broad sash which looked like it might be a quilt or a blanket was tied securely so that when and if our Solemn Old Judge Ripper leaned against it, he wouldn't fall out of his last judge's seat.

"No, it won't be long before your judge will have to stand before God's Great Judgment Seat and be judged," he said. "This thing of judgment is a serious matter, I realize now more than at any other time of my life. I know it because maturity has come to me as the years have passed. My days of judging men and women, boys and girls, have passed, because the lengthening shadow of time has spread over my world. Before I reach the Great Judgment Day, I must make a few confessions to you."

More people had come, joining the outer rim of the circle of Judge Ripper's friends and followers and those who had come, perhaps, to jeer at him because of some of the decisions he had made. More than a thousand stood jam-packed in a wagon-wheel circle under and beyond the giant elm with a half-acre spread. Judge Ripper had selected the right tree, where he could look down from his rocking chair on the faces, both familiar and unfamiliar, looking up at him. He had chosen this giant tree among the smaller trees as a symbol comparable to his being the human giant among his constituents living in Greenwood County, which constituted the limitations of his judgeship for the past fifty-four years.

"Last December 31 I served my last day," he spoke down to the eager faces packed in the wagon-wheel circle beneath him. "I have waited for this first day of June, which brings the fairest weather and plenty of green leaves to our fair county-seat town of Blakesburg, where our courthouse and our seat of justice is, and where I have served you over half a century.

"Do I hear the hum of whispering down there? I have no gavel today. You must get quiet and listen to what I have to say. My voice is not what it used to be, not with the wind blowing up here and with the rustling leaves all around me. I cannot talk against this wind in the leaves. They are trying to speak to me while I am trying to speak to you. We must let the wind and the leaves make noise, while you silence yourselves down there."

"All quiet down here, Your Honor," said Willie Potter. "Go ahead! We want to hear what you have to say."

"First, I must confess to you that Ripper is not my real name," he said. "I gave up a better name than Ripper. My real name is John Jamison, a very old pioneer name in Greenwood County. It's not Honest John, Big John, Good Old John, or Father John Ripper, either. All these prefixes to my first name were added in an earlier day to woo the voters. Honest John is a good name to get votes. And, of course, Father John came when I was running for circuit judge beyond retirement age. I was old enough to be the father of ninety per cent of this county's population."

"Tell us how you got the name Ripper, Your Honor," said a woman looking up from the crowd.

The hissing sound of low whispers was going through the crowd beneath the tree: "Well, I never knew that!" "I always thought his name was Ripper." "Well, I knew his name was Jamison," whispered an old man. "But I never norated the story, for he's a man of my party." "What's the matter with him?" whispered another old man. "It's better to let sleeping dogs lie. He must be in his dotage to make such a confession and ruin our party." And there were more whispers, mingled together in an indecipherable profusion of words.

"Order down there," said the Solemn Old Judge. "This is my day, and I want to speak the truth. Now, quiet, so I can tell you how I got the name Ripper."

A stillness came over the crowd.

"As a young attorney in Blakesburg, I was both a schemer and a dreamer," our Solemn Old Judge continued. "I had ambitions of being circuit judge. But in those days Greenwood and Lantern Counties were joined in one judicial circuit. Since Lantern County had enough plurality of votes in the minority party to elect a circuit judge, I got another idea. I ran for representative of Greenwood County, where the only election I had to watch was the primary in my own party. I had a battle in my party, but I came through with flying colors, while the man we ran for circuit judge, Lawyer Ephraim Gullett, who has long been dead and gone to his reward, was defeated by a prominent attorney of Blakesburg, Oder Timmons. Now Oder Timmons, too, has gone to his reward.

"My friends, I have to pause a minute here," continued our Solemn Old Judge as he pulled a leaf from the elm, took a pencil from his front coat pocket and laid the leaf on the rocking-chair arm. "I shall write the name Oder Timmons on this leaf," he said. "I'll write it on the white belly of the leaf, where it will be legible. And here it goes."

He threw the leaf to the wind and the wind carried it away.

"I'll say for Oder Timmons he was a fine lawyer, an honest and good man. He was old enough to be my father. I had gone to him when I was a very young lawyer, for we had graduated from the law school at State University. He was an experienced Blakesburg lawyer when I hung out my shingle. He helped me like a father would help a son. But I had my dreams, and I couldn't help doing what I did, though I knew it would be extra expense to our state, which has suffered from poor economy for more than a century. Oder Timmons was elected circuit judge of Lantern and Greenwood Counties, but I knew he would never serve. Why had I fought through a long, hard primary in my party to be elected representative of our county?

"My constituents thought I would get better roads for them, and buildings in the state park, as I had promised," he continued. "But the first thing I did when I got to the legislature was to present a ripper bill to make a new district. I'm the one who separated Greenwood and Lantern Counties. I knew if I told our boys in the legislature, a majority of two to one over the minority party, that I'd vote for anything they asked me to vote for and would ask for nothing in return—no roads, no building for the state park—they'd tallyho for any bill. How could it be otherwise when the governor and I were classmates? Now, when we sent Oder Timmons from our Greenwood County, where he was born and grew to manhood to become circuit judge of Lantern County, who do you think Governor Boston appointed? Not Ephraim Gullett, who had been defeated. I was the man appointed.

"Excuse me a minute until I write old Ephraim's name on a leaf and toss it to the wind! Good old Eif! He lived fourteen years after that defeat and double-cross, and died of a broken heart. He always thought he had been betrayed, and he worked hard against me when I ran the first time. I was barely elected, but by being a good party man, I kept my election pluralities gaining from 'Big John,' 'Honest John,' 'Father John,' to the 'Solemn Old Judge.' When I came to be your 'Solemn Old Judge,' no man dared run against me."

"Your Honor, why did you write Oder Timmons' and Ephraim Gullett's names on the leaves and toss them to the wind?" asked a man with a sun spot on his face where sunlight had filtered through the leaves.

"Are we not as grass?" Judge Ripper asked. "Don't even the lawyer and the circuit judge pass and are forgotten like the rest? Aren't we leaves on the wind? As I now look upon the past, I wonder just how fit I was to judge the people after routing Oder Timmons from his county, which was my county and your county, and he must have loved this county then the same as we do now. And then, look at what I did to Ephraim Gullett! No wonder he accused me of betrayal. He was in line for appointment as judge of the newly created district. So, it was he or it was Oder Timmons who named me Judge Ripper, and it went from constituent to constituent until I became Judge Ripper. By having one name consume the other name and by due process of law, I discarded Jamison, my real name, and I accepted the name Ripper that the people had given me. I have found it better, dear friends, to obey the wishes and desires of the people if I wanted to stay in office, and I did!"

"Honorable Judge, I never knew your real name was Jamison," said a man standing very close to me. "I have always believed your name was Ripper. I didn't know you inherited your name by such devious methods."

"Well, I did, and I think of the promises I made to the people about bringing them better roads back there in 1963 and when I ran for the office of representative," he said. "I never got one foot of road for them. I can tell you now that the mind of the voter is fickle. He wants a promise. And he accepts a promise and votes for it even when he knows he'll never get it. In my younger days I was a climbing man. I had dreams of being appointed to the State Court and maybe, if I was lucky, to the Supreme Court of the United States."

"Your Honor, that was not an honorable thing to do to Oder Timmons, even if he was not in your majority party," spoke the man who had asked him the last question. "And you did betray Ephraim Gullett, the man in your majority party who ran against Mr. Timmons and lost."

"I admit to all you have said," Judge Ripper replied as his rocking chair rocked and his long white hair rode on the wind like a horse's flaxen mane when he runs to meet a blowing wind. "Today I sit above you, an honest man looking down upon you. And this day is just beginning for me. Will you call off the names to me, Cyrus?"

"Your Honor, shall I call off the names beginning with your first term in the spring of 1964?"

"Yes, begin with the beginning," he replied. "See, I've explained about my name and how I became the youngest circuit judge ever to sit on the bench. I was twenty-eight when I became circuit judge of this district, which was before many of you were born. I am now eighty-two and when a man becomes my age, when he is so near the last and final judgment by the great Master Judge, it is time for him to confess and be an honest man. I cannot face my Great Judge until I have made these confessions to you, my friends and my former constituents." Our Solemn Old Judge Ripper stopped briefly to clear his throat with a feeble cough. Then he continued, "Of course it is impossible to mention all the men, women, boys, and girls I have passed sentence on or have given instructions to the juries who have passed judgment. I shall mention a few of the many, those I was never sure about and those where I leaned a little for personal gain."

"Has he lost his mind?" said Bailey Elswick. He was our sheriff of Greenwood County. "He'll ruin our majority party."

"I heard what you said, Bailey Elswick," Judge Ripper spoke up in a high voice. "Don't worry about our majority party in this state and all the other Southern states. It has been tried. It has been killed, cooked, and eaten, but never digested. It comes to life and is as good as new. I used to think it would hurt when our majority party was disowned by other areas of our great country. But, torn into parts, our party always got back with the others before a state or national election. And we became a living, united whole again, ready for another assault on the helpless minority party. We always rode the Victory Horse. The minority party's horse we named Defeat."

"All right, Your Honor. The first name on this scroll is Willie Allcorn."

"Convicted on circumstantial evidence and given life for cutting Horam Gullett's throat with a razor," he said. "Two others could have been guilty of this hideous crime. But I was a young judge then. No votes were subtracted from me when I passed sentence, for he belonged to the minority party. Bear with me, dear friends, while I pull this leaf."

When the Solemn Old Judge wrote "Willie Allcorn" on the leaf, he spelled the name for all to hear. "Poor old Willie grew old and died in the pen, and may God rest his soul." He threw the leaf on the wind and it went sailing above the treetops and over Big River. Our judge watched the leaf until it disappeared, and then he said, "That's the way of man. He's here, a leaf, a blade of grass today and he's withered and gone tomorrow. Not any decision can be wrongfully right or rightfully wrong. Who ever hears of Willie Allcorn today?"

"Your Honor, only I," spoke a feminine voice below. "I am his granddaughter, and my father, God rest his soul, always said his father died in the pen and was never guilty of the crime of which he was accused."

"No one is sure whether he was or not," said our Solemn Old Judge Ripper. "He might not have been, and he might have been. But I write his name on a leaf from the Tree of Life, since I am not sure."

"But what you are doing is crazy, Your Honor," protested Sheriff Elswick.

"You are young and party-minded," the judge said. "Wrong decisions, getting what we think is somewhere too fast by any means to an end, doesn't pay. This trying men in newspapers for crimes they are merely accused of doesn't pay."

"Judge, I belong to the minority party, and I just came here today to be coming," said Mike Hansford. "But I'm glad I came. I'm glad you're doing this. It takes a big man to do what you are doing."

"Thank you, Mike Hansford," the judge said. "The world has changed so much with so many people in it that it is so much with us now we had better play life's game with honest intentions."

"Your Honor, are you ready for another name?"

"Yes, Cyrus, I am."

The voice was familiar to me. I looked around the tree, and there stood Cyrus Middleton, reading off the names to the judge. He had served forty years as Greenwood County Circuit Court Clerk. He was the man who put the jurors' names in a wheel, turned the wheel, and took out the names. He had been accused by many in both parties of stacking the jury with names that would either convict a man or clear him, whatever happened to be the wish of the judge, the party, or those in power. He was wearing a tight-fitted checkered suit and a ribbon tie like Judge Ripper wore. He always had been a close friend of our judge.

"Your Honor, George Felty."

"I regret very much that George Felty died on the hot seat," Judge Ripper said. "It was proved that he killed Buzz Johnson . . . a trial I will never forget. But life was dear to him, even if he had taken a life. And had he been sentenced to life, he would have been punished more by thinking of the crime he had done."

Then our Solemn Old Judge Ripper wrote George Felty's name on a leaf and tossed it on the wind. The leaf turned over and over, just as thoughts of murder must have turned over in Felty's mind and thoughts of his sentence had turned over in Judge Ripper's mind.

"Will you please hoist my chair up so I can reach more leaves?" Judge Ripper asked.

His attendants on the ground pulled the rocking chair up by pulley ropes to another cluster of leaves.

"Reckon there'll be enough leaves on that tree for him to write all the names he has sentenced?" asked an elderly woman standing near Nadine and me.

"No, there won't be enough leaves on that big elm for all the people he's sentenced," said an elderly man standing near her.

"Another name, Cyrus," said our Solemn Old Judge, who was now perched higher in the tree. "We must move along faster if we get to all the names listed on that scroll."

"Walt Whitefield."

"Sentenced to three years for nonsupport of wife and

seven children," the judge said. "Three children didn't belong to him, since another man stayed there, too. His wife, old Effie, should have been sentenced."

"Janice Traylor, for killing her husband, Bill, with a butcher knife. I commuted her sentence, since she was the mother of two children. She should have served."

He scribbled her name on a leaf and threw it to the wind.

"Now Janice has been judged by the Supreme Judge, for she has gone to her reward. Cyrus, please keep the names coming."

Well, there were many names read by Cyrus from the scroll and many leaves tossed by Judge Ripper's cadaverous hand from the elm tree, which represented the Tree of Life to our Solemn Old Judge. These leaves brought comments, sighs, and cries from the crowd beneath. A fight started, but Sheriff Elswick put an end to it. I never heard anything like the confusion beneath the elm. Maybe the people got tired of standing, but they wouldn't leave. They waited to hear the next name called, and there were many called, written on leaves, and tossed to the wind—leaves for only those who now had gone with the wind from Greenwood County, which had been their Tree of Life, to their last resting places in Greenwood County earth, in prison burial grounds, state or federal, and in potter's field.

Names recorded on leaves and tossed to the wind included Worldly Fritz, possessing illegal licker; Dudley Kearns, armed robbery; Aleck Chaffin, shooting his brother-in-law, Mooney Cotswold, six times at close range with intent to kill; Mary Pennix, accessory to armed robbery; Pert Pennix, armed robbery; Cottle Abrahams, detaining a female against her will; Wilford Seymour, carnal knowledge of a female under sixteen; Thaddeus Stevens, stabbing with intent to kill; Roscoe Blevins, breaking and entering; Benton Remines, third offense of making illegal whiskey; and other names for similar offenses—Don Sibene, Redbelly Seagraves, Arnold MacNutt, Dollie Stump, Martin Hillsdale, Ernest Howard, Wiley Wilson. He went on calling names as he pulled leaves from the elm and recorded their names for the wind. When leaves around him were used, his attendants below hoisted his rocking chair up to new clusters. There was a hole up through the center of the elm where all the leaves were plucked clean. Now our Solemn Old Judge Ripper was climbing higher and higher up into his Tree of Life. And the wind continued to blow up Big River, the usual direction from which the winds and the rains came.

"Boy, am I tired," said Art Mullins. "It's awful interesting to hear His Honor, Judge Ripper, call them names and tell what they have done and say what he thinks about them now. Maybe his successor, Honorable Clifford Harper, ought to have one of these tree-sittings once a year and invite all his constituents out to hear him. Maybe it would be better for the law."

All the time Art was mumbling his words to the man who stood beside him, our Solemn Old Judge was spelling out more names and recording names on leaves for the wind to carry hither and thither over Big River and up the valley.

"What does it matter that their names are written on leaves now?" said a young woman standing near Art Mullins. "They are gone with the wind. They have served their sentences. They have no stones with recorded names and dates. How much will recording their names on leaves help them now, when they are gone and forgotten and sleep in unmarked graves?"

"But His Honor, our Solemn Old Judge Ripper, is making an open confession," said a woman over beside the tree. "Open confessions are good for the soul."

"If I were in his shoes when I stood before the Master to be judged, I'd have fears," Art Mullins said. "I've never been anything but a farm laborer, but I won't have to answer for what he did to Ephraim Gullett and Oder Timmons. Think back in the middle of the twentieth century! Ah, his sins have found him out. His soul is hungry and crying. I hope he will come clean, and God will rest his soul when he comes to that final judgment all men must face."

"My ears are good, and I heard that, Mr. Mullins," Judge Ripper raised his feeble voice from midway up in the elm. "And you, sir, are exactly right. But it is not too late for a man to get forgiveness for his mistakes. It is good that he can recognize his mistakes and make his confessions before the kin of those he wonders about wonder about some of his decisions, and know that some of them were made because of other pressures and interests, party affiliations, and other things of the day and time of their trials."

"Judge, I admire you for what you are doing," Art said. "But I can't stand here and listen, for I weigh two hundred fifteen pounds, my shoes are hurting my feet, and I'm hungry."

"Go eat, Mr. Mullins, rest yourself and return," he said. "I'll be going strong here all the day with the list of names on the scroll that must get a leaf from this Tree of Life. All right, another name, Cyrus."

"Nadine, I'm tired of standing," I said. "I'm hungry, too, like my friend Art Mullins. Let's go eat and rest and come back. I see that is what others are doing."

Still there were as many around the tree as come to Blakesburg when we have a street carnival. Nadine and I walked back to the car, where we still could hear Judge Ripper reading names as he sent them away on currents of wind.

We drove down to Blakesburg and ate in Pennington's Cafe. I was tired enough to drop, too, but I still could see and hear our Solemn Old Judge up in that tree. His ripper bill, introduced in the middle of the twentieth century, just to redistrict a county to give himself a position, at extra expense to our state, would never die. Not even in the year of 2019 A.D.

"Nadine, as soon as we are rested enough, I want us to go back to the park to see if our Solemn Old Judge Ripper will still be up in that elm," I said.

"You know he will," she said. "I don't see much use of going back there and hearing the names of those sentenced and seeing him write another name on a leaf and throw it to the wind. I don't see the point of standing under that tree in that curious crowd of lookers and listeners. But I'll go back with you if you feel compelled to return."

"I'll bet he's got a hole cleaned nearly to the top of that giant elm by now," I said. "Think of that, won't you! There's never been another day here like this one. It will be talked about after our Solemn Old Judge Ripper has been judged by the Great Judge and when he sleeps out on Lonesome Hill with a tall stone, maybe twenty feet high, above his final resting place."

"He'll run into a problem on Lonesome Hill," said Nadine. "Will his name on the stone be Jamison or Ripper?"

"I can't answer that," I said. "Let's get back to the park. It's getting late in the afternoon."

Back inside the park, we parked and looked over to the elm. There sat Judge Ripper in his rocking chair almost at the top of the tree. All the leaves up through the center of the tree that had been in reaching distance of the Judge's long arms had been plucked. A great crowd was still gathered beneath the tree, and the sun was setting.

"Well, I see you're back," Art Mullins said. "We went away, ate lunch, but I had to come back. I can't forget this, can you?"

"No, I can't," I said. "How much longer will it go on?"

"Until all the names on the scroll are read," Art said.

"Where is he with the names now?" I asked.

"Up in the twenty-first century," he replied. "There's been fighting here. Relatives of the people whose names he's read off are here. Sheriff Elswick has had to call in a couple of his deputies to help him handle the situation."

The barren branches up through the center of the tree gave us a good view of Solemn Judge Ripper reaching up toward the topmost twigs, pulling the last leaves he would be able to reach as the names were called. We heard names called. We watched people pushing and shoving and heard them swearing at each other in the crowd beneath the tree.

"I've been here all day," said Bonnie Madden. "I've waited to hear the name of my husband called. Don't guess his going to the pen and spending ten years of his life for a crime he didn't do was important enough for Judge Ripper to consider. I feel like going over there and cutting one of the ropes and letting the chair fall with him."

"You just try that, lady," Sheriff Elswick said. "Clear out now before I arrest you."

Solemn Old Judge Ripper was calling off names—Carrie Dravenstot, Marshall Sprouse, Winnie Skaggs, Arville Deer, Charlie Coon, and Denton Kirby.

"And now call no more names," Judge Ripper called down to Cyrus. "I am pulling the last leaf. This leaf is for myself. The sun has set. It's time to come down."

Our Solemn Old Judge Ripper pulled the last leaf from the topmost twig he could reach and began to spell his name. We listened to see how he would spell it. And he spelled it out loudly for us to hear: "J-u-d-g-e J-o-h-n R-i-p-p-e-r." Then he looked down to us and said, "It's the name I've earned. I know it's false, but there's no escape now."

He threw the leaf on the wind and at that time a great gust, like wind before rain, came up Big River Valley and swept the leaf out over Big River. We watched it zigzagging on the wind-swirl until it was a speck, and on and out of sight.

"That's the way it is, my friends," Judge Ripper said. "Lower my rocking chair."

When his attendants let the chair to the ground and Cyrus untied the sash, our Solemn Old Judge stood up.

"My day is over," he said. "You have seen and heard. I have no gavel to dismiss you. I have only the sound of my voice. You are dismissed. Go in peace and administer honesty and justice to your fellow man, so that when you stand before the Supreme Judge you will not shake and quiver. Goodbye and good luck to all of you."

The Rightful Owner

It wasn't the same at our breakfast table. Everybody was silent. We'd always done a lot of talking to each other across the table at breakfast time. And, after we'd finished eating breakfast, we sat and drank an extra cup of coffee as each talked about his plans for the day. Pa would talk to Mom. I'd talk to Sophia. And we'd talk to Mom and Pa. But this morning it was different.

Maybe it wouldn't have been different if Scout had kept still in the woodshed. He was barking for his breakfast. Every time he barked I could see new color flash into Pa's face. Scout was my dog. Maybe I'd better tell you about 'im. I'd better tell you how I got him. And after I got him what happened to me. And then you'd understand why Pa was silent at the breakfast table.

A young stray hound came to our farm and stayed. He had

a short piece of rope around his neck. I tried many times to get near him so I could get hold of the rope. But he was too wild. He didn't stay around our house. He didn't even come near the house. But he took up with the cattle and lived in the pasture. When the cattle lay down under the trees on cool spring nights he would sleep with his back against a steer. And all the time the piece of rope stayed around his neck. This worried me, for I thought when he hunted wild game for food the rope might get foul somewhere on the vast pasture lands where there wasn't a house for miles and this pretty hound would die of thirst and starvation before anyone found him.

Pa helped me make a trap so I could catch the dog without hurting him. I had tried every way in the world to coax him to me with bread. But he wouldn't come. I'd tried to get him acquainted with other dogs that were tame and toll him to the house. But I couldn't. He wouldn't leave the cattle. He had gone wild, and the only way to catch him was in a trap. I bought heavy-meshed wire, strong enough to hold a wild dog. Then Pa helped me build a big trap with a funnel going in at the main entrance. And beyond this entrance I baited the trap with fresh meat and left it near where the cattle slept on the highest point of the highest hill in our pasture. They slept here at night under the big bushy-topped oak trees.

The first night I set the trap I caught the young hound. Pa and I took the mules and sled to the pasture and hauled the trap home. For the trap we'd made was big enough to keep him in until we'd tamed him. I kept him in the trap three weeks before I gave him his freedom. Then I had a tame hound dog. And I knew he'd be a good hunting dog, for he had been wild and had to forage for food. I knew he'd be a wonderful hunting dog. I called him Scout. Wherever I went

Scout went with me. He was a pretty black and tan hound with dots above his eyes.

Summer passed and autumn came. When possum-hunting season opened in November, I took Scout possum-hunting one night. As I walked along Seaton Ridge I came upon a group of fox hunters. They were sitting around a big open fire listening to their hounds chase the fox circles around the long ridge. Scout was walking along with me when I reached this group of men. And just as soon as I walked up to the fire, Freeman Abdon, an old fox hunter with a long red beard, claimed my dog.

"That's my dog you've got thar," he said. "How come you with 'im?"

"How long has your dog been gone?" I asked.

"I lost him in these woods over six months ago," he said.

"He's my dog now," I said. "I've had him over six months."

"Where did you get 'im?" Freeman asked.

Then I told Freeman how I got the dog. I told him how I'd tamed the dog.

"It's strange," I said. "If he's your dog, you didn't know his bark. He's lived in these fox-hunting woods and you've been hunting here all spring, summer, and autumn Scout's been here. He's caught his own food and has done a lot of barking on tracks, in holes, and up trees!"

"But he's my dog," Freeman said. "I know my dog when I see him. He's the dog I lost. And I'm a-goin to have 'im."

"He's my dog," I said. "And I'm goin to keep him!"

"Now you're pretty young, son," Freeman said. "I wouldn't do anything to you but throw sand in your eyes. I don't want to have to do that. But I'm going to have my dog."

I couldn't help but crying when Freeman pulled a chain from his pocket and snapped the link into Scout's collar.

"Now you go home before I throw sand in your eyes," he warned me.

The fox hunters sitting around the fire didn't open their mouths. They let Freeman take my dog. They didn't say whether Scout was or was not Freeman's dog. But I could not keep from crying. I went straight home and told Pa and Pa got out of bed, dressed, and came back to the Seaton Ridge to see Freeman about my dog, but the fox chase was over and the hunters had gone home. The big open fire they'd built was now a heap of gray-charred embers. Pa came home at daylight without his ever seeing Freeman.

Next day while Pa and I dragged logs from the timber woods with our mules, Pa planned how to get Scout back for me. He worked silently all day. He asked me about every hour in the day to repeat the exact words Freeman had said to me. He'd have me repeat what Freeman said about throwing sand in my eyes.

"I'll have that dog back if I have to go to law about it," Pa said when we drove the team home at quitting time.

But when we got to the house Scout was there. He was back with us.

"Freeman turned him loose too soon," Pa said. "He won't be getting him again."

Then Pa put Scout in the woodshed and put a padlock to the door and locked it. That's the story about how I got old Scout and why he was barking in the woodshed. He was wanting out to get his breakfast. He was wanting the freedom of the hills that he had enjoyed when he ran wild and hunted his own food. He didn't like the padlocked woodshed where Pa put him so Freeman Abdon couldn't get him if he came while we were in the timber woods.

"I couldn't sleep a wink last night for thinking of Scout," Pa said as he took an extra cup of coffee. "This sort of thing worries a man. Let an old red-bearded fox hunter like Freeman Abdon tell my boy he's a-goin to throw sand in his eyes if he doesn't give up his dog to 'im. I'm not a-takin that sort of thing!"

"Pa, a hound dog is not worth this much fuss," Sophia said.

"Scout's worth this much fuss to me," Pa said. "Let a man talk to one of my children like Freeman Abdon did. What kind of a man am I to let him to get by? I won't do it! There'll be trouble first! He'll be in the timber woods to see me today about the dog. I know he'll be there."

"I'd like to have the dog back, Pa," I said. "But I don't want you to hurt Freeman Abdon or to let Freeman Abdon hurt you over him."

"Let him have the dog," Mom said.

"I will do no such thing," Pa snorted. "What kind of a man do you take me to be? I have more honor in my bones and pride in my heart than to let any man do one of my children like this."

While we talked at the table Mom got up and went into the house. She wasn't gone very long until she came back, sat down at the table, and poured herself more coffee.

"There's not any use of having a lot of trouble over a worthless hound dog," Mom said.

"Worthless," I said.

"Worthless," Pa repeated. "Best dog in the county."

"Not a fox hound," I said. "Scout is a real hunting dog. I've kept him most of last spring and all summer and now hunting season is here and I want to do some hunting with him."

"You'll hunt with him, Shan," Pa said. "If Freeman Abdon takes that dog he'll do it over my dead body."

Mom looked at Sophia and I looked at Mom. We knew that Pa meant what he said. There would be trouble. Then I got up from the table, walked over to the stove and picked up a dozen hot biscuits for Scout.

"Be sure the woodshed is locked when you leave," Pa told me.

"I will," I said.

I unlocked the woodshed and gave Scout hot biscuits for his breakfast. I gave him fresh water. And I did what Pa told me. I locked the padlock so Freeman couldn't get the dog if he came to the house while we were gone.

"It's funny something would happen to my pistol," Pa said to Mom when I went back into the kitchen. "And at the same time, the bolt be missing from my rifle and the lock that holds my single barrel onto the stock be gone."

Pa's face was red as a red-oak leaf in October. Mom didn't say a word.

"I tell you that Freeman Abdon will be in the timber woods to see me today," Pa said. "And he'll have a gun. I'll be without protection."

But Mom didn't answer Pa.

"You know we've got to work," Pa talked on. "We've got to get the logs down for the sawmill. Mill will be moving in next week."

Mom sat at the table and looked into her coffee cup.

Sophia looked at Mom and Mom looked up from her coffee cup at Pa.

Then Pa left the house and I went with him. We got the mule team at the barn and we were soon on our way to the timber woods. As we drove up the log road that wound through the dense undergrowth, Pa asked me to hold the mules. While I held the checklines Pa took my ax and cut down a straight sourwood. And he cut him a club about three feet long. He could grip the little end with his big hand. But the big end was like a fence-post maul.

"Freeman had better not fool with me," Pa said. "I'll hurt 'im."

We drove the mules to the high hilltop above Coonden

Hollow. And here the red-oak logs lay on the ground where the young sawbriars and the mountain tea grew thick as clover. And the October sun hit first here of a morning and the white frost went up toward the sun in streaming vapor, and it was good to see.

I cut a road through the brush for Pa to get to a log. He hitched to it and dragged it down to the logpile. And while he was gone and I was cutting another road, I saw something that made my heart go up into my throat and choke me. Freeman Abdon came around a fox path with a double-barrel shotgun across his shoulder. With one hand he held the gunstock that was balanced across his shoulder, with the other hand he wiped away the mountain vapor from his long red beard. Behind Freeman walked Oliver Abdon, his tall son, with a clean-shaven face, a pair of big blue eyes, and a shock of hair on his hatless head the light-gold color of October poplar leaves. He was well over six feet tall and he didn't carry a gun or a club with him. He was empty-handed. I clutched my double-bitted ax handle. I raised it across my shoulders.

"Good morning," Freeman spoke.

"Good morning," I said.

"Where's your Pa?" he asked.

"Went over the hill with a log," I said. "He'll be back shortly. You want to see him?"

"Not exactly," Freeman said as he took his double-barrel from his shoulder and stood it on the leaf-covered ground beside him. "Thought I'd come out in your Pa's woods and kill a few gray foxes. And I thought while I's out here," Freeman talked on as he wiped the morning mist that was shining like dewdrops in his red whiskers with the back of his big fire-shovel hand, "I'd stop a minute and see old Mick about a little matter. It's about a dog."

"You've not brought that gun out here to kill gray foxes," I thought. "Freeman Abdon, you wouldn't kill a fox. You were never known to kill a fox. You love them too well. That's why you're called "Fox" Abdon. You're a friend to the foxes. You brought that gun out here to use on Pa."

"You won't have long to wait to see Pa," I said. "He's coming up the hill now."

When Freeman looked down at the log road, he saw Pa driving the mules with one hand on the checklines and a big sourwood club in the other. Then he lifted the double-barrel that he had standing beside him and was leaning on like it was a cane to his shoulder. Then Oliver Abdon picked up a club and leaned on it like it was a walking cane. I didn't take my double-bitted ax from my shoulder. Not yet.

"Pa, Mr. Abdon is here to see you," I said soon as Pa got in shotgun range. "He's out here killin gray foxes and stopped to see you about a dog."

Pa didn't say a word. But I knew he'd heard what I said. He drove the mules up beside Freeman and Oliver. Then he dropped the reins and he stood with both hands on his club. He held it with a firm grip. And he stood close enough to Freeman that he could strike before Freeman could get the long double-barrel to his shoulder to shoot. Then Oliver Abdon came in close with his club. When he came in close, I stepped up close with my double-bitted ax across my shoulder.

"If there's going to be trouble between us," I thought, "let it come and let us soon be over with it."

"Freeman, I'd like to know who gave you permission to hunt on my land?" Pa spoke the first words. "I didn't send for you to come out here and kill gray foxes. Did you know you are violating the law?"

"Gray foxes aren't any good to chase," Freeman said. "They're a nuisance. Our hounds can't chase the red foxes for these devilish gray ones."

"Is that all you came out here for?" Pa asked, and his beardy lips were trembling.

"I thought while I's out here I'd see you about a dog," Freeman said. "My boy, Oliver, raised the dog and we lost him in a fox chase. Next time I saw him your boy had old Fiddler out here possum-hunting!"

"That's my dog, Mr. Powderjay," Oliver said. "Shan's not got any right to take him."

"He's not your dog," I said. "He's my dog."

I guess my hands got a little nervous on my ax handle.

"Old Fiddler loves me," Oliver said. "When Pa brought 'im back home the other night and he saw me, he jumped high as my head and tried to kiss my face."

"That's the gospel truth, Mick," Freeman said. "It's a shame to take a dog from his rightful owner when he loves his master like that. I saw it with my own eyes. Old Fiddler cut all kinds of capers when I took him home the other night."

"Then why did he come back to our house?" I asked Oliver. "Soon as you turned him loose, he came back to me, didn't he? Now answer that one for me!"

"But just a minute," Pa broke in. "I don't care so much about the worth of the dog. It's not that, Freeman. It's the way you talked to my boy the other night."

"How did I talk to him?" Freeman asked Pa as his big hand played nervously up and down the gunstock that was laying across his right shoulder.

"You know what you said, Freeman," Pa said, looking Freeman straight in the eye. "You told him if he didn't give Scout to you, that you'd throw sand in his eyes. Didn't you use these very words, Freeman?"

"I did not," Freeman said.

"Mr. Abdon," I said as I gripped the handle of my ax. "You did say them. You know you said them. I can prove you said them by a dozen fox hunters whose names I didn't know but whose frozen beardy faces I'd know if they were here at this minute."

"If I said them I don't remember," Freeman said.

"If you ever throw sand in one of my youngins' eyes," Pa said, "then you and I will throw a different kind of sand in one another's eyes. It's good that you don't remember and that you don't own to the rightful truth."

As Pa talked Freeman was looking at Pa's club. And I was watching Oliver's club. If he had raised it to strike I was ready. My ax handle was shorter than his club, too. I could have reached him by inches before he reached me. And Pa's club was about the length of Freeman's double-barrel. And I wondered if Pa was thinking that Freeman might try to use the double-barrel like a club instead of trying to put it to his shoulder to shoot if trouble came. For Pa took another half step closer to Freeman. I thought sure trouble was going to start, for Freeman's hand that was fingering his gunstock was nervous as a white-oak leaf in the autumn wind. And they weren't drops of morning mist gathered in Freeman's red whiskers. They were drops of sweat that had come from little streams that were oozing out all over Freeman's face. And sweat drops were trickling down the long red beard like raindrops after a storm run down the little barren twigs on trees. Now they were shining in the autumn sun, like white corn grains on a velvet night.

"Listen, Shan," Oliver said, "you called my dog Scout. I want you to know his name. It's Fiddler!"

"It's Scout to me," I said. "It'll always be Scout."

"If you'd have called him Fiddler when you found him wild," Oliver said, "he would have known his name and he would have come when you called."

"Don't talk so damned crazy, Oliver," I said. "I had to trap that dog to catch him."

"Don't come any closer to me, Mick Powderjay," Freeman said. "You are close enough. You're as close as I want you."

"This is my land, Freeman Abdon," Pa said. "I never sent for you to come out here this morning. I've never sent for you nor a one of your fox-hunting crowd that hunts on my land and builds fires on my land. Remember, I'll step where I please on my own property. If you don't like it, be off to Shinglemill Hollow where you belong."

"What did you do with my boy's dog?" Freeman asked. "That's what I've come after. That's what I want."

"Why didn't you tell the truth in the first place?" Pa said. "I knew why you'd come. You didn't bring that double-barrel for a gray fox. You brought that double-barrel for trouble. You brought it for me. But it won't be safe to raise it to use on me, Freeman. It won't be safe, I tell you. I don't want trouble. I'm not a man who hankers for trouble. But if trouble comes, I'll stand my ground!"

"But where is Oliver's dog?" Freeman asked.

"My dog, you mean, Mr. Abdon," I said.

"Pa means what he says," Oliver said. "He means my dog."

"He's locked in the woodshed," Pa said. "And there's a padlock on the door. I defy anyone to break it."

Oliver was facing me. And I was facing west. I was facing the direction away from home.

"There's Fiddler, Pa," Oliver almost shouted. "Look, coming up the hill!"

But I didn't take my eyes off of Oliver to look. I thought it might be a trick to get me to look away. Pa didn't take his eyes off of Freeman. We stood there and faced our foes.

"I won't believe it's Scout until I see 'im here," Pa said, looking Freeman in the eye.

"I won't either," I said.

"But it is Scout," Pa said as he came running up to all of us.

But he must have smelled trouble, for he didn't run in and jump upon either one of us. He stood off to the east of us and barked a few times.

"Wonder who turned that dog out?" I said.

"I don't know," Pa said. "The same one who took the bolts and screws from my guns, I guess."

"See how he knows me," Oliver said. "Listen how he whines to me."

"He's whining to me," I said. "It's not you!"

"That dog knows me so well he's trying to talk to me," Freeman said. "Way he used to fox-hunt with me. Then you try to take my dog!"

"Don't say that again, Freeman," Pa said. "The dog is trying to get to me. He knows you. If he'd 've wanted to have stayed with you he would have. He had his chance."

Pa's lips stopped trembling. And Freeman's hand stopped playing with the gunstock.

"If you think Fiddler likes you better than he does me," Oliver said, "I'll tell you what I'll do with you. I'll get over on that hill and call him and you stay on this hill and call him. And if he goes across the hollow to me, then I'm his rightful master. If he goes up this hill to you, then you are his rightful master."

"Oh, I'll do that," I said thoughtfully.

It didn't take me any longer to make the decision than it did to speak the words.

"What do you think about it, Pa?" Oliver asked Freeman.

"That's all right with me, son," he said. "For I know where the dog will go."

"Do you agree to this, Pa," I said, for Pa was still clutching his sourwood club in his big strong hands. "We'll never get anywhere like this. We'll be here until nightfall. I won't give an inch of ground."

"Then you both agree?" Oliver asked.

"Yep, I do, son," Freeman said.

"I'll agree," Pa spoke reluctantly.

"Then you'd better lay your weapons down," Oliver said.

"Lay your gun down first, Freeman," Pa said. "My honor that I'll lay my club beside your gun. My honor that I'll abide by the dog's decision. Since we can't select the rightful owner, then let the dog select the rightful owner."

"I think, Mick," Freeman said as he laid his double-barrel on the leaves, "that the hound should select his owner."

"That's a sensible way to do it," Pa said as he laid his big club beside Freeman's double-barrel. "It will save further trouble."

"Then we lay our weapons down too, don't we, Oliver?" I said.

"Sure," he said as he laid his club down beside Pa's.

Then I laid my ax down on the other side of the double-barrel.

"Now is everybody willing to abide by this decision?" Oliver asked.

"I am," I said.

"My honor," Pa said.

"My honor," Freeman said.

"Then I'll go to yon hill," Oliver said.

"And I'll go to the top of this one," I said.

"Freeman and I will take the dog betwixt you," Pa said. "And when you both are ready and start calling, we'll turn him loose."

Freeman lifted Scout into his arms. And Pa walked beside him down the hill. Oliver ran down the hill and I went up the hill. I climbed to the top of the hill. And then I heard Freeman shout from the hilltop on the other side of the little hollow, "Are you ready, Shan?"

"Ready, Oliver," I shouted back.

"Then start calling," Freeman yelled.

"Heah Fiddler, heah Fiddler," Oliver began calling.

"Here Scout, here Scout, here," I began calling.

And we called to the tops of our voices. We couldn't see the dog each of us claimed, for he was turned loose down in the hollow. And neither of us would know to whom he belonged until he came running through the brush to one of us. Neither Oliver nor I let up calling with all our might. A thousand thoughts lashed through my mind as I called. "Here, Scout, here, Scout, here!"

"Oh, my dog, my Scout," I shouted as loud as I could when Scout came running through the brush to me. He jumped up and kissed my face time after time and I let him do it for the first time. I knew then he was my dog. There wasn't any question now. Scout was his name, not Fiddler. And he was my dog. Scout had decided his rightful owner.

A Stall
for Uncle Jeff

$\mathbf{S}$han, I want you to go after Brother Jeff,"
Mom said. "You'll find him over in Thompson's barn."

"How can I ever get 'im over that mountain, Mom?"

"You'll haf to haul 'im on a sled," she said, wringing her
hands. "Get Finn to help you."

"All right," I said.

When I started to harness the mules Pa walked inside the
barn; Finn walked behind him.

"What're you a-goin to do with the mules?" Pa asked.

"Uncle Jeff is over in Thompson's barn," I said. "Mom told
me to go after 'im."

"Is she sendin you across the mountain with my mules to
get that old sot?" Pa asked, his face getting red as a turkey's
snout.

"That's her orders," I said.

173

"It'll be an awful trip on my mules," Pa said.

"It won't be a feather bed for Uncle Jeff," said Finn.

"That will serve Jeff right," Pa said. "He ain't been to my house but three times in his life. I've been married to his sister thirty-three years. Twice we've had to haul 'im here; once we had to tote 'im. I'd rather have a copperhead in my house as to have your Uncle Jeff."

"But Mom is worried about 'im," I said.

"She's worried about 'im," Pa said, "but he don't think much of her. If he did he'd come to see her while he's sober."

Finn harnessed Dick; I harnessed Dinah. Pa stood watching us as we hooked the trace-chains to the singletrees and fastened the well-worn checklines to the bridle bits. We were ready to bring Uncle Jeff home.

"You'd better take a rope with you," Pa suggested.

"Why?" Finn asked.

"You'll haf to tie Jeff on the sled to keep 'im from rollin like a log."

"Okay," Finn said, laughing. "We can tie Uncle Jeff so he can't roll off."

Finn brought two rope plowlines from the corncrib. I slapped the mules with the checklines. We were off over the mountain to get Uncle Jeff.

"God Almighty, a-bringin that old sot here," Pa grumbled as we drove away.

When we climbed the mountain with the empty sled we had to let the mules stop to rest. It was so steep that it was all our big mules could do to pull the empty sled up the mountain across the sawbriar clusters, gullies, and big rocks. When we reached the ridge road it was better, for the road was wider. And when we started down the mountain to Thompson's barn Finn had to tie a rope to the last round in the sled and pull back to keep the sled from running upon the mules' heels. When we reached Thompson's barn our mules had gobs of foamy lather dripping from their bellies.

"It's hell on mules to pull a empty sled over that mountain," Finn said.

"But what about goin back?" I asked.

"How much does Uncle Jeff weigh?" Finn asked.

"Three hundred and seven pounds!"

"Goddamit, how'll we get 'im on the sled?"

"Just put skids upon the sled and roll 'im on, like you would a barrel of salt."

Dick and Dinah were glad to get their wind while we went into the barn after Uncle Jeff. There was a crowd standing around Uncle Jeff's stall looking him over.

"I'm glad ye've come to git 'im, boys," Effie Thompson said. "I can't keep people from comin to this barn to see 'im. It's been full of people ever since he's been here."

"How long's he been here?" Finn asked.

"He's been in that stall a week tomorrow," she said. "I didn't know who he was. Just come here and put up with the cattle. He took one of my cow's stalls and I've had to let her stay outside the barn. Soon as I found out he was yer Ma's brother I sent her word."

"God, what a man," Finn said.

"Oh, he's a mountain of a man," Effie Thompson said as she stood there looking at Uncle Jeff.

Uncle Jeff was laying down on a bed of cornstalks; his eyes were closed; his mouth was open, showing two rows of gold front teeth. His hair was gray where it showed beneath his cap. Uncle Jeff had one empty gallon jug beside him. Near his mouth was another gallon jug half full. He had a hollow weed from his mouth to the jug's neck. He'd been sucking moonshine from the jug through a hollow weed since he was too drunk to lift the jug to his mouth. His overall pants were mud-caked and his overall jumper was ragged at the sleeves and messed with cow manure.

"Can you help us get 'im on the sled?" I asked.

"We certainly can," Effie Thompson said. "I'd be glad to get 'im outen my barn so I can git my cow back to 'er stall."

Finn got Uncle Jeff by one arm; I got him by the other. Effie Thompson got him by one leg. Two boys got his other leg—and several small boys lifted along his body. One held his head up, for his neck was limber. We carried him through the stall door, out at the barn door—everybody grunting under the strain of the lift; finally we got him onto the sled.

"He'll weigh over three hundred and seven," Finn said, getting his breath hard and wiping sweat from his red face with a blue bandanna. "He'll weigh nearly four hundred pounds."

"He's a fine-lookin big man," Effie Thompson said. "Hit's sich a shame he drinks!"

Finn tied the half-filled whiskey jug to a sled standard while I wove a spider web of ropes around Uncle Jeff with the plowlines. I tied them to the sled rounds and standards; I fastened him until he couldn't roll—he couldn't move even if we turned the sled over. Uncle Jeff didn't know what was happening to him. He just moaned. Finn took hold of the lines; we started up the mountain.

"Do you reckon it'll hurt Uncle Jeff when the sled stands on its front end and Uncle Jeff's heels are in the air?" I asked Finn.

"Hell no," Finn said. "He's drunk and he don't know anything about it."

Sometimes the sled went over on its side; sometimes it stood on one end and then on the other. Twice it turned over; but the ropes held Uncle Jeff. There was a new moon in the autumn sky that made us enough light to drive by.

When we finally reached home, Mom and Pa were waiting. I think the jolting on the sled had sobered Uncle Jeff a little, for soon as we untied the ropes Ma and Pa helped Uncle Jeff in the house while Finn and I took the mules to the barn. When we came back to the house Mom was giving Uncle Jeff hot coffee.

"Bad trip from Lennix County," Uncle Jeff said over and over, waving his big hand.

"It must've been," Pa said. "You ought to 've come sober."

"It's a hell of a ride to rope a man to a sled and haul 'im over a mountain," Uncle Jeff moaned, gesturing with his hands.

"It serves you right," Pa said.

"You don't talk like that atter you've been drunk, Mick," Mom reminded Pa.

"When I get drunk I stay at home," Pa said.

"But Jeff don't have a home," Mom said.

"Whose fault is it but his own?" Pa asked Mom.

Mom didn't say another word. She carried chicken broth to Uncle Jeff that she had made soon as we'd gone over the mountain to get him.

"We're stuck with a copperhead in the house," Pa grumbled as he left to go to bed.

"Your pa will see Jeff's a worker," Mom said to Finn and me, soon as Pa had gone to bed. "He's jist got one bad fault; it ain't wimmen nor pistol-totin. Moonshine's got a hold on 'im."

When Finn blew out wisps of burley tobacco smoke from his pipe, Uncle Jeff fought the clouds of smoke away from his nostrils with his big hand.

"You're a-makin Jeff sick, Finn," Mom said.

"You mean to tell me that terbacker smoke makes 'im sick atter the way he can drink that rotgut moonshine with gnats and flies in it?" Finn asked Mom.

"That's right," Mom said.

Finn emptied his pipe and went upstairs to bed while I

watched Mom feed Uncle Jeff hot chicken broth with a big spoon. Uncle Jeff nodded his head like a sick chicken gulping the broth Mom fed him. I went to bed while she was still feeding him.

When Pa got up at five next morning, Uncle Jeff was up with him. I heard them talking while Mom rattled the pots and pans in the kitchen. Then Pa called Finn and me to get up and wash for breakfast. When we went downstairs Uncle Jeff was sitting before the fire with Pa, talking about cattle, farm, and crops. He didn't look like a man that had ever been drunk. If his face had been shaven he'd have been taken for a small-town businessman.

Uncle Jeff ate a hearty breakfast of a dozen hot biscuits, a half-dozen fried eggs—besides the ham, hot gravy, jelly, butter—and he drank five cups of black coffee. When Finn and I left the table to feed and milk, Uncle Jeff was leaning over the table explaining the harmful effects of alcohol on a man's body. He was explaining to Pa what it did to different parts of a man's body. He talked to Pa as if he were a member of the W.C.T.U.—and from the way he talked he was warning Pa never to take another drink.

That day when we went to build a fence, Uncle Jeff showed Pa how to do it. "Never put the butt-end of a post in the ground," he told Pa. "It won't shed the water like the tip-end will. That's why your fence posts have been rottin off at the top of the ground." He showed us new ways to brace the fence to keep the wire from getting slack.

"I'll tell you Jeff is a fence builder," I heard Pa tell Mom. "He beats any man I ever saw workin. He can do as much work as three men. I can't he'p it if he is sixty years old."

That winter when we cut wood, Uncle Jeff could bury a double-bitted ax to the eye every lick he struck. He could cut as much wood as Finn, Pa, and I put together. Then Uncle Jeff shod the mules; that was something none of us could do.

Uncle Jeff was a good mule driver too. Pa liked the way he handled our mean mules. They didn't run away with Uncle Jeff. They seemed to like Uncle Jeff. He could go into their stalls the darkest night and they wouldn't kick at him. My dog left me and took up with Uncle Jeff.

"I'll tell you there's no wonder Jeff goes to a barn when he gets drunk," Pa said. "He's got a way with 'im that livestock, mules, horses, and dogs like."

Uncle Jeff was glad to get a place to spend the winter. He didn't ask Pa for any money for his work. And I heard Pa tell Mom that he was glad that Uncle Jeff had come, for he was getting a lot of work done for nothing. He told her that Jeff ate as much as three men but he did four times as much work as any man he'd ever worked with. He told her Jeff was such a powerful man that he could sink a posthole with a digger fast as the digger could lift the dirt.

When spring came, I heard Pa tell Mom that Uncle Jeff wanted a dollar a day, three hot meals, a good bed, and his clothes washed and mended. And Pa told Mom that since Jeff had quit his drinkin rotgut moonshine that he would pay him his price. Mom agreed with Pa that Jeff was a changed man, for every evening Uncle Jeff would explain to Mom for hours at a time what moonshine whiskey would do to Pa if he drank it. He had Pa afraid to drink a bottle of beer when he went to town on Saturdays. When Uncle Jeff talked to Pa he looked like the picture of health. His cheeks were red as roses, his eyes bright—his face smooth—and I'd say Uncle Jeff weighed over three hundred and seven pounds. He wasn't fat; he was just a big man.

It was the middle of spring when Pa first paid Uncle Jeff. Uncle Jeff said he'd take the Saturday off and go to town with Pa. Said he wanted to buy a few little things. When Pa came home from town he asked if Jeff had come. We told 'im Uncle Jeff hadn't come home. "I'll bet he's on a bender," Pa said. "He can buy rotgut moonshine for two dollars a gallon."

Monday morning Pa was forking hay from the loft before good daylight. He stuck something with a pitchfork prong and a man hollered. He had stuck Uncle Jeff in the leg.

"What are you a-doin here, Jeff?" Pa asked.

"I've been to see my boy, Bledsoe," Uncle Jeff told him. "And I didn't want to come in late and disturb you."

"That's nice of you, Jeff," Pa said.

Uncle Jeff ate a big breakfast that morning and worked all day in the cornfield. When he got through explaining to Pa that evening about the harm a bottle of beer could do to a man, Pa told Mom that he didn't believe that Jeff had been drunk.

Every Saturday Pa paid Uncle Jeff and he took off to town. Pa always found him in the hayloft on Monday morning. Pa said it was all right since Jeff didn't smoke; there wouldn't be any danger of his settin the barn on fire. Uncle Jeff always said he had been to visit one of his children.

When September came and our big crop had been laid by, Uncle Jeff went away one Saturday and stayed away a week. Finn walked across the mountain to the post office. And as he walked along the path that wound among the tough-butted white oaks he heard singing. Under a rock cliff he found Uncle Jeff beside his two gallon jugs. After Finn came home we took the mules and sled and hauled Uncle Jeff home. Uncle Jeff explained to Pa that he'd been to see one of his boys and that he was away from the good influence of our home and was persuaded to tip the jug.

That winter Uncle Jeff did some work, but mostly he sat before the fire and talked about the evil influence of whiskey. He didn't charge Pa for the work he did about the place. But when spring came he started charging Pa three gallons of moonshine per week. That spring we planted a big crop, for we expected Uncle Jeff's help. Maybe Uncle Jeff knew that we'd have to keep him even if he did get drunk every week end.

Once Uncle Jeff was locked up in Greenwood jail. Pa heard that Uncle Jeff was cleaning the streets in Greenwood to pay his fine. He laughed, but Mom didn't. She told Pa to go pay his fine and let him work it out in the cornfield. Pa and Mom had a little fuss but finally Mom won, since we were crowded with weeds in our corn. Pa paid a twenty-four-dollar fine for Uncle Jeff and Harlan Jaggers, Greenwood's "town marshal," told Pa that if he had known the big man was his brother-in-law he wouldn't have arrested him. But Harlan told Pa that Jeff was liable to get shot, since he'd opened Jim Sinder's door and walked into his house when they were all asleep. Said Jim's wife opened her eyes and saw a big man standing over her bed—said she screamed and Jim reached under his pillow and got his .38. But said he lit the lamp and saw that the big man was drunk and didn't kill 'im. Said Uncle Jeff was clawing in the dark with his big hands.

During that summer Uncle Jeff opened the doors of two more houses. He found an empty bed in Horace Didway's house and went to sleep. When Uncle Jeff woke next morning he explained to them that the front of their house was so near like the one where he lived that he had made a mistake. He told them that it looked like a man was drunk when he did a thing like this. Uncle Jeff apologized to Florence Didway about getting into the wrong house and soon as he had his breakfast he came home. And then Uncle Jeff got into Spittie Hexter's house and slept on the floor. He explained to Spittie the next morning that the house looked so much like the one where he lived and that the night was so dark that he made a mistake. And that the reason he slept on the floor, he thought his sister had moved the bed. And he told them it looked like that only a drunk man would do such a thing. He ate breakfast with Spittie before he came home.

The town people talked about this big man, Jeff, that was making mistakes and getting into people's houses. The men talked about the way he had scared their wives when they found him in bed the next morning or when he was standing over a bed clawing in the dark. Pa heard the talk every time he went to town and he told Mom that he had had enough of Uncle Jeff. He told Mom that Uncle Jeff had come into his home and that he was trying to run his farm. Said Uncle Jeff had just taken everything over as if it belonged to him, telling him how many times to plow his corn, how many times to take hoes through it and chop the weeds. He said that Uncle Jeff was telling him how much wood to cut for winter, how to worm and sucker his tobacco and telling him the way to hang it in the barn. He told Mom Jeff had to go.

"Where can Brother Jeff go?" Mom asked him. "What would a man like Jeff do if you turned him loose on the highway?"

"I don't give a damn what he would do," Pa told her. "He ought to stay with one of his own youngins."

"I ain't so shore that a one of his youngins will have 'im," Mom said.

"I can't blame 'em atter the way he's carried on," Pa said. "He's glutted a small fortune down his gullet and deposited it out on the fence posts. One of us has to leave here."

"Jeff's not a-leavin," she told Pa. And Uncle Jeff didn't go.

Pa packed his suitcase to leave.

"Where you goin, Mick?" Mom asked with a scrutinizing look.

"Back to Big Sandy among my people," Pa said.

"When will you be back?" Mom asked.

"When Jeff high-tails it down this road," Pa said.

Then Pa told Finn and me to do the best we could if he

never got back; but we knew that Pa would be back and that he would clean house if the house hadn't been cleaned. He told us his home wasn't his home any more. Pa said Jeff was a man too big for him to fight fair, and he didn't want to hurt Jeff. Then Pa said, "I won't be missed here until I'm gone." We watched Pa walk slowly down the road, a small sun-tanned man leaving his own home.

Pa hadn't more than left the hollow until Uncle Jeff went to town. Mom sat weeping, saying that both Pa and Jeff were gone.

"Don't worry, Mom," Finn said, "Uncle Jeff will be back."

That evening Uncle Jeff came home drunk. He didn't go to the barn loft either. He sat on the porch with the flies lighting around his mouth where he slobbered. Mom stopped weeping when she saw us trying to do the work and Uncle Jeff sitting on the porch drunk.

"Git out of here, Jeff," Mom screamed, with a sled standard in her hand. "Take your duds and git outen this house!"

Uncle Jeff pulled out with a turkey of clothes flung over his shoulder and a gallon jug in his hand. We watched him stagger over the hill toward the sunset.

"He's gone," Mom wept. "What will happen to 'im?"

"Don't worry, Mom," Finn said, "He'll get along all right."

"I wonder how Pa's gettin along?" I asked Mom. But Mom wouldn't say anything.

Summer passed and the September leaves had started turning. We hadn't heard a word from Pa. Ma heard that Uncle Jeff was back in Lennix County. We remembered Pa's last words had been to us that Mom wouldn't miss him until he was gone. And Pa was right. Long suckers had grown on the tobacco and it hadn't been topped. Tall weeds grew in our cornbalks. Hay rotted in the meadows. October came and our potatoes hadn't been dug. Finn and I were worked to death.

Mom often asked us when we thought that Pa would be home. We told Mom that we didn't expect him. Her face got as desolate as the mountains after the leaves left the autumn trees.

It was early November when we saw Pa coming up the road. Pa hurried up the path to his home as Finn and I ran to meet him. Mom stood upon the hill watching us meet Pa. We had expected him to be mad, but he was laughing. We walked beside him up the path toward the house; Finn carried his suitcase. When Pa got to the house, Mom wanted to kiss him but Pa was leery.

Remember
the Sabbath Day
and Keep It Holy

It was Sunday morning, the day the Lord rested from making the earth, and I rested from working in the little coal mine on my farm. I dug coal and farmed to make a living. I raised enough to feed Myrtle, my wife, and our four youngins, and the truck- and wagonloads of coal I sold when I was lucky made extra money to buy our clothes and pay our taxes. I owned a hundred acres of Plum Grove hilltops, which was poorer soil for crops than the Plum Grove Valley land. But my hilltop land had a vein of coal that the Plum Grove Valley land didn't have. So the Lord had evened everything up for the valley and the hill people at Plum Grove.

I had eaten my breakfast, milked the cows, and turned them out on the sawbriar pasture, and I had fed my mules and turned them onto their steep sassafras hillside pasture

185

where it was too steep for the cows to graze. Sunday was a day of rest for the mules and cows too. I'd fed the hogs their corn nubbins so they could take off to their smaller pasture where the sandbriars and greenbriars grew. My valley neighbors didn't know my six hogs looked better on less feed than their hogs. But I knew hogs would root down and eat the greenbriar and sawbriar roots. So each year I fenced a new pasture to get more roots for my hogs. And by doing this I got rid of the greenbriars and sawbriars that were trying to take over my farm.

With the cows fed and milked and the mules and hogs fed and off to enjoy the Sabbath behind fences in their small worlds, I figured I might as well be off too. I'd walk out to the Old Line Special dirt road where people passed on Sunday. Maybe I'd see somebody. Maybe we would sit under the shade of one of the oaks beside the road, and I could find out something I didn't know that was going on among our neighbors. There was always something going on.

As I walked along the little road that led from my little coal mine, I looked back once at the big blue-slate dump just below the gaping hole. The mouth of my coal mine looked like an open mouth, and the slope of the hill it was on looked like a face. And the sawbriars, greenbriars, and sassafras sprouts looked like beard on the face. The two old mines farther up on the slope looked like two old eyes in wrinkled sockets. My father before me had worked these mines.

The mine props in the mouth of my coal mine looked like discolored front teeth in the mouth of an old man. Well, it made me think of my father's face ten years ago before he died. He'd worked his lifetime on this hill and I'd work my lifetime here while time flowed on like a river of wind.

When I stopped looking at the mouth of my mine I picked up a stick to whittle that was lying across one of the tracks Old Red Brady Callihan's coal wagon had made. There were two yellow streaks his loaded wagon had made when his bay mules got down sometimes to their knees to pull forty bushels of coal from my mine. Red Brady, now seventy, had always had the best mule teams in the Plum Grove hills. He had red tassels on their bridles, red trimming on the shoulder pads under their collars, and he had the trace chains wrapped so they wouldn't rub the hair from his mule's sides. Old Red Brady had hauled coal with mule teams all his life. Where the mines were out in good places, trucks came now and hauled the coal. But my mine was the place for Old Red Brady and his mules.

He was called Old Red Brady, now, for he had a son Young Red Brady.

Then there was a White Brady who worked back under the hill digging coal where the sun never shone on him. And he had eyes about the color of shallow water in a fast-flowing stream. His hair, eyebrows, and beard were as white as field-daisy petals. Then there was Slim Brady, Big Brady, and Little Brady. There were so many Brady Callihans that they had to have additions on their names to tell them apart. The reason for so many Brady Callihans was that old Doc Brady had delivered all of them but Old Red.

I thought about these things as I whittled on my big stick. I had to pick up a big stick, for I carried a hawk-bill knife and it sliced wood like a drawing knife. This morning the sun rose over the lazy Plum Grove hills and dried the morning dewdrops on the Queen Anne's lace that grew on either side of the wagon ruts. The sun's warm rays came down splintering the lazy morning wind. They sliced the wind like steel colters sliced the new ground earth on the steep slopes. But the sun splinters were prettier than the colters in the cutter plow. I was having fun just whittling splinters and leaving a trail of them along the road from my coal mine. I didn't know why it was fun to watch the brown-oak splinters roll from the oak limb.

I stood for a minute to watch a snail inch his way to get

under the bark of a log that lay beside the road. The sun was driving him to the shade. I'd never seen anybody slower than a snail unless it was Young Sherd Jason. Young Sherd was about twenty-five and he wouldn't work in a pie factory when he was hungry. If he'd been willing to work no one would have hired him. When the sun got hot he went for the shade like a snail. Still, Young Sherd had an easy life. He lived about three days with each family among the Plum Grove hills so he wouldn't be a burden too long for any family. He had to stay with people no kin to him, for his kinfolks wouldn't have him. Many people called him "Snail" Jason. But I never called him that. He'd sat before my fire in winter telling big tales that kept us laughing until bedtime.

"Good morning, Dewey," Old Red Brady greeted me. "I'm glad to see you on this Sunday morning."

"Good morning," I greeted him.

Old Red Brady was sitting upon the bank above the Old Line Special road. He was sitting in the shade of a tough-butted white oak fanning his red sweaty face with his hat.

"It's goin to be another scorcher," he sighed, looking at me and blinking his little beady blue eyes. "Thank the Lord for givin us Sunday, but I wish He'd not have sent so much heat."

"But we can't have it all our way," I said.

"You're right about that," he said, blinking his eyes and fanning faster. "Come up and sit awhile. Maybe we'll see somebody go by. Come up and sit and fan yourself and let's make the Lord's Day a holy one."

"Don't mind if I do," I said.

My brogans gathered particles of dust that rose from each step where I dug in with my toes as I took a run up the dry weedless bank. Before I sat down beside Old Red Brady I gathered a few dry last year's leaves so I wouldn't get dust on the seat of my Sunday pants. Then I sat down on the

leaves and pulled my red bandanna from my pocket to wipe
the sweat from my face. Above us the leaves on the tough-
butted white oaks were wilted and hanging in pods. A crow
flew over very slowly with something in his bill. A redbird
lighted on the branch of a red haw beside the road but he
didn't sing. His bill was opened and his tongue was showing
like a thin wild crabapple leaf on a hot summer night. Two
gray lizards ran up and down the scaly bark on the white
oak.

"It's mating time for the lizards," Old Red said, swinging
his hat back and forth in front of his hot face. "They don't
know anything about the Lord's Day. Now I'm an old man
and I have learned one must keep it holy."

Old Red's white eyebrows were holding little beads of
sweat that shone when the lazy wind moved the branches of
the tough-butted white-oak branches back and forth to let
the pencil strips of light break through between the wilted
pods of leaves. Old Red was a little man, about one hundred
thirty pounds and five feet six inches tall. His little mustache was as white as a daisy petal over his pink hot face.
The hair on his head, a bit long, was as white as the shirt he
had on.

"Dewey, I got hot a-climbin that hill," he said. "I'm hot all
the way through."

"Who's that comin around the bend?" I asked.

"Sherd the Snail," he said. "That's who he is, all right. And
he never dresses up any more for the Lord's Day. He used to
wear his peg-legged blue pants and a white clean shirt with
a high collar and a bow tie every Sunday. He used to dress
like we're dressed now," Old Red whispered so low Young
Sherd couldn't hear him.

Young Sherd was six feet tall and weighed one hundred
sixty pounds. He was as slender and lean as an oak sapling growing on a poor slope of a Plum Grove hill. His

eyes were as blue as a deep hole of water shaded under a cloud of green leaves. His hair was as red and tangled as a mass of love vines twining around a decaying stump in a new-ground cornfield.

"Come up and jine us and enjoy the Lord's Day," Old Red invited him.

At the sound of Old Red's voice Young Sherd looked up.

"Don't mind if I do," he said. "It's better up there in the shade than it is a-breathin the dust."

When Young Sherd left the road to make a run for the bank as I had done, he stopped abruptly and looked at the ground. Old Red stopped fanning and looked over the bank to see what had caused him to stop. I looked too but I couldn't see anything. I saw Young Sherd standing there dressed in his brogans and tight-fitting overall pants with the brass screws below the side pockets and on the four corners of the hip pockets. His pants fit as tight across his swiveled hips as the tough-butted white oak's scaly bark clung to the body of the gnarled, scrubby tree. And his blue work shirt, now dark with sweat, was as wilted as the pods of leaves above us. His red beard was almost as heavy and tangled as the hair on his head. Beneath his heavy brows his eyes sparkled, but there wasn't any sign of his mouth. And when he spoke the beard muffled his words and made them sound like echoes coming from a deep hollow.

"What do you see, Sherd?" Old Red asked.

"I see what you didn't see," he said. "I'll fetch him up and let you see what you missed." Then he bent over and put his hand down. "Now don't you try to run," Young Sherd said.

He made a quick grab and came up with a blacksnake. He held the snake's head up level with his own and its tail wiggled on the dry ground.

"You're not going to kill him," I said. "That's a pretty old bull blacksnake. And he's harmless, too."

"No, I ain't goin to kill him," he said. "But I could kill him easy enough. I could take him by the tail and crack him like a whip and his head would fly off. I ust to do that for fun. But I quit that. Becoming a man, I put away childish things." Then he laughed louder than the rising wind that was becoming wider awake as the day wore on. The wind was now frolicking in the wilted pods of leaves on the white-oak tree. "I think you ought to wear him around your neck for a tie, Red Brady," he said, "since you have such pretty white hair, eyebrows, mustache, and pink cheeks. Besides, you're all triggered up for the Sabbath in a white shirt. This blacksnake would make you a pretty necktie. You'd really be dressed up for the Sabbath if you had a blacksnake necktie. Somebody might pass here and see you and think you're right pretty."

"You're just a-gabbin' Young Sherd," Old Red said, grinning and blinking his little beady eyes.

"No, I mean it," he said. "We've got to have you dressed up with a blacksnake tie."

"I've always been afraid of any kind of a snake," Old Red Brady said. "And I'm sure not a-goin to wear one around my neck for a tie."

"What if I put this one around your neck?" Young Sherd said.

"If you mean what you're a-sayin and you put that snake on me, I'll go home and get my rabbit gun and I'll fill you full of shot!"

"You're a-funnin, Old Red Brady," Young Sherd said. "You know you are. You've not shot a rabbit in twenty years."

"Yes, but my old gun will still shoot," he spoke in a resolute voice.

"But you must remember Sunday is the Lord's Day and we ought to keep it holy," Young Sherd mocked. He was still standing down below us holding the squirming snake up with his hand around its neck. "Look what a long nice black tie you'd have to match all that white. You'd look mighty nifty. Some young gal might come along and look at you with her pretty peepers."

"No young gal for me," Old Red told him. "Grace has been dead ten years now. I could've had one, near my age, but I didn't want her."

Then Young Sherd laughed louder than the lazy wind among the wilted leaves. He ran up the bank with the snake in his hand. Red Brady thought Young Sherd was joking. He never even moved from where he sat. When Young Sherd reached the top of the bank he wrapped the big snake twice around Old Red's neck. Then he turned and scooted back down the bank to the road. Old Red's face turned almost as white as his shirt. He wouldn't touch the snake with his hands but bent his head over and let the snake fall onto the ground. The big snake was as glad to get from around Old Red's neck as he was to have it off. The bull blacksnake crawled away in a hurry with his head up and his forked tongue sticking out. He disappeared among the greenbriars, sawbriars, and wild huckleberry bushes. The snake was gone while Young Sherd bent up and down and slapped his thighs with his hands, laughing louder than the noises the frolicking summer wind was making in the treetops.

Old Red Brady got up slowly with his hat in his hand.

"It's not funny," he said. "It's not a bit funny! You couldn't do anything that's lower to a man old enough to be your father than to put a snake on him. It's the worst thing that anybody'd ever done to me in my life."

Young Sherd was still laughing when Old Red Brady walked out the hill and went over the bank into the Old Line Special road. He didn't come down where he would have to face Young Sherd. He looked back a few times but he kept on walking.

"He won't go home after his gun," Young Sherd said. "He's bluffin. Don't you think he is?"

"I don't know," I said.

"Now I'll come back up and sit beside you and shade awhile," Young Sherd said. "I've laughed so hard it's made me sweat more than if I had worked. I've never had more fun in my life. Old Red will allus remember his blacksnake necktie."

Young Sherd came running up the bank again and he dropped down on the same pile of dead leaves that Old Red had gathered to keep from getting the seat of his Sunday pants dirty. He pulled a soiled blue bandanna from his side pocket and pressed it against his beard to absorb the sweat.

"If you'd shave that beard off, your face would be a lot cooler," I said. "How can you stand that red crow's nest on your face in this hot weather?"

"Used to it," he told me. "Why shave my beard? Why comb my hair? Why change my clothes until I have to? I like to have fun and take it easy. No ust to hurry life to its end among Plum Grove hills. I've found life so easy and good here. 'Take it easy and live long,' I say to myself every day. I could lie down by the branch and drink the water and eat sassafras leaves and blades of grass if I got hungry and just lie there and love being lazy and looking up at the sun by day and the moon and stars by night. Why worry about anything? Never get in a hurry. Just take life easy and have fun."

Then he absorbed more sweat from his red beard with his sweat-soaked blue bandanna. I wiped more sweat from my clean-shaven face with my red bandanna.

"Dewey, I can't remember when I've ever run as fast as I could," Young Sherd said. "Talk about the Sabbath for the day of rest and to keep it holy! Every day is the Sabbath for me if it means rest. But I've not exactly kept it holy!"

"There comes Old Red Brady up the road," I said. "And he's got his shotgun."

"He's a-bluffin," Young Sherd said. "He ain't goin to shoot me."

"Look, he's comin closer," I said. "You'd better go."

"I'm as good as my word," Old Red shouted. "When I tell you something I mean it. I aim to sprinkle you real good with number eight shot."

He raised the shotgun to his shoulder.

"Just a minute, Red Brady," I shouted. "I'm too close to Young Sherd. I don't want to be sprinkled. Let me move out of the way."

I jumped up and ran down the bank. When I reached the road I ran back toward Old Red Brady. When I turned to look back because Old Red Brady was moving his gun barrel, Young Sherd had scooted down the bank and was walking fast up the road.

"A blacksnake around my neck for a necktie," Old Red shouted.

Then I heard Young Sherd laugh but his laughter was drowned.

"Pow," and a stream of black smoke came slowly from the gun barrel.

Young Sherd jumped two feet high and slapped his hands on the seat of his tight-fitting pants while Old Red reloaded. Young Sherd turned in time to see him raise the shotgun to his shoulder again. Then he ran as I'd never seen a man run before.

"Pow." A stream of smoke came from the gun barrel.

Young Sherd never looked back, for he looked like his feet were on the wind moving faster than the pistons of the Old Line Special engine when it came down the grade on its thirty-six miles of tracks pulling a passenger coach, a mail car, and a freight car.

"The number eight shot burnt him good," Old Red Brady said, "Throwin a snake on a man old enough to be his father on the Holy Sabbath Day."

He put the shotgun across his shoulder.

"I'll go pray for forgiveness for what I've done," he said. "Then I'll go home and talk to my mules. It's a-gettin so a man can't trust his friends."

"It's too bad neighbors can't get together and have fun," I said. "I wanted to rest and talk."

He turned and walked slowly down the dusty road while I walked up the road and over the hill the way Young Sherd had run. I was going back home too. I wondered how many shots Young Sherd had in his seat. The second time Old Red shot, Young Sherd hadn't jumped too high, since he was running faster than a racer snake from a new-ground fire.

When I reached the other side of the hill, just before my lane road turned off, I heard someone moaning and groaning over under the wahoo bushes that shaded a deep gully. I looked through a little window among the leaves. Down there sat Young Sherd with his pants down craning his long neck to see the little red spots while he fanned his face with wahoo leaves.

"Are you all right, Young Sherd?" I asked.

"About a hundred little pellets went in skin-deep and they're a-smartin somethin awful," he said. "I didn't dream he'd go home and fetch a gun. After he brought it I thought he was tryin to bluff me. What do you think's come over Old Red Brady?"

"I don't know," I said.

"He's not followin me, is he?"

"No, he went to pray for forgiveness for shooting you," I said. "Then he said he was going to spend the rest of the day talking to his mules."

"Well, I forgive him," Young Sherd said. "I've been a

thinkin as these shots burn like fire that I ought not to have put that old bull blacksnake around his neck. Gee, I'm smarting so much I might have to get out of this wahoo shade and start running again."

"Can I be of any help to you?"

"No. Remember the Sabbath Day and keep it holy," he sighed.

Here

It seemed to Jason that he stood among strangers when Huey, the engineer, pulled his train through the Dial's Cut. Huey waved to him as his engine passed and slowly came to a stop. He greeted Huey by waving back. But all of these strangers around him waved to Huey, too. He watched Conductor Brady Black help an old man down the steps. The passenger was a stranger, and the only one to get off. This old man was as tall and straight as the Prince Albert on a tobacco tin. Only he wasn't wearing that kind of coat. But he did have the beard and he wore a high hat and walked with a cane. He wore a high celluloid collar and a colonel bow tie. He acted like a man who knew where he was going.

There was no rush among the strangers to get on the train first. They were polite and very silent. Both men and women were oddly dressed, Jason thought. Conductor Brady Black helped two elderly women first. Younger women with babies in their arms climbed on unassisted. Young boys waited until the older men were on. Biggest crowd I ever saw get on Huey's train at Three Mile, thought Jason. He turned to look at the baggage coach just ahead. The slide door was half open, and he could not help noticing the long pine box with the wreaths of flowers lying on top. The box was close to the open door.

"You'd better watch that box," the Prince Albert passenger warned the baggageman.

"We'll put it off at the next stop," said the baggageman. "That's why I have it near the door."

"W'y, the next stop is Nellavale," said the old man. "Who's dead?"

"Jason Stringer," was the baggageman's reply. "He's taking his last ride with Huey to the Howeland Cemetery."

I am Jason Stringer, he thought. That can't be me. I'm here.

Jason was a little confused as he watched Conductor Brady Black signal Huey. The engine's high drive wheels spun on the rusted T-rails and the sparks flew. Huey's train—a coach, baggage car, and a freight car—began to move up the grade on spinning wheels. The baggageman stood in the open door beside the box as the train slowly gained speed over the two red streaks of rust toward the dark and gaping mouth of the Barney Tunnel. Jason watched until it disappeared under the hill, leaving its trail of black curling smoke behind. The old man had turned and was walking up the wagon road tapping his cane gently.

Jason Stringer started walking up the track where the cowcatcher on Huey's train had shorn the grass until it was even with the rusted rails. He looked at the little crossties half hidden in the grass. He didn't see a good one. Huey needed sound timbers under his rusted T-rails if he was to keep his train on time. Wonder what was wrong with Bill Kaiser and his three section men? Why didn't they replace these decayed ties with sound ones? Bill had only twelve miles of track to keep repaired, ditches on either side to keep cleared out, and fallen slate and rock in five tunnels to watch for.

When he had heard Huey blow two mournful shorts and a lonesome long for Nellavale, he looked at his watch at Three Mile, but he had been among those strange people. Their outdated clothes and polite, silent ways had made him forget to look. Bird Norris had been the last to clean and set his watch. Bird had done a good job, too. Ten till eleven. His time was right on the dot with Huey's train. For thirty-six miles along the track, farmers within the sound of Huey's train whistle set their watches when Huey passed. Housewives set their clocks by the sound of his mournful whistle. Huey, the engineer, always kept his head sticking out of the cab window. The wind pressed his long white beard against his face. He wore a small pin-striped cap with jumper to match and a red bandanna tied around his neck. Huey wore goggles to protect his eyes from the cinders. Old Huey, the engineer, never changed a bit.

Jason remembered when he was a boy he had wanted to grow up and be an engineer like Huey.

Huey's engine had never hit a person in the half century he had been at the throttle. He had never hit a horse or a cow that had escaped its shorter pasture for the lusher grass that grew along the track. These thoughts flashed through Jason's mind as he took long steps from tie to tie. And why had he stopped at Three Mile among those people he thought were strangers? Like everybody else along the track he'd just walked to the flag stop to watch Huey go by.

Jason stepped upon the narrow T-rail. He wanted to see

how many rails he could walk before he stepped off. He remembered how he and Jack Dysard had tried to walk these narrow rails through the Barney Tunnel and not step off. He knew he was never able to do it, but Jack claimed he had. He never knew whether Jack did or not, because he couldn't see Jack's feet in that midnight darkness. He thought of the times, too, when he and Jack had run through the tunnel to beat the train. After they'd been to Tom Fitch's country store they had always come back through the tunnel instead of walking over the hill. It was a shorter and cooler walk, even if it was dangerous.

Jason had balanced himself and was holding on until he thought about Walter Phelps. How they used to put a cinder on the T-rail, hide in the tall horseweeds beside the track, and watch Huey's engine crush the cinder. That was fun, too! But the thing he hated to think about was how he and Maurice Sinnett used to stand on top of the Barney Tunnel and throw rocks down on the train when it came through. He remembered the feel of the wind from a bullet that passed between them when somebody shot from the vestibule. Maurice said he felt the wind, too.

Not too much to see, he thought, as he came to the crossing where the road turned to Plum Grove. Not much to see, but a good walk on an August morning. The fresh wind on his face felt good. He stopped to look at the old crossing where the long boards crisscrossed. On each board in large black letters were: STOP! LOOK! LISTEN! Here he, Aaron, Little Ed, and Penny used to throw rocks. Each tried to center the O with a cinder. Each, in those days, wanted to be an engineer and pull a train like Huey's or to be a baseball pitcher. The big O's were catchers' mitts and each pitcher tried to put the ball right in the center. But Bill Kaiser caught them one morning rocking the crossing when he came suddenly out of the dark tunnel on a handcar. He reported them to their parents. Never any more baseball practice at the O's on this crossing. . . . Why had he thought of this?

Then he walked on the soft sand along the Plum Grove road. He leaped Shacklerun Creek to keep from getting his shoes muddy. He used to wade this creek on his way to and from Plum Grove. This road hadn't changed in all the years he could remember. He walked up the steep, and thought of the way he and Aaron used to roll their hoops to school there. This was the place that tried their skill. Only he and Aaron had been skillful enough to push their hoops to the top of this steep without having them fall over. At the top of the steep was the same old tree leaning over Shacklerun waters where he had once done something Aaron was never able to do. There was a big blacksnake lying on this tree sunning himself in the September sun. He threw a rock from the road and killed the snake the first blow.

Down in the hollow below the steep was where old Henry Wheeler, the Dutchman, kept a tall stack of hay with a pole down through the center to steady it against the wind. Old Man Wheeler had got after them many times for climbing his haystack and sliding off. But he'd never chase them off again. Not now. Henry Wheeler slept at Plum Grove. Jason decided he'd stop if he thought about it while he was at Plum Grove and see where he was planted.

He turned the little point and started down where the road dipped and the water ran across. In this ravine Henry Wheeler used to have a big hewn-out log for a watering trough. When Lis, Siani, Jim, and Rufus Young rode by they could water their horses. Henry Wheeler knew how to do things with his hands all right, even if he did wear thick wool clothes in summer. He believed what would keep out cold would keep out heat. Wonderful man! Jason could almost see him now cutting out a fence row. He never could forget him.

Beyond the watering trough was Henry Wheeler's tall

house with the steep roof. Above his house, on a finger of the hill, were many buildings. These had steep roofs, too. There stood unchanged the same cow stable, woodshed, toolshed, lumber shed, mule stable, cornbin, wheatbin, and a ketch-all. And beyond this, on another hill, were the Plum Grove School and Church spires. And west of all this were the meadows on the rolling slopes. Beyond these meadows were the giant trees where Henry Wheeler had cut the under-brush for wood to burn. Each autumn he raked and hauled the leaves from under these trees. He hauled them to his creek bottoms and plowed them under to grow better food another season for his children and better feed for his cattle. What a land, Jason thought. His land. It had never been pret-tier than on this morning. He had never appreciated it more.

He climbed the steep Plum Grove hill where the black haws were ripe and inviting. But he didn't have time to eat them. He passed the place where little Bob Griffee found a hen's nest with a rotten egg and eased it into Roy Perkins' hip pocket. When the bell rang and Roy sat down he crushed the egg. Calvin Clarke, their teacher, smelled the egg, and when he started to paddle Little Bob he found a spelling book in the seat of his pants. Jason never could for-get that.

He looked at the big honey locust covered with thorns and with the ripe red honey-locust beans hanging on its long bending boughs. He remembered how they used to split the beans and run their tongues over them to get the honey-locust sugar. Once when they were shoving each other under the trees trying to get the beans, Timmie Phelps ran a thorn clear through his bare foot and Mr. Clarke pulled it out.

Calvin Clarke was a good teacher, Jason remembered, as he climbed on to the big white oak that grew in the corner of the schoolyard. Here the ground had been worn away by his own and his classmates' bare feet, and the exposed roots were big and gnarled like coiled cow snakes. It was on one of these roots that elbowed up that Mr. Clarke used to have the boys sit while he cut their hair. He brought clippers and scissors to school the same as books. He wanted his pupils to look neat.

The school and the church faced each other, and the ground sloped away in all directions. What a pretty place this was! He was glad that he had come. Not anything had changed from the first impressions embedded in his memory. The smell of Jim Young's silking corn in August had come through the open window where he sat. In September he had looked at the jays more than he had looked at the pictures in his books. He watched them fly up to the tops of the tall oaks with acorns in their bills. He had listened to them scolding other birds away. Now he laid his hand on the window sill where he had sat, and he thought about Calvin Clarke, his first teacher, and Earl Riley, Nora Riggs, Rosie Maggard, Eva Hilton, James Stephenson, and Everett Hilton, his other teachers. He wondered where they were now.

But Henry Wheeler's stone. He mustn't forget to see it. Henry Wheeler used to say he liked to get into a quiet place where he could sit and think through steel. He was in that quiet place now, but he wasn't thinking through steel. He'd been planted like the yuccas on this hill. Jason remembered he used to be afraid to walk barefooted among these yuccas because he was afraid of copperheads. But now he went straight to Henry Wheeler's stone. He stood with his hand on the warm stone remembering the double-breasted brown corduroy suit, with rows of black buttons up the front, which Henry Wheeler used to wear on Sundays through the summer months. And he wore a heavy, autumn, oak-leaf-brown wool shirt to match, which he kept buttoned at the collar.

The sun was dropping now. It was over the Putt Off Ford in the Little Sandy River, a place he planned to visit later. This was where he had learned to swim. And there were a lot of people he wanted to see, too. But he didn't have time. Not now. He had to start home. So he ran from among the gray and white Plum Grove stones and leaped over the schoolyard fence as he had done when after a hard-hit ball at Plum Grove. He kept on running across the meadow toward the giant oaks and under their overlapping branches that formed a canopy between him and the sky.

At the stile between the Wheeler and Collins farms he paused and thought of what his father told him once: "More courting has been done at this stile than in any parlor among Plum Grove homes." He wondered how many lovers had embraced and how many lips had met on this spot. It was hidden by trees in all directions, and a grove of wild plum shaded the stile. He wondered if the old man, who looked like Prince Albert and got off Huey's train, was one of these. He wondered how many of them remembered, and if any of them now slept at Plum Grove with regrets. Jason kept thinking about what his father had told him until he had reached the top of Collins' Hill and had walked past the twin persimmons.

Now he was in the orchard where he used to get pears on his way to school. He got them until his first cousin told his mother, and she whipped him all the way to Mrs. Collins' home and made him confess he had stolen her pears. He never could forget this. His mother's whipping made him feel very miserable then. But not later. He knew it was an important lesson along his way.

At the east end of the pear orchard he stopped under a familiar oak. This was a spot dear to his heart. His memory wasn't vague about this oak and the rock beneath. He used to stop here on his way to school to write his themes. He remembered he could study better here than at his home or in the schoolroom. He thought of how many times he had sat on this rock solving problems when he heard the Plum Grove school bell. How afraid he was to go to school unprepared! That time wasn't far away and long ago to him. It was almost now—because these things had become a part of him, as had every person he had met in his lifetime, everything he had read, everything he had seen, and every voice he had heard.

The beauty of the wild flowers he had observed in their seasons had become a part of him too. And the songs of the winter winds in the pine needles and the soft summer wind's rustling in the oak leaves had left in his memory a wild soft music.

The tiny seedling at his feet was interesting. It was four inches high with six leaves, growing from barren ground under the shade of its giant parent. He bent over to touch the leaves with his fingertips.

An acorn had fallen from this tree, he thought. Winds blew autumn leaves to cover it. Rains fell and roots sprang from it and went down, and a living shoot went up through the leaves to the air, sun, wind, and rain to get nourishment from them too. *But this is plant life. This is not my life. A tree can't think and remember. I can. I was created differently. My creation was above and beyond the natural laws governing plant and animal life.*

There was no doubt in his mind about this now.

Jason Stringer had always believed simply in his Creator. He had followed divine guidance for the promised reward of everlasting life.

The husk of a living tree, he thought, digging for the acorn with a little stick. He found it, all right. It was barely embedded in the ground. He picked up the thin hull and examined the remains of the seed that might grow into a giant tree.

This husk doesn't end all, he thought, as he threw it back on the ground.

He looked up into its giant parent's towering branches that blotted out the sky. Here was the growth and maturity of the tree. He listened again to the slow-moving August winds rustling the soap-bellied leaves. He had heard these same sounds of soft, wild music years ago, and there was not anything vague in his memory about them. Rustling oak leaves in August wind was music embedded in his active memory.

But who was that baggageman? he kept thinking. He should have known the man. He knew or had known everybody who worked or had worked on Huey's train from 1882 until 1929. He stood searching in the horizon of his memory for a clue to remember the face and the sound of that voice. The clue just wasn't there. He was certain he had never seen the man before. Where was Zebo Campbell? He was the only baggageman he had ever known on Huey's train.

Old Huey, the engineer, he had known and loved since he could remember. That was from 1882 until 1929.

Strange light, he began to notice, was filtering between the oak leaves. The sun had long been down beyond the Putt Off Ford. Huey, vaguely stirred in this outer horizon of Jason's memory, didn't pull his train any more. Again Jason was a little confused. He had just seen Huey a few hours ago at the throttle in his pin-striped cap and jacket, the red bandanna around his neck, and goggles over his eyes. He had set his watch by his train. He had waved to him and Huey had waved back.

But three years beyond the living impressions sealed in his mind, they had torn up the E. K. tracks and sold the rusted

T-rails and spikes for scrap iron. Jack Dysard and Timmie Phelps had said that Huey's losing his engine and thirty-six miles of track speeded his life to its close.

That life. Huey was hauled to Lindsay's Holy Chapel. That's where he slept. The husk of him might be there, but the real old Huey was still at his throttle pulling his train. Jason had just seen him and his train. He knew. No one could tell him differently.

Jack Dysard and Maurice Sinnett? He didn't know about them. Not after they left Plum Grove. But Zebo Campbell, two years after Huey, fell over. That quick. And Walter Phelps, working on a C. & O. section, ran his handcar head-on into a freight train coming through the fog. A crowbar punctured Walter's lung. He slept at Three Mile, on the hill, above where the stranger got off the train. Timmie, Walter Phelps' brother and a baseball pitcher, was smoking when he moved a haystack. The stack got on fire and he was surrounded by flames. He came through, flaming himself, threw his pocketbook one way and his watch another. They didn't burn. Timmie's charred husk, remade by expert undertakers, with false hair and painted lips, was planted at Three Mile. Aaron, Little Ed, and Penny must still be in the years beyond his impressionistic ones.

He stepped softly from under the oak to his school path, which wound serpentlike down Collins' Hill. He looked at his valley. He had been born here and had grown to manhood. In this valley he had played with Walter, Timmie, Jack, Little Ed, Aaron, Penny, Maurice, and Zebo. But he had never seen light over his valley as brilliant as now. The sky reflected a beauty such as he had never known. In the distance, framed in the colors of a sunrise, he saw the three-room house where he was born.

Walking down the school path, he passed the blue slate dump at the mouth of the coal mine where his grandfather and his father had dug coal. The dump was beautiful and shining in this new light. Trees, hills, rock, and landscape were the same. At the foot of the path the two-story Collins house was painted as white as new snow, with trimmings as green as the needles on the two giant firs that had grown a century to shade it. Where the path met the valley road Jason Stringer stopped suddenly. He saw an old man walking up the road.

Could he be the Prince Albert-looking stranger? He was wearing a high hat and walking with a cane. He looked like the same man Brady had helped from Huey's train that morning. He was walking toward the old Daugherty house. That house was an old-timer, all right. Made of yellow poplar logs hewn from virgin giants.

Vaguely he remembered sitting on his father's knee and his telling him about W. W. Daugherty: tall and straight as a stick of yellow poplar, and the valley's first settler. He had come to this valley when there wasn't a stick of timber amiss. He was eighty the first time he rode on a train. And he rode with Huey, a young man to the Daugherty house. There he stopped. He had to be old W. W. He couldn't be anybody else.

I'm proud of the years I have lived, Jason thought, as he started walking again. I'm pleased with my reward. My investment in life was the best I ever made. And it was easy. First, the promise. Then, the way. One can't miss if one believes. . . .

Jason hurried happily toward the house framed in the colors of a morning sunrise.

Nearly Tickled
to Death

My father threw his bean basket and took off running across the field like a wild turkey. He was slapping the side of his face with his straw hat as he went over two bean rows every time he leaped.

"Did you get in a yellow jacket's nest, Pa?" I shouted.

"Not like a yellow jacket's sting," he yelled back. "It's worse!"

On the far side of the bean patch was a high bank. He was going so fast toward this forty-foot drop-off I thought he was going over. He had to stop so suddenly and brace himself he tore up two bean rows. He was still slapping the side of his face with his straw hat.

"What is it, Pa?" I screamed.

He was now running down the field between two rows. "Pa, can I help you?"

He didn't answer but kept on running, hitting his face with his hat. Every half dozen steps he let out a wild scream.

"Pa," I shouted. "Pa!"

Pa's not a big man. Not much bigger than I am. He's forty years old and I'm fourteen. I didn't know a man as small and as old as my father could stretch his legs so far and run so fast. I went after him. The way he was screaming, hollering, and running scared me half to death.

It took something to make him run. I'd seen a man try to bluff him once over a line fence. He came at Pa with a double-bitted ax and I ran that time. Pa picked up a rock and stopped him. Pa wasn't afraid of fighting bulls, biting dogs, yellow jackets, hornets, or any man. Once I saw him pick a copperhead up by the tail and wrap it around a tree. That finished the snake that struck at me but missed. He was small, but he'd stand his ground. I'd never seen him run from anything before.

Now, he was circling the two-acre bean patch and I was trying to catch him.

"Pa—"

"Don't talk to me," he shouted. "I don't know what it is. It's something powerful! It's tickling me to death!"

He circled the bean patch twice with me cutting corners trying to catch him. He was fighting something I couldn't see and screaming like a laughing hoot owl. I tried to get close enough to see what was after him. I tried to head him off but I couldn't.

The bean patch wasn't a big enough place to hold him. He took off down the lane toward the house. I lost more ground trying to keep up with him on this straight road. His legs were stretched out until he looked like he was running on the wind. I was doing my best to keep in sight. He didn't stop to open the barn-lot gate. He went over it like a young mule.

When I opened the gate he was almost to our yard. I guess Mom must have seen him through the window, for she ran out on the porch. She jumped from the porch and came running to meet him. Mom had never seen him run like this either.

"Bud, Bud, what's the matter?" she screamed.

Dave Royster, a meddlesome neighbor who lives in sight, dropped his hoe in his garden when he saw Pa running. He took off running across the little meadow between our houses.

"What is it, Bud?" Mom screamed with her hands high in the air.

"You tell me what it is, Faye," he shouted.

"I can't see anything," she said in a high voice.

"I've never seen anything either," he shouted, and kept on running. "But it's there!"

He sidetracked Mom and started around the house.

"Acts like a dog with a running fit," Dave said, running up. "I've never seen a man run like that before. I've seen dogs!"

Pa was coming around the house now, and Dave tried to head him off. Dave made an awkward grab for his arm but missed it as Pa ran between us. I thought about a shoestring tackle.

I'd made third-string football team in Maxwell High School, but Pa was lifting his feet so high he'd have got me with one of his brogan shoes.

"Just have to let him run down," Dave said. "He's wound up like an eight-day clock. I've never seen a man run like him before!"

"No, we won't let him run down like a clock either," Mom panted as she came around the house after him. "There's something after Bud! Help me catch him."

"You go around after him, Faye, and I'll go this way and meet him when he comes around," Dave said with a trembling voice. "Maybe I can hold him. He might be off in the head."

"He's not off in the head," I said. "Something is tickling him to death."

"Tickling him," Dave said. "Then why doesn't he laugh?"

Dave went around the house the way Pa was coming and was close behind. When Pa came around the corner he hit Dave head-on, and Dave hit the ground. I dove for a shoe-string tackle but the legs I tried to grab just weren't there. I scooted ten feet on my stomach over the grass. My head was within two inches of the wall when I got up slowly.

"He knocked the breath out of me," Dave said, getting up slowly. "He's crazy!"

"He's not crazy," Mom said, getting her breath fast. "There's something after Bud."

"I'd like to know what it is," Dave said.

"I'll get him next time," I told Dave.

I figured Pa would be slowing down and I could tackle him.

"Don't let Bud run into Faye," Dave warned me. "He's a wild man!"

"Tickling me to death," Pa panted as he turned the corner full-speed toward us.

"Watch out, Mom," I shouted.

I didn't have to tell Dave. He got out of the way. I dove at Pa's feet and I caught his ankle with my hand. I couldn't hold on, but he went end over end. His straw hat rolled like a barrel hoop.

"Get hold of him, Dave," I said. "Help me hold him! Let's see what's after him."

"Are you hurt, Bud?" Mom said, running up.

Dave was down beside him now.

"I don't see a thing," Mom said.

"But it's something," Pa moaned.

"It's a running fit," Dave said.

Mom and Dave were both looking at the side of his face.

"It's there," he said, slapping his face with his hand. "It's after me!"

"Bud, I don't see a thing," Mom said.

Pa was on the ground doing all kinds of didoes.

"Must be in your ear," Mom said.

"That's exactly the way my hounds acted when they had running fits," Dave sighed as he watched Pa, who was rolling like a dog toward the house. "My hounds acted like they had something in their ears. A racehorse couldn't have kept in sight of one."

"I never heard of a man having a running fit, Dave," Mom said, disgusted-like. She followed after Pa when he rolled against the house. "What on earth is wrong, Bud?"

"Don't ask me again, Faye," he spoke like a laughing owl. "It's tickling me to death."

"Stay still long enough until I can look in your ear," Mom told him. "Quiet, now Bud! Quiet!"

He shook his head there on the grassy ground, but Mom held his head and looked in his ear.

"I don't see a thing," she said. "Let me send Bill after a doctor."

"Oh, no," he said. "Maybe it will stop tickling me. That tickling has eased up some now."

"Exactly like a running fit," Dave said. "The spell eases on one of my hounds after he runs until his tongue almost touches the ground."

"Dave, that's crazy talk," Mom said. "Don't go away from here and tell Bud had a running fit."

"He's had something, Faye," Dave said. "I never seen him act like this!"

"Well, I've never either," Mom said. "I know something is after Bud."

"Sometimes it's just in the mind," Dave grunted.

"It's not my imagination," Pa said. "This trouble is real!"

"Did you see anything, Pa?"

"Not a thing," he told me. "I just felt it. Now, let me stay right here and not move. It's stopped tickling me."

We stood over Pa, looking down at him. His face was red and sweaty.

"You hollered, Bud, just like a dog with a running fit," Dave told him.

"Stop talking about Bud's having a running fit," Mom told Dave. "It's something in his ear. I'm going to look again."

"Don't you stir it up again," Pa said. "Let me lay right here and rest while it's not tickling."

"I thought I saw something move in there," she said. "Honest I did! Looked like a little white ball."

"Well, it might be," Pa said. "But I don't feel it now."

Pa lay there on the cool green grass looking up at us. He got his wind back, then he got up on his feet.

"Still some tickle there," he said, putting his hand on his ear. "But I feel much better now."

"Maybe whatever it is got tired too," Dave said. "Maybe that little white ball is resting to get a fresh start. I've seen one of my hounds rest from one running fit and then go right into another one."

"You're not helping Bud any to talk that way," Mom said. "Maybe you'd better go back to your garden."

"No, I'm hanging around to see if Bud takes off again," he said. "You need me here, Faye. This thing isn't over yet!"

"Bud, if that's something in your ear, I'll fix it," Mom said.

"How, Faye?"

"Kill it with heat!"

Leave me be now, honey," he told Mom. "Don't bother it as long as it's just tickling a little. I can't stand to be tickled to death."

"But, I'll heat the smoothing iron," she said. "I'll put a cloth around it so it won't burn your ear. I'll fix whatever it is."

We went into the kitchen and Mom plugged the cord in and turned the juice on like she was going to press my pants.

"I think steam would do it better," Dave said. "It's soft and can get up in the little earhole."

"We'll try the smoothing iron first," she said.

Mom had her own way. She wrapped the iron with a cloth. She had Pa lie down on the divan and she put the smoothing iron to his ear.

"That heat's stirring that little white ball up," Pa said. "Maybe it's trying to get out!"

Then Pa threw the iron off on the floor. He jumped up and started running wild over the living room. He kicked over chairs and leaped the divan.

"I told you steam would be better," Dave said. "Let's catch him, Bill! Faye, put water in the teakettle and turn the stove up high."

Mom ran to heat the water while I dove for Pa's legs. I liked tackling in football. This time I made a perfect shoe-string tackle and brought Pa down before he broke up every stick of furniture in the living room.

"I told you how my hound rested before he took off on another running fit," Dave said.

"Hold his body down, Dave," I told him. "I've got his legs."

His legs were hard to hold. He was taking on again something awful.

"While the water heats why not use the Flit gun, Faye," Dave said. "A little Flit in Bud's ear won't hurt him."

"Bee-smoker would be better," I said. "The bee-smoker will push the smoke up in his ear."

Mom came with the Flit gun. She pumped it into Pa's ear.

"That thing's trying to dig deeper," Pa shouted. "I feel it. It won't work, Faye. Don't drive it deeper! It has to come out."

"I'll try the steam," Mom said. "The teakettle is singing now."

Then she came with the teakettle while we held Pa, who was kicking something awful. She put the spout up close to Pa's ear. Steam shooting out of the spout shot up into his ear.

"It's hot," he shouted. "It's making that little white ball go deeper! It's tickling!"

"The bee-smoker," I said. "That rag smoke blown in there will kill it."

"What do you say, Bud?" Mom asked.

"Anything to stop this thing," he said. "Rag smoke will addle a bee. I don't know what it will do to that little white thing!"

"Pa, if you'll lay still I'll get the bee-smoker," I said. "I can have it in a jiffy."

"I'll try," he promised me.

I went after the bee-smoker. It was in the smokehouse, loaded and ready to use when we robbed our bees. I fired the rags. I ran in and put the smoker to Pa's ear.

"Smoke is getting in there all right," he said. "It's not hot like that steam, but that thing is digging deeper."

"Must be as big as the earhole is wide," Dave said. "It's closed up the place so smoke can't get to its nostrils."

"I'm worried," Mom said. "What can we do now?"

"Leave Bud alone," Dave said. "You stirred that thing up once, Faye. Don't stir it again."

"Leave it alone and let it tickle me to death?" Pa moaned. "No, it has to come out. It feels as big as a bird egg in there! Only it's alive and kicking!"

"It has to be pulled out, Mom," I said. "We're pushing it deeper."

"That makes sense, Bill," Pa said.

"We've got to get a doctor," Mom said.

"While you're getting one here I'll be tickled to death," Pa sighed.

"Maybe it does have to come down," Dave said.

"But how?" Mom said. "We don't have anything that will pull it out."

"Yes, we do, Mom," I shouted. "That new floor sweeper! It's got a little tube that sucks up dust. That will fit over Pa's ear."

"Oh, yes," she said, pleased. "That sweeper Bud fussed so much about me buying from a salesman."

Mom ran to hook up the sweeper. Pa was about to wrestle Dave under until I grabbed his legs again.

"Hurry, Faye," he said.

It was awful the way my little father kicked and carried on. I didn't know he was so strong. I wondered now if he had gone off in the head, but he still talked sensible. And I wondered if he had what made a dog have a running fit. I wondered if it was catching and he'd got it from one of Dave's hounds. I was glad when Mom plugged the sweeper in and pushed it over where we held Pa down on the floor. This ended my wild thoughts. In a jiffy she had the tube hooked on and had the sweeper buzzing like a bee swarm.

"Do you reckon it will hurt your ear, Bud?" she asked Pa.

"It can't hurt it any worse than it's tickling me now," he said. "Put it on!"

Mom put the little tube over his ear.

"It's trying to hold on," Pa said. "It's digging and scratching. Keep it on! He's losing his toe holds. I felt it turn loose! It's gone! Faye, Glory, glory, I'm a new man!"

A big smile came over Pa's face. Mom took the tube from his ear and he jumped up from the floor.

"I want to see what it was," Pa said.

Mom opened the end of the sweeper and removed the dustbag. She gave it to Pa.

"It's sealed," she said. "You'll have to tear it open!"

"Good, for it can't get out," he said.

He tore the bag open. We looked into the dust.

"There it is," Pa said. "See it moving in the dust!"

Pa reached down and got it between his thumb and finger. He blew the dust from over it.

"Its one of them hard-backed, white bean beetles that lays the eggs!" he said.

"You were at the right place to get one down there in the bean patch," Dave said. "Maybe that one was trying to find some place to lay her eggs."

"She'll never lay any more," Pa said, crushing the bug between his fingers and thumb. "That little white thing will never tickle me again."

"I'm glad it's over," Mom said.

"I'm glad I thought of that sweeper," I said.

"I'll get my wife a sweeper now," Dave said. "She's been wanting one. And when one of my hounds has a running fit, I'll know what to do."

Uncle Jeff
and the Family Pride

Pa, Uncle Jeff, and I were in the front room sitting before the fire when somebody knocked on the door.

"Open the door, Shan," Pa said. "See who it is."

"It's my friend," Uncle Jeff said. "He's come after me."

Uncle Jeff didn't move. He didn't even turn his head to look back. He gazed steadily at the flames leaping from the dry wood.

I got up and went to the door. When I opened it, there stood Sheriff Bill Acherson.

"Is your Uncle Jeff here?" he asked.

"Come in, Bill," Uncle Jeff invited before I could speak.

"What is it this time, Jeff?" Pa asked. He looked disgustedly at Mom's big brother, who had come uninvited three years ago to live with us. He didn't live with us all the time. He didn't like to stay winters when we had wood to cut, fifty

219

head of livestock and three teams to feed, and barn stalls to clean and bed. In spring and summer, when days and nights were warm, Uncle Jeff loafed in Blakesburg.

"I've got a warrant for your arrest, Jeff," Sheriff Bill said.

"What, again?" Pa said, looking up at the pink-cheeked sheriff.

Sheriff Acherson was Pa's third cousin, but he was not in Pa's political party. Since blood was thicker than water, Pa never let him down at election time.

"I've just been settin here a-waitin on you, Bill," Uncle Jeff said. "What's kept you so long?"

"The Greenwood Grand Jury was a little slow about this indictment," he replied.

"What's the matter with 'em?" Uncle Jeff said, looking up at Sheriff Bill with a big smile. "This is the first of November. It's getting late. What's they get me fer this time?"

"A horse," Sheriff Bill chuckled.

Pa looked hard at Uncle Jeff. Mom, who stayed in the kitchen, couldn't help hear what we were saying. She was ashamed of Uncle Jeff. But she wouldn't run Uncle Jeff away from our home because she was afraid something worse might happen to him. She wouldn't let Pa run him off, either. And, since my father loved my mother, if she wanted her brother to stay with us regardless of how he carried on, Pa let him stay.

"Well, Bill, I'm ready," Uncle Jeff said, getting up from his favorite chair. "I've been packed for the last two days waiting for you. I'm ready for my winter home."

"It's awful when a man ain't got no more pride than you got, Jeff," Pa said, getting up from his chair.

Uncle Jeff was a big man. He stood beside my one-hundred-thirty-five pound father. He was six-two and weighed three hundred seven pounds. His shoulders were broader than our corncrib door. He had big hands, feet, and head, and a full set of teeth, white as blackberry blossoms.

"Well, Mick, little feller," Uncle Jeff said to Pa as he walked over to pick up his battered suitcase, "I won't be seein you until spring."

"All summer you've had a place to sleep here, Jeff," Pa said. "You've danced like the cricket. You've not laid anything away and you've paid no taxes and now the people will feed you all winter. It's a nice life, Jeff."

"Uncle Jeff doesn't look like a man goin to jail," I said to Pa as he walked away beside Sheriff Bill Acherson. "He looks like the governor of Kentucky ought to look."

"He's not in jail yet," Pa said. "He has to have a trial."

Uncle Jeff had on his dark Sunday suit and a light-blue shirt that Mom had washed and ironed so slick a fly couldn't light on it. He wore a necktie the same color as his suit. His big shoes were polished until they shined like mirrors in the sun. He had spent some time getting in his clothes and shoes.

"Pa, I'd like to hear Uncle Jeff's trial," I said. "Maybe he'll come clear and won't have to go to jail."

"Your Uncle Jeff is a smart man," my father said. "He's figured out some way to get indicted over that horse he bought and didn't pay for. See, he was indicted in the October term of court, just before winter. He'll manage to get a speedy trial."

The door opened and Mom walked in.

"Poor Jeff," Mom said, wringing her hands. "I'd like to know what's happened to him. I'd like to know how he lost his pride. There's never been a Shelton like him."

"Jeff might find his pride again," Pa said.

Mom turned and went back into the kitchen. She was tall and handsome like Uncle Jeff, only Mom wasn't very big. She just weighed one-hundred sixty-nine pounds. She had light blue eyes, black hair, and was smooth-complexioned like Uncle Jeff.

"It's a shame, Shan, your ma has a brother like Jeff," Pa

said. "Don't try to walk in Jeff's footsteps when you grow up. Take a lesson from a man who has lost his pride."

Sheriff Bill arrested Uncle Jeff on Wednesday. On Thursday Mom talked to Pa and cried about how embarrassed she was to have her brother in jail again. She said she'd hate to go to Blakesburg and look the people in the face. She wanted Pa to do something about it. Friday she was still talking to Pa and crying about Uncle Jeff. And on Saturday Pa and I walked five miles over the hill to Blakesburg to see about him.

When we reached the courthouse yard, Sheriff Bill was hunting six jurors for the Quarterly Court. Uncle Jeff had timed his arrest just right. Sheriff Bill was picking good citizens to serve. He picked men who had no use for one as wayward as Uncle Jeff. Two of the men, Amos Skaggs and John Crider, owned riding horses.

"Jeff and Sheriff Bill work together," Pa said. "Jeff votes for Bill too. If Jeff wants to go to jail for the winter, Sheriff Bill will select a jury that will put 'im there."

We watched the well-dressed man Sheriff Bill had summonsed going up the courthouse steps. A few minutes later, we saw Jailer Thomas Hartley walk from the jail toward the courthouse with Uncle Jeff.

"You go listen to the trial, Shan," Pa said. "Tell me what it's all about. I want to go see my old friend, Dave, the blacksmith. Later, after the trial, I'll want to have a word with Judge Burton."

Pa took another look at Jeff, all dressed up and smiling as he walked along with Jailer Hartley, who had a bad limp. Jailer Hartley had a leg which never gave him any trouble when he was a young man at the square dances. But after he got into politics, he started walking with a crutch. He beat all other candidates in the primary. In the final election he beat Shade Miller by a landslide.

"It's awful, Shan," Pa said, watching Uncle Jeff come up the street. "Your Mom is right. Jeff needs something to seize and shake 'im."

Pa turned and walked toward the blacksmith shop, shaking his head. I waited for Uncle Jeff and Jailer Hartley.

"Shan, I'm glad to see you," Uncle Jeff said. "Come up and listen to my trial."

"That's where I'm goin," I said. "Uncle Jeff, what did they indict you for?"

"You'll have to listen to the trial," he said. "They've got me. I'll be boardin here with Sir Thomas all winter, I'm afraid."

Not many people had gathered to hear Uncle Jeff's trial. No one was mad at Uncle Jeff but John Ainslow. His face was as red as a turkey snout as he sat staring at Uncle Jeff. Judge Burton was sitting on his golden-knobbed chair. A young lawyer, DeWitt Armstrong, was appointed to defend Uncle Jeff. He had never won a suit. Seldon Braiden was Blake County's prosecuting attorney.

When County Judge Burton read the indictment, I listened closely. Uncle Jeff was indicted because he had brought the horse back to John Ainslow and turned him into a dry pasture. There was a law in this state where no animal could be put in a confined place without water.

"But Uncle Jeff, you carried—" I started to say.

"Ssshhhh," Uncle Jeff interrupted, with a sweep of his big hand.

"Order in the courtroom," Judge Burton said, pounding with his gavel.

After Uncle Jeff's lawyer, DeWitt Armstrong, got up and stated his case, telling what a kind man and a fine gentleman Uncle Jeff was, John Ainslow was sworn on the witness stand. He was then asked to tell the story to the jury about his selling the horse to Uncle Jeff.

John Ainslow told how Uncle Jeff wanted to buy his horse, and he sold him for fifty dollars. Uncle Jeff paid ten dollars down and was to pay the balance at ten dollars a month, but never made another payment. He told how Uncle Jeff wanted him to take the horse back and refund his ten dollars. John Ainslow said he was a man of his word and didn't do business that way.

Then, one dry October morning, two weeks ago, John said he found the horse in an abandoned pasture where all the waterholes were dry and the horse was almost famished for water. John Ainslow was cross-examined by DeWitt Armstrong, who was shaking like a leaf in the wind.

When Uncle Jeff was given the oath, he told the jury the same story John Ainslow had. Only he said he didn't know all the waterholes in the pasture had dried up. The lawyers agreed not to argue the case. They put the evidence in the hands of the jury. The jury was gone only a few minutes. When they returned they found Uncle Jeff guilty, and Judge Burton set his fine at one hundred dollars and gave Uncle Jeff twenty days in jail. Uncle Jeff smiled and started counting on his fingers.

"Along in March," Uncle Jeff whispered to me. "Not a bad time to get out. Spring will be almost here."

Uncle Jeff couldn't pay his fine, so for each dollar he was fined he had to stay a day in jail. That made one hundred twenty days in jail for him. I could understand a few things now about my uncle. Last year he had bought a pair of shoes from L. W. Madden and had charged them. After he had worn the shoes a few times, he had taken them back. He waited until L. W. was out of the store and, since Uncle Jeff was so large, the little clerk, Ernie Porter, was afraid of him. L. W. Madden talked of having Uncle Jeff arrested, but he didn't. That year Uncle Jeff got in jail for disorderly conduct. He came to Blakesburg with an empty suitcase and

talked to a tree on the courthouse square. And the year before that Uncle Jeff had bought an expensive pair of big
gloves at Blakesburg Dry Goods. He had charged the gloves.
He wore them a month and took them back. Ellis Earwood,
manager of the store, talked of having Uncle Jeff indicted,
but he was afraid he'd offend us. Uncle Jeff finally got in jail
for putting a bridle and a saddle on one of Pa's large steers
and riding him to Blakesburg.

When Uncle Jeff was boarding with Sir Thomas, as he
called him, he got three meals a day. He played rummy all
day and into the night. And for a breath of fresh air, and to
see his old friends, he got to walk out into the town, get the
mail, and often buy groceries. He could be sent as a trusty.
He was one that wouldn't leave. Not during the winter anyway.

Uncle Jeff had been lodged in his winter home a couple of
hours before Pa walked down from Judge Burton's office.

"Uncle Jeff put that horse in a pasture where there wasn't
any water," I said. "He'll be in his winter home one hundred
twenty days."

"Jeff never starved an animal for water in his life," Pa said.
"Jeff's too tenderhearted to kill a chicken. He's just smart. He
knew how to get himself a good bed and free grub for the
winter. I think in another month Jeff'll be a changed man.
He'll wake up. If he's got any Shelton pride left in 'im, it'll
rise up like sap in a spring tree."

When we went home, I told Mom how it had all happened
and how Uncle Jeff walked so proudly to jail.

"Think of it!" Mom said. "And he's a Shelton. No more
pride in him than that. Our ancestors, long departed, are
restless in their graves."

Uncle Jeff was happy in his winter home for two weeks.
Sir Thomas fed him three good meals a day. And Uncle Jeff
sat behind the bars with the boys and played set-back,

hearts, bid-trump, and rummy almost all the day. He was treated a little better than the other prisoners in the afternoon. He was chosen again by the jail's "kangaroo court," because of his "seniority rights," to go after mail in the afternoon. He'd walk down the street to the post office, meet old friends, shake their hands, and tip his big black umbrella hat to the women. He was making the jail a very popular place. Often Uncle Jeff was sent on a special mission for Jailer Hartley.

Late November came, and something happened to the prisoners.

Uncle Jeff, because of his seniority, was the first it happened to.

Ty Coons, our neighbor, who lived on a one-horse farm on Coal Branch, stopped by our house on his way home.

"You know what's happened to Big Jeff?" he said, laughing.

"I'd like to know," Pa said. "Tell me."

"I saw Jeff in Blakesburg and he's sweepin the city streets and wearin a ball and chain," he said, roaring again. "Funniest sight you ever saw!"

"Wait until Mom hears about this," I said.

"They tell me Dave, the blacksmith, is makin six more balls and chains," Ty said as Pa squirmed to keep from laughing. "He's makin 'em for Jailer Hartley's winter boarders."

"Jeff was the man to start this winter-boardin idea with Sir Thomas," Pa said. "He made it so popular others have followed."

"Now they'll wear the ball and chain and sweep the streets like Jeff," Ty said, laughing and slapping his thighs with his skinny hands.

"How big is the ball hooked to Jeff's chain?" Pa asked Ty.

"Made out of a piece of T-rail from an old railroad switch,

they tell me," Ty said. "It's about all Jeff can carry. About everybody is a-coming up tryin to lift it. Big Jeff's a worried man. He ain't got that smile on his face now, Mick."

"Gee, I hate that," Pa said, turning his head to laugh. "Who sentenced 'em to the ball and chain?"

"They say in Blakesburg that Judge Burton had a lot to do with it," Ty replied. "They tell me Big Jeff's picture with his ball, chain, and broom has been in a lot of papers. Judge Burton made the statement that the jail was still a jail and not a winter resort to keep 'em in and feed 'em on the taxpayers' money."

"I hope Uncle Jeff picks up that ball and runs all the way home," I said.

"He can't do that when deputy sheriff Tim Constable is standin not ten feet away," Ty said. "That ball they've got chained to Big Jeff's ankle is a man's load. I tried to lift it and couldn't."

"What'll Mom say now?" I said to Pa, who was grinning like a lizard.

"She'll really be plagued," he said. "She won't go to Blakesburg now. Not your mother. She's got that Shelton pride!"

"But I'm goin to see Uncle Jeff," I said. "I'm not ashamed. That's awful, to put Uncle Jeff in a ball and chain."

When Pa told Mom about it she laid down across the bed and wept.

"There were well-to-do farmers, lawyers, schoolteachers, and doctors among my people," Mom said. "They were a respectable line of men until they got to Jeff. If he could get his pride back again!"

November dragged on and Mom wept over Uncle Jeff day and night. Pa didn't offer to go to Blakesburg to help get Uncle Jeff free from his ball and chain. All the news we had about Uncle Jeff was what our neighbors told Pa and me.

They'd been to Blakesburg and had seen him sweeping the streets. They told us how people followed, looked him over, and tried to lift the ball chained to his ankle. They talked about the prisoners of old wearing the ball and chain.

Martha Hinsland, our friend and neighbor, stopped to tell Mom she had just come from Blakesburg, where she had seen Jeff carrying his big ball and shoveling snow from the streets.

"Jeff's a slave," Mom cried, running to Pa. "Mick, can't you help Jeff?"

"He wouldn't help me," Pa told her. "He sat around here and talked about his winter home just like he had a mansion in the skies. He's got what he wanted. I'm gettin along feedin the teams, livestock, cleaning and bedding the stalls, and cuttin wood without Jeff's help. I'd as soon leave him be. Let Sir Thomas board 'im."

"They've turned the clock back in Blakesburg," Mom said. "But why should my brother be the first sent back to the Dark Ages?"

"Jeff will think twice next time before he buys something and takes it back," Pa said, looking at Mom and never batting his eyes. "Jeff's been making a joke out of our laws. When a man enjoys wintering in jail, there's no shame left in 'im!"

"Shan, you go to Blakesburg tomorrow and bring me news about Jeff," Mom said. "Your father won't do it!"

That warm December day when I walked over the hill to Blakesburg I thought of the times Uncle Jeff had walked this same way. How once he had carried an empty suitcase and talked to every tree along this road. Then he'd talk back to himself for the tree. Uncle Jeff had fun in those days. Now it was different.

When I got to Blakesburg I looked across the street from Lantern's Drug Store where a big crowd had gathered. They were around Uncle Jeff. He carried the ball that little men were showing their strength by trying to lift. Uncle Jeff didn't look like a Governor of Kentucky ought to look now. I saw his handsome Shelton face above the crowd. It had a worried look. I walked across Main Street and pushed through the crowd to Uncle Jeff. He was carrying a long stick with a sharp nail in the end and picking up scraps of paper and putting them into a satchel like I carried schoolbooks in.

"Uncle Jeff," I said.

"Shan!" He stared at me and avoided the questions people were asking him. "Where's Mick?"

"He's at home," I said.

"Why haven't Mick and Millie come to help me?" he asked.

"Mom's ashamed to come. She's about to grieve herself to death."

"I'm ashamed too," Uncle Jeff said. "I've never been as ashamed in my life as I am now. I was never treated this way by friends before. I want to pick up this ball and chain and leave this place."

Tim Constable walked up close to Uncle Jeff. He carried a revolver in the holster on his hip. He wore a bright badge on his coat lapel.

"Big Man, let's pick up the paper on the street near the depot," Tim told Uncle Jeff.

Uncle Jeff picked up the ball and chain and carried them across Main Street. The crowd followed. I went too. I felt sorry for Uncle Jeff.

"Shan, this is an awful winter," Uncle Jeff said. "I thought I'd have a good one, and this is what I got. I've kept the dirt swept from the streets of this whole town. I've kept the snow and sleet cleaned off too. A trusty for two winters and now I'm in a ball and chain."

"All right, let's pick up the papers," Tim told Uncle Jeff. "This town is dirty. Clean it up!"

"I'd rather be dead," Uncle Jeff said. "Maybe I'll find a way."

"All right, let's pick up papers," Tim spoke harshly to Uncle Jeff.

Then Uncle Jeff went to work and I started to help him. Tim made me throw the papers back on the street that I had gathered up.

"You wouldn't take the work away from the man who needs it," he said. "That's not right."

I followed beside Uncle Jeff and looked up into his sad face. The crowd followed too, and watched Uncle Jeff pick up papers to the length of his twenty-foot chain. Then they watched Uncle Jeff go back, and they listened to him heave and groan as he picked up the big iron ball. He lugged it to where there were more papers scattered on the street. Then he set it down again and went to work.

"I'm ashamed of this, Shan," he said again. "But I got you a horse last summer, didn't I?"

"Yes, you did," I said.

"But I'll never get you another horse like I got that one," he said, spearing an empty Red Horse tobacco sack and putting it in the bulging satchel. "Not if it costs me like this one has. Something is happenin on the inside of me. I don't know what it is."

Uncle Jeff worked while the deputy sheriff trailed us a few feet behind. The crowd of people looked at Uncle Jeff and kept on following him.

Number Three passenger train, westbound, whistled for the curve above the railway station. "I used to come out here and watch her pass this station," Uncle Jeff said sadly. "She's one of the crack liners that won't stop at this little town."

Then Uncle Jeff looked up like something had come over

him. There was a new light in his eyes. He went to get his heavy ball so he could pick up more paper. The train was in sight when Uncle Jeff threw the satchel from over his shoulder quicker than I could bat my eye. He threw down his stick. He made a beeline toward the tracks, carrying the big ball and the chain.

"Hey, hey, Big Man," Tim Constable shouted. He fingered for his revolver, but didn't take it out. "Stop before I shoot!"

"It's a suicide!" a woman screamed.

"I don't want to see it," said a young man as he turned his head.

"Uncle Jeff," I screamed, running after him. "Don't do it, Uncle Jeff!"

Many of the women and men stood stunned as Uncle Jeff ran toward the tracks to beat the train. He got there just before the train rounded the depot. He threw the iron ball onto the tracks and the chain rested on the T-rail. There was a screeching of wheels and Uncle Jeff pulled backward like a big ox until he went end over end and came up with a piece of the chain in his hand. When Tim Constable saw what Uncle Jeff had done, he started to pull his revolver. Everybody was on Uncle Jeff's side and they started screaming for him to run faster. He ran behind the old flour mill and down beside the railroad tracks and disappeared over the Little Sandy River bank into the tall dead horseweeds. He was out of sight when Tim got to the other side of the flour mill.

"Don't you dare to shoot my uncle!" I screamed.

"I wouldn't shoot 'im for anything," Tim said, grinning. "Jeff Shelton's beginnin' to get some pride. The taxpayers won't have to feed him this winter. Maybe they'll never have to feed 'im again."

Then Tim laughed as I had never heard a deputy sheriff laugh.

Before his laughter died on the chilly wind, I heard

splashing in the Little Sandy River. I knew something had come over my uncle. I knew he'd never liked cold water. He had always washed his face and bathed in milk-warm water. Now he had plunged into an icy river.

I took off again as fast as my legs would carry me to overtake him on the other side. Loud screams and laughter got fainter as I ran across town so I could cross the bridge and circle back. "Pa'll have somebody to help 'im now," I thought as I ran like a deer upon the bridge. I looked up the river to my left and saw Uncle Jeff going up the bank, wet as a scalded chicken. He'd lost his big black umbrella hat and he was running up the river bank with the short chain in his hand. I increased my speed to reach him where the road junctioned for home.

Another
Thanksgiving

The morning stars were still in the sky when Pa walked down the rough-stone walk, dressed in his brown hunting suit and boots and leading Rags and Scout. They charged against their chains, barking pleasantly, for they knew the big hunt was on. I carried our single-barrel shotguns. Finn walked ahead of Pa, silhouetted against the morning sky.

"Ever since I've been big enough to hunt," Pa said soon as we reached the car, "I've always taken a hunt Thanksgiving morning. Pa used to hunt on that day. Grandpa used to hunt Thanksgiving morning. We always hunted while the womenfolks fixed a big dinner."

"And now you're going out with your boys," Finn said, stepping on the starter.

"A-goin out with you boys to show you how to shoot," Pa said, as he climbed into the back seat with Rags and Scout.

233

"If Grandpa was alive and a young man, I'd like to go hunting with 'im," Finn said.

"He's the best shot I ever saw shoot a gun in Lawrence County," Pa said. "Son, don't get it in your head you can shoot like the old men."

I put our guns in the back seat where Pa was sitting between Rags and Scout. I sat on the front seat beside Finn. We were off to Batten County, where there were plenty of rabbits. The headlights showed the ground was white with frost. The air was cool and crisp.

"Don't get in a big way, Finn," Pa said. "We've got to pick up the other boys."

"Don't worry, I won't forget," said Finn as he left the frozen dirt road and pulled onto the highway. "'I want to see how these city doods can shoot!"

"I'll tell you they can shoot, young man," Pa said. "I've hunted many a Thanksgiving with Art Saddler. He's a fine shot on the run."

"That's the only way I ever shoot at a rabbit," Finn said. "I like to give the rabbit a chance!"

"Don Saddler's a good shot," Pa continued, "and there's none better than Sam Akers. Son, you'll never get a shot if you stay near Sam Akers. He's quick on the trigger."

When we reached Greenwood Finn drove the car past the railway station, then he stopped suddenly.

"Reach me my gun, Shan," he said quickly.

"What is it, Finn?"

"Never mind, Pa," he said as I reached over the back seat and got his gun.

Finn ran across the railroad tracks, fell to his knees, aimed at something under the baggage wagon.

"What does he see, Shan?" Pa asked me.

The gun barked, and a rabbit rolled kicking from under the wagon.

"I never saw that rabbit!" Pa said.

"I never either!"

"That's one for me," Finn said as he put the rabbit in the car amid the bellowing hounds.

"It's a wild rabbit all right," Pa said, examining the rabbit. "But I didn't know you'd find one in town."

"I killed one on Main Street once," Finn said, starting the car.

Art Saddler was waiting for us on his porch. He carried his single-barrel across his shoulder, smoking his pipe, walking proudly to the car. He got in the back seat with Pa and the hounds. Then we crossed Main Street to the other side of Greenwood to pick up Don Didway and Sam Akers. Don got in the front seat with us and Sam got in the back seat with Pa, Art, and the hounds. We were loaded now and we were heading for Batten County.

Finn drove the car with his single-barrel across his lap.

"Now everybody's got the same chance on this hunt," Sam Akers said. "Of course, it never bothered me much to have a single-barrel and let the other fellows hunt with pump guns and automatics. I've always managed to get my share of the game and then some!"

"I've just been tellin my boy Finn what a good shot you were, Sam," Pa bragged.

"I always like to let the other fellow do the bragging on me, Mick," Sam said in a pleased tone of voice. "You've hunted with me and you know how I can shoot."

"I've just told Finn that the young men nowadays can't hunt like the old men could."

"You're right, Mick," Sam Akers agreed, puffing his pipe. "I don't know what's wrong with 'em. They can't see er something. Seems like their nerves go to pieces. They just can't hunt with the men of my generation! I'm only forty."

"If the young men can't shoot," Finn said, "I guess that leaves me out. I'm just seventeen."

"You're pretty young to hunt with us old-timers," Sam

Akers said, then he laughed and slapped his knees with his big hands.

Finn brought the car to a sudden stop on the highway, jumped out and aimed at something down the streak of headlight. "Pow!"

"What's he shootin at, Mick?"

"Don't ask me, Sam," Pa said. "He's killed one rabbit in the railway station this mornin."

"I never saw anything down the road," Don said as Finn walked back to the car.

"Never either," Sam said.

"What was it, Finn?" Pa asked.

Finn didn't answer until he stopped about eighty yards down the road. Finn stopped the car to get his rabbit.

"Do you get game for every shot?" Finn asked Sam.

"I miss one shot out of every eight," Sam said. "I don't try to be perfect!"

"That beats me," Finn said.

Pa, Art, and Sam talked about the great hunts they had taken on former Thanksgivings and the great hunters they had hunted with. And to hear them tell it, they had beaten these great hunters of former days.

As the morning stars left the sky, Pa and Sam switched from great hunters and great hunts to the fine Thanksgiving dinners that they had eaten. They bragged about how their wives could cook and what big dinners they expected soon as they killed their game. I thought about something I'd read in one of my books at school about the first Thanksgiving, how the men had hunted while the women cooked.

Pa directed Finn over the turnpike in Batten County to the "rabbit country." Pa had hunted here before. And he had bragged about what a great hunting ground it was. "It will test the kind of shot you are," Pa told Finn and me, "when you see three rabbits running at once and you're huntin with a single-barrel."

It was light enough to see to shoot a rabbit when we pulled before a farmhouse.

"There's George Bracken now," Pa said.

When he saw our car he stopped. Pa got out of the car.

"I'm back for a Thanksgiving hunt on your farm," Pa said. "I have five men with me."

"You know my rules," Mr. Bracken told Pa. "Kill all the rabbits you can. Just watch about shooting too close to my barn."

"We'll watch that," Pa assured him.

Never was there a finer morning to hunt. The air one breathed into his lungs tasted good enough to want to hold it and breathe deeper and deeper. It was fresh, crisp, intoxicated with spicy perfumes of dying summer-farewells, goldenrods, ironweeds, and leaves. We breathed deeply of this good air before we led the hounds toward the ragweed field that was white with late November frost.

"What a morning for a hunt," Sam said, inhaling and exhaling a full breath of good morning air. "I feel like I can knock the cottontails this mornin."

"Now boys, it's seven o'clock," Pa said, looking at his watch. "We'll hunt until eleven. That will give us time to get back home for our Thanksgiving dinners."

"That gives us four hours to see what we can do," Sam bragged.

"Now everybody be careful and not shoot toward the other fellow," Pa instructed us, since he was the oldest man in the crowd.

We started toward the ragweed field. Pa led Rags and Scout and I carried the guns. Soon as we reached the field Pa unsnapped the chains and the charging hounds took off, whiffing the frosted earth as they went. I gave Pa his gun and he started behind the hounds. Finn walked on Pa's left and Sam Akers walked on Finn's left. Finn was cupped between Pa and Sam—two good shots. Art Saddler walked on

Pa's right, Don Didway walked to Art's right, and I walked along to Art's right. I thought that if I took the outer rim of the fan-shape we were moving in I would get a chance to shoot a rabbit.

"Wow-wow-wow!" our hound dogs barked.

"*Pow—*"

"*Pow.*"

"Sorry, Pa," Finn said. "Maybe it was too close to you."

Finn walked out and picked up the rabbit, put it into his hunting coat. Sam Akers watched as Finn reloaded his gun. Before Finn had walked ten steps his gun discharged harmlessly into the air.

"What's the matter, Finn?" Sam Akers asked.

"Playin with the trigger and my gun went off," he told Sam.

"That's a dangerous thing to do," Sam said nervously.

I had never known Finn to let his gun go off before. I thought maybe he was a little tense, since six men were hunting, each wanting to kill the most game. Then I noticed Sam hunted farther to Finn's left. I knew that was to Finn's advantage, for it gave him more space made him cupped less tightly between Pa and Sam. I thought the reason Sam was edging over was that he was afraid of Finn's gun.

"*Pow!*" I aimed at a running rabbit and missed. The rabbit went to my left, facing the other hunters' guns. Don Didway shot and missed. Art Saddler knocked the rabbit down, picked it up and put it in his hunting coat with a smile on his ruddy cleanshaven face.

"*Pow!*" Pa shot again and missed. Finn waited for Pa to shoot before he shot, and he upended the rabbit.

"It's this gun," Pa said. "After you hunt with the same gun thirty-five years the barrel gets thin. But maybe it's my eyes."

"You're shootin too quick, Pa," Finn told him.

"Never mind, young man," Pa said, "I killed rabbits long before you were born."

It was a beautiful stretch of land that we were hunting over. The ground was level and we could see the other fellow shoot at the rabbits. The sun peeping over the eastern ridges on this level frost-white field—and the gray-brown rabbits running over the white frost made excellent targets. It took a good eye and a steady nerve to hit the small fast-moving targets, since they were excellent dodgers.

"Pow!" Pa shot again. The rabbit turned over and over.

"Just started shootin now, Finn," Pa said in a happy tone of voice. "Take keer, young man. Your old dad will show you how to bag the cottontails!"

But before Pa had his rabbit in his hunting coat, Finn had killed another rabbit and reloaded his gun. Before Finn picked up his rabbit Scout jumped a rabbit that came straight toward Finn at full speed. It was a quick shot that Finn made, upending the rabbit.

"That's good shootin, young man," Sam Akers complimented him, "when you hit a rabbit coming that fast right at you."

"I never like to shoot one up," Finn said before he picked up the rabbit. "When I make a shot like that I always like to clip the rabbit's nose."

When Sam Akers saw that Finn had just clipped its nose, he wheezed harder on his pipe.

"Pow!" Don Didway got a rabbit. At the same time Art Saddler shot another rabbit, and Pa killed another. Their guns barked almost at the same time. Neither Sam Akers nor I had killed a rabbit.

"Pow!" Finn killed a rabbit after Sam had shot and missed.

"That was a lucky shot you made then," Sam said, examining his gun as if there were something wrong with it.

"Yes, it was lucky," Finn repeated, picking up the cotton-tail.

Now the hounds had jumped another rabbit. And it was good music to hear these barking hounds running across the field toward me while small clouds of melted frost ascended toward the sun. I saw the rabbit, aimed, fired. It was my first rabbit.

"*Pow!*" Pa shot and missed. Art Saddler got the rabbit.

"What's the matter with the rabbits?" Sam Akers asked Pa. "Why do they always break your way, Mick?"

"They know Pa won't hit 'em," Finn said, laughing.

Before we had reached the far end of this long field Finn had killed eleven rabbits; Pa had killed four; Sam Akers had only killed one and had missed nine shots. Art Saddler had killed three, Don Didway had killed two, and I had killed three.

"I don't know what's the matter with me," Sam said. "I've been nervous since Finn let that gun go off; I can't hit a thing!"

"I know what's the matter with me," Pa said, as he walked toward me.

"Here, Shan, take a chew of this twist," he said, reaching me a twist of light burley.

"What for?" I asked.

"Spit ambeer in my eyes," he said. "It's my eyes the reason I'm not shootin no better!"

"But that tobacco will make me sick."

"Come on! Chew it," he commanded me. "You ain't no better to do it for your old pap than I was to chew it for mine. I had to chew and spit ambeer in Pap's old eyes to make 'im see to bark squirrels from the tall hickories with his rifle. It helped Pap's eyes and it will help mine."

I chewed the tobacco and spat in Pa's eyes. It smarted his eyes but he squirmed around and stood it. The burley was so strong I could taste it long after I spat my quid on the ground. It nearly made me sick.

"I'll show Finn how to shoot," Pa said, soon as his eyes had quit smarting.

Now we crossed a little knoll where there was a tough-butted white-oak grove. The November wind rattled the leaves still clinging to the white-oak trees. The sound of the wind in the trees and among the ragweeds on the empty autumn fields, the cracking of the guns, and the barking of the hounds were good sounds to hear.

Finn killed two rabbits on the knoll and Sam Akers killed one. The hounds ran one rabbit into a hollow tree, another rabbit into a groundhog hole. And soon as we crossed the knoll we came upon another ragweed field as big as the first one we had crossed.

"Here's where the rabbits are, boys," Pa said soon as we waded among the dead dark weeds where the frost had evaporated into thin white clouds toward the sun. "Here's where we finish the hunt!"

"Rabbits will be harder to hit now that the frost has melted," Don Didway said. "They are almost the color of the dead weeds."

"*Pow!*" Finn got a rabbit soon as we'd walked onto the field.

"Lucky," Pa said. "Rabbits just run toward you!"

"I can't help that," said Finn.

I noticed that Finn was getting a load of rabbits. Big, tall Finn swaggered under the weight of his bulging hunting coat. The rest of us managed to carry our game very well, since we had much less than Finn.

It was like a battle the way we shot in this ragweed bottom. We had as many as five rabbits running at one time. Our hounds didn't know which rabbit to run. They would start after one rabbit and jump another. I had never seen as much excitement in my life. But Finn kept picking up more rabbits and putting them in his bulging pockets. Only once did he miss a rabbit, then Sam Akers shot at the same time at the same rabbit and claimed the rabbit. Finn let him have it. Only one had shot the rabbit, since it was coming toward them and its nose was clipped off.

"Ten till eleven, boys," Pa said when we reached the far end of the field. "We'd better mosey back toward the car."

The day was warmer and we had sweated through our hunting coats. The sun had dried the dead leaves, grass, and weeds, and they were loose and fluffy beneath our feet. The white-oak leaves rustled dryly now on the bough-butted white oaks—and the wind whined over the fading-russet autumn fields. The hunt was over, and what a hunt it had been!

When we reached the car Finn took twenty rabbits from his hunting coat. Pa had killed five; I had killed three. Sam Akers had killed four rabbits; Don Didway had killed three; and Art Saddler had killed five. We had killed forty rabbits and Finn had killed twenty. He had two in the car that made him twenty-two rabbits. Finn didn't brag about it; he looked at Pa and smiled as Pa chained Rags and Scout and put them in the car.

As we drove toward Greenwood Pa rubbed his eyes with his hands. I knew they had started smarting him after the sweat had touched where I spat the ambeer. He didn't brag about the old men of his generation, his father's and his grandfather's generations, outshooting the men of the younger generation on Thanksgiving hunts. Sam didn't talk about what a shot he had been; he talked to Pa about the big dinner awaiting him soon as he got home.

Soon as we had reached Greenwood and had let our hunting companions out at their homes, Finn turned and whipped the car across the railroad tracks.

"This is not the way home, Finn," Pa said.

"But we don't need thirty rabbits, Pa," Finn said. "Four will be plenty for us. And I know a lot of families over here too poor to buy a turkey, and I'm giving 'em these rabbits."

"Glad you thought of it," Pa said.

"Why did you let that gun go off, Finn?" I asked. "Was it an accident?"

"It did what I wanted it to do," he said, laughing. "It made Sam Akers nervous. Don't guess he'll go around braggin now."

"Is Finn as good a shot as Grandpa was?" I asked Pa.

He didn't answer me. He sat between his hounds, his face serious in thought. Maybe he was thinking of the big Thanksgiving dinner that was awaiting him; maybe he was thinking of the big Thanksgiving dinners Grandma cooked for the hunters of long ago when Grandpa shot wild turkeys for Thanksgiving—Grandpa with his long rifle and his raccoon-skin cap, with burley tobacco spittle in his blue eyes, climbing the steep Kentucky hills, scratching his boots on the brush and briars as he knocked the wild turkeys from the trees and from the air with his trusty rifle.

About the Author

Jesse Stuart is recognized as one of the most important voices of America. Poet, short-story writer, and novelist, he has written over twenty books, all of which have immortalized his native Kentucky hill country. Besides being one of the best-known and best-loved regional writers, he has taught and lectured extensively. His most recent book *Daughter of the Legend,* an idyllic love story, also published by McGraw-Hill, appeared in 1965. *My Land Has a Voice* is the eighth volume of his collected pieces.